ine

What About Me?

Kate Figes

What About Me?

The Diaries and E-mails
of a Menopausal Mother and
her Teenage Daughter

W F HOWES LTD

This large print edition published in 2004 by
W F Howes Ltd
Units 6/7, Victoria Mills, Fowke Street
Rothley, Leicester LE7 7PJ

1 3 5 7 9 10 8 6 4 2

First published in the United Kingdom in 2004
by Macmillan

A CIP catalogue record for this book is available
from the British Library

ISBN 1 84505 694 9

Typeset by Palimpsest Book Production Limited,
Polmont, Stirlingshire
Printed and bound in Great Britain
by Antony Rowe Ltd, Chippenham, Wilts.

Friday June 15. Nothing worth watching on TV, no one's picking up the phone, so I thought I'd start a diary.

Dear Diary,

It's my 14th birthday tomorrow and I'm going shopping with Mum. Actually I'd rather go shopping with Ruby, Fran, Nat, Hayley, Saskia and Serena, but I need her credit card to get anything worth having. I can't wait. I want a new pair of jeans, some little T-shirts, a skirt perhaps, some flip flops, a new jumper, a hoody. I need at least three shades of lipstick, mascara, eye-liner, a bag, a belt, spot concealer, stuff for my hair, a padded bra so that it might look like I've actually got some tits and don't have to stuff loo paper down my front any more to make it look like I've got some, and I'd really, really LOVE to have a really sexy long dress for parties and film premieres, and some of those boots with high heels and pointy toes. I wonder if I'll feel any different when I'm 14. It's got to be better than 13. And when you're 14 it's only two years until you're 16 when you really can do what you like. All I REALLY want for my birthday is tits. Hopefully, by the time

I'm 16 I'll have some, otherwise I'll have to get a boob job. Mum'd never let me, so I'd better start saving now, just in case.

From: Sue James
Sent: Friday 15 June 20.06
To: Angela James
Subject: I miss you

Darling Ange,

I know you're on the other side of the world
and probably (hopefully) fast asleep, but
shopping is a feeling that unites women all
over the world. Imagine then how excited I
was when Frankie said that she wanted to go
to Oxford Street with me for her birthday
(which is tomorrow). I know she just needs
me to pay for things, but spending some time
alone with her these days is precious, even if
that clocks in at around £50 an hour. She
spends every minute of her free time either on
the phone to her friends or with them. She's
all giggly, cocky and chatty with them and
then totally silent, surly or rude to me. Like
Jekyll and Hyde. With one of her friends the
relationship seems only just short of being
sexual. They're always hugging and kissing
and Frankie's face lights up in her company,

3

it's as if she's in love. We had a huge row about it last week. I can't believe it but I actually found myself telling her that I thought this friend was a bad influence on her, and then remembered how Mum had said exactly the same thing to me when I was a teenager, and felt sick. Frankie just screamed insults, said I had no right to criticize her friends, stormed off to her room and wouldn't speak to me for two days. She's right, but so am I. I do have a right to comment on who she spends her time with, I'm her mother. For all I know Ruby could be smoking dope and taking her to under-age drinking clubs. I know she's just a teenager and that all this will pass, but it just makes me feel so sad, all this distance between us. She used to be affectionate like that with me. Now it's clear that she doesn't even want to touch me. All I get is selfishness, the strops and a clear indication that she finds me deeply irritating or embarrassing to be with.

It's a cliché but they really do grow up so fast Ange, so you make the most of those nephews of mine because in ten years' time you'll hardly see them. I look at Frankie sometimes and wonder what happened to that adorable, cuddly child. When she was small I really used to notice the roses and honeysuckles of June,

4

because they had completely passed me by in the year when she was born, I was so wrapped up in her and the aftermath of birth. Now that's gone and Blooming June doesn't hold that same magic any more and I can really chart the years flying by as she's got older. They are so heavily punctuated by terms and things like sports day and the Christmas Carol concert, and now Lola is coming home with exactly the same homework and I'm sitting at the kitchen table AGAIN doing projects on the Ancient Egyptians and the Greek Myths and wondering why we never kept the old ones. It feels as if life with them is spinning away, faster and faster. Frankie seems so different now, so tall and grown up, so withdrawn and private. She comes in looking ashen from school, hostile, critical, and slumps in front of the TV or gets on the phone. It's like living with a completely different person. I'm afraid I'm pinning a lot of hopes on tomorrow's trip to Oxford Street (which will of course be Hell). I'll ping you tomorrow night and let you know how it went. We've got the entire gang coming for a sleep-over tomorrow night (aaaarghh!!!). Cheap (all they seem to want is 18-rated scary videos and pounds of chocolate) but it's certainly not hassle free. Masses of love from Big Sis Sue xxxxxxx

Dear Diary,

Saturday June the 16th, MY BIRTHDAY AND
I AM NOW OFFICIALLY 14!!!!!! I feel
different, older, but when I looked in the mirror
this morning, disappointingly I looked exactly
the same. All I actually really want for my
birthday is some tits.

Mum has put on sooooooo much weight. I
think if I ever got to look like that I'd have to
kill myself. And SHE had the nerve to tell ME
in Top Shop that that skirt made my bum look
big just because it was short and she didn't like
it. She and Dad are always criticizing the way I
look when it isn't any of their business. It's my
body, and when I'm out no one knows I'm her
daughter wearing these clothes, so what difference does it make?? It doesn't reflect badly on
her. She tried on some clothes in the changing
room and I was shocked by how large her
stomach has got, there were these disgusting
rolls of fat over the top of her knickers. How
does she even get that big without noticing?
Why doesn't she go on a diet? And she doesn't
even seem to care who sees her that way. When
we go swimming I just want to die! I hide away
in the cubicle, because why should anyone want
to see my body, but she's happy to walk around

completely naked with her thighs and pubes
flapping and nothing on but her flip flops
because she's neurotic about veruccas. She just
doesn't seem to care who sees her like that. She
managed to open the curtain of the changing
room three times today when she went to get
things in a bigger size, so that EVERYONE,
ABSOLUTELY EVERYONE could see me in
my bra and knickers, and she didn't even seem
to notice. Anyway . . . didn't seem much point
in arguing with her about the skirt when she
was paying and we were in such a public place.
She didn't buy me nearly enough stuff AND
she forgot about the padded bra, even though I
reminded her about it like a hundred times. I
really REALLY need a proper bra, one that
might make my tits look bigger, but she doesn't
understand that. She did buy me this fantastic
top that I'm going to wear next Friday to
Saskia's party (I hope Toby comes, he's
SOOOOOOOO GORGEOUS!!!!!), but
she made me buy this purple dress which I
HATE, when what I really wanted was this
sports top. She wouldn't let me have it, said it
was much too expensive just because it was
branded, but that's why it's nice. She said that
in two weeks' time it wouldn't be cool any
more, but what does it matter what anyone
thinks in two weeks' time? Who can even think
ahead to two weeks' time? I could be dead in
two weeks' time. What matters about life is

today, now, enjoying this very minute, not the future. She thinks nothing of spending more money than I get for my entire allowance in a year on designer clothes in Selfridges. She dragged me in there and bought one small black jumper (hasn't got enough already) and it cost more than she spent on me the whole day. I suppose she thinks that if she spends enough on the clothes, nobody will notice her body.

From: Sue James
Sent: Saturday 16 June 22.59
To: Angela James
Subject: Re: I miss you

Please don't worry about forgetting, Ange, you have enough to cope with at the moment with the twins. I gave her £20 and said you had sent it. Nothing thrills her more than money these days, so you're still in there as the loving aunt.

Top Shop is living Hell! Loud music, fluorescent lights, and masses of branded cheap clothing that is never bigger than a size 12 – teenage heaven I suppose, unless you're on the large side. It's been a ghastly, exhausting and difficult day. Next time I think I'll just give her £100 and be done with it. Everything that she wanted to buy was either hideous or obscene, and when I said so the only thing that stopped her from shouting at me was that we were in a public place. So she scowled at me instead. I've spent far too much money on a whole load of rubbish that she won't be wearing in a month's time, and she hasn't even thanked me for it. I thought that by doing something together we could feel closer,

9

that somehow she would feel like my daughter again, but I fear it's just driven us further apart. It's probably all my fault, I've handled it wrong, but you should see what she's like these days Ange, it's unbelievable!

And then being with this lovely, lithe young body in a changing room just made me feel fatter and older, so that wasn't much fun either! There was this amazing moment in Miss Selfridge when we stood side by side in the changing room just in our bras and knickers and looked at each other in the mirror. She looked gorgeous – thin, flat stomach, tiny little perfect breasts. I bulged everywhere. Awful it was: bare white legs covered with dark hairs and dimpled cellulite; much too small knickers so half my public hairs fell out and I remembered how I used to loathe Mum's enormous stomach when I was Frankie's age and wondered how she could bear to look at me. Then I said something about how awful I looked, and immediately felt terrible about doing myself down in front of her, because it's supposed to set such a bad example for young girls. How is she supposed to accept her body if I can't bear mine? But it is hard pretending that you don't mind hairy legs when they so clearly look awful. She said something about hormonal slowdown and

10

gaining weight being inevitable, and I said something like what on earth could she know about that when her hormones had only just begun to pick up, and then she stormed off saying that she was only trying to help, and it took me half an hour to find her again.

Everything she tried on in every single shop looked fab, but she hated most of it and complained that her breasts were non-existent when they're absolutely gorgeous, and everything I tried on was too small because I can't quite believe that I am definitely a 14 now and not a twelve (I swear 12s are smaller these days). You know how anorexics are supposed to look in the mirror and see a body that is fatter than it actually is? Well, I think I have the reverse condition. I delude myself that I am smaller than I actually am and then can't get anything on, which is just depressing. So all those skimpy little tops – fantastic if you've got no tits but when you're fulsome like me, forget it. She looked fantastic in this amazing dark pink T-shirt dress but refused to believe me, said it hugged her hips too tightly and showed off the fact that she didn't have any anyway and that it would look better on me. I tried it on in a larger size and looked rather like a raspberry, bulging over the knicker and bra lines in every possible direction, but she

11

insisted it looked fine, which just smacked of revenge because I wouldn't buy her this hideous branded top. Funny how it doesn't matter how old you are – if you're female you seem to hate the way you look.

The whole gang are downstairs screaming and hugging each other in front of a vampire movie. They resemble very noisy bees, or perhaps locusts would be a better comparison. They swarmed into the house, deposited a pile of massive trainers behind the front door and then swarmed through the fridge and the larder. Whole jumbo sized packets of crisps and chocolate biscuits disappeared, and I had to send Matthew out for more juice and a bumper-sized packet of loo paper! Then they sat down to watch the video of the play they did in their last year at primary school, while I cooked. (Chilli con carne – F's favourite meal.) They shrieked with laughter at how silly they looked. I cried silent tears into my chilli. My little Frankie, she was so small and pretty and innocent then, so cute compared to the young woman that towers over me now at 14. How, in just three years, did we go from that to this? It's incredible, more miraculous than the way that babies change into toddlers and so, so sad, Ange, I just couldn't stop crying. It was the way that I could see her on the screen, moving, talking, singing, at the age of 11, and yet I couldn't remember how she really WAS then. That got to me. How she sounded, the things she said, the way she moved, it's all gone, just like that. I've always regretted the fact that we've never had a camcorder like Her Next Door, but this evening I realized that even if we had one, even if we had cupboards full of footage capturing magic moments, they never really could capture the essence of who that child was. Only your mind can do that, and that tricks us with false memory and amnesia. You watch a ghost of the child you once knew on the screen, that's all, and in some ways it's better not to have that at all. So now I'm quite glad that we never wasted money on that camera – it's bad enough having ten years of photographs that have never been lovingly filed into albums with the dates written beneath them, and where would we store all that tape?!

Anyway must go. Matthew's stomping round the house like a denied child because he can't watch *Match of the Day*. Dying to hear your news. Has Stan stopped teething? Hope so for your sake.

Masses of love S xxxxxxxxxx

Dear Diary, Sunday. I'm 14 years old and 1 day.

My birthday has been the best ever, although Mum did get the food slightly wrong. Three of my friends are vegetarian (she says I never told her, but I know I did) and we ran out of things to munch through the movies. Fran and Ruby argued over the choice of film. Ruby wanted a cosy musical because she got scared by the vampires, but Fran said that was wet. Saskia insisted on sleeping right in the middle, said she got scared at the end (how pathetic is that) AND those mattresses are unbelievably uncomfortable, so we hardly got any sleep and I woke up with a stiff neck. Honestly, Mum is so selfish. We had hardly any pillows or bedding. She wouldn't let her friends sleep here in these sort of conditions. I think she may be right about the purply dress though, the colour does suit me, and the dress is OK I suppose, if I remember to pull in my stomach and eat nothing but grapefruit for a week. I might just wear it to Saskia's party.

From: Sue James
Sent: Sunday 17 June 15.02
To: Angela James
Subject: Re: I miss you

You poor thing, it really is a complete bugger when they cry through the night like that – and you've got two teething at the same time – damn it! Can you get those homeopathic teething granules there? They were brilliant for Lola – I don't think Frankie even noticed her teeth coming through. Otherwise, try a large mallet over their heads when you're ready to drop with exhaustion.

Yes I will keep working on Matthew about Christmas, although getting to talk to him about anything is hard at the moment, we pass like the proverbial ships in the night. But how about you doing the same with Spike? Surely he fancies the idea of a little snow and jingle bells rather than the beach?

I'm completely hungover from Frankie's birthday party and I didn't touch a drop of drink. They shrieked and indulged in horseplay until at least three in the morning, and I had to sleep with a pillow over my head, and then when Frankie woke up she came into my bedroom and had the nerve to complain about the hotel accommodation, and that they hadn't got any sleep because the mattresses and pillows were uncomfortable, and how come I had all the good pillows in the house! I was so livid I nearly smothered her with one. The fact that there were seven of them cooped up in one room, frolicking about the place until three in the morning, had of course nothing to do with it, she maintained. How many of her friends' parents let them all stay over like that?? She doesn't even say 'Thank you.' Anyway, I shouted at her and then felt guilty, so I made them pancakes for breakfast and they were quite polite and sweet really, and then they sat in a circle in Frankie's bedroom and sang along to *Grease* and the Spice Girls' greatest hits at the tops of their voices and they were all so happy and having such fun, getting high on the music and being with each other. Do you remember all that Ange? Remember how much fun we used to have, just being together as a gang, nothing mattered more. Then I cried some more, but out of happiness this time. Honestly, middle age is pathetic, I think even the Mother Superior singing 'Climb Every Mountain' in *The Sound of Music* would make me cry when I'm in this sort of mood. Anyway, gotta go to Sainsbury's. There's absolutely nothing to eat in the house. Matthew's sulking and Lola's playing happily with Clare next door, probably eating her way through a mountain of crap. Must have an early night. Yawn. S xxx

Dear Diary

Friday, 22nd June (Saskia's Party!!!!!!!!!!)

What am I going to do? I've tried everything
on, in every combination and nothing seems to
look right, on me anyway. My new purple
dress is too dressy when everyone else is
bound to look grungy, and the top's OK
except that I haven't got anything that really
goes well with it. I've been through all of
Mum's clothes and Lola's and now Mum's in
a state because they're all over the floor. What
does it matter, when this is a real crisis?
Saskia's party is in TWO HOURS' time AND
Toby's going to be there, and all my clothes
are just crap CRAP. And I look CRAP CRAP
CRAP CRAP! I've rung Ruby and she's going
in jeans and a strappy top. She thinks I ought
to brave it and wear the purple dress, says I
look great in it, but I'm not sure I dare.
Perhaps it would be better not to go at all
than to go looking like a bag lady or, worse
still, like Mum. She just doesn't understand
how important this is. She keeps saying things
like, 'What about this top, it's lovely?' when it's
no good at all, which is why it's on the floor –
and then she picks this moment to have a

18

moan about the state of my room. What is the point of making a bed when you just get into it again? And then she gets all upset when I tell her to leave me alone. Honestly, I can't win. She's SOOO grumpy and tired at the moment, the sooner she gets over the menopause the better.

From: Sue James
Sent: Saturday 23 June 04.29
To: Angela James
Subject: Insomnia

Ange, Darling

I can't tell you what a night I'm having.
Frankie is more grumpy and tired than I've
ever known her. Threw such a fit at about 6
o'clock, screaming and shouting that she had
nothing to wear for Saskia's party when she's
got far more to wear than I have. If this is
pre-menarche-tension then the sooner she gets
her period the better. She refused to come
down for dinner, refused to tidy up her room,
and then stormed out of the house at about 7
looking like a cross between a streetwalker
and Judy Garland in the *Wizard of Oz* with
black fishnet tights, trainers, and a short, tight
denim skirt, with her hair in bunches and a
blaze of red lipstick. Matthew then stirred
things up by saying 'Hoping to make some
money tonight?' and she flew into a rage, used
every expletive in her vocabulary and told him

20

that she hated him and that he had no right to criticize her clothing when she's spent ages getting ready. She then stormed out of the house, slamming the front door so hard behind her that the house shook. Actually she was being so revolting that it was a relief to see her go.

But now that it's 4 a.m. and I haven't slept with worry, I'm beginning to wonder whether I should have let her go at all. She drives me mad half the time when she is here . . . *always* on the phone, never really telling me what she's planning, moaning that there's nothing to eat, arguing with Lola and stealing her clothes, but then again she creates such a huge presence that when she isn't here I miss her dreadfully. The house seems so silent, so eerily quiet and I worry . . . God how I worry. I know she's probably fast asleep by now, amongst a heap of girls on Saskia's bedroom floor, but it was so awful to have her leave in such a furious temper, and hating us that much, that I just can't sleep. Matthew is of course snoring . . . I thought I'd worry about my kids less as they got older. Do you remember when Frankie was about eighteen months and I saw the tail end of that glass reindeer hanging off the Christmas tree disappearing into her mouth? As a doctor I knew that there was nothing to be done but wait anxiously for it to come out the other end, but as a mother I was convinced she was going to end up lacerated with permanent irritable bowel syndrome. The rest of Christmas was spent monitoring her nappies and sifting through the shit for tiny pieces of glass. I even pieced the whole reindeer back together again to make sure that nothing had been left inside. Even though I worried all the time when she was small about whether she was all right, at least I could see her. Now, God knows what she gets up to away from home. There are boys at this party . . . . could she be sleeping with them, at fourteen?? The mind boggles. And is she drinking booze yet? I didn't at her age, but, judging by the gallons Matthew consumes, who could blame her if she did? You just don't know what they're up to, Ange, and you can't ask, and they don't tell you, and now I'm half deranged from lack of sleep.

AND I've had a perfectly frightful day with Her Next Door. Her real name is Fuchsia which I always manage to get wrong somehow and call her Freesia (Matthew says they're both horrible flowers anyway, so what does it matter?), so it's safer just to refer to her as HND. It's not other people's children who are the problem, it's their mothers. Lola and Clare are as inseparable and in love as ever, in and out of each other's houses as if they were their own and I love that, but Clare's mother just goes from bad to worse. She seems to buy her a new toy for each day of the week, her clothes are always new, without a stain or a crease in sight, and every time Lola comes home from her house she's clearly eaten nothing but junk food and a ton of sweets. She's the sort of woman who piles crap into her child to compensate for everything she denies herself. She's a stick insect, permanently on a diet, malnourished and NEVER eats pudding. Can you imagine the torture of having to deny yourself one of life's greatest pleasures EVERY DAY? All she ever does is complain. When it's not the school or some minor incompetence from the teacher, like she can't spell, it's her 'Daily Lady', because she has the time I suppose to hover over the poor woman and check the corners, while I'm just grateful that someone comes in and cleans for me at all. But what really turns me into heart attack material is that she is so competitive over the kids. Do you know that when Clare started reading before Lola, she actually said, 'Oh well, every child has different strengths I suppose.' What a patronizing put down! I could have hit her.

Still could, in many ways, because she never lets up. Funny how the gripes just build up when I ought to have let them go years ago. She's always on about how important she feels it is to be at home for Clare when she gets back from school, when she knows what a nightmare it is for me at the moment without an au pair, particularly when I'm on call. (The other GPs cover for me, but I can't go on like this indefinitely; the agency has to come up with somebody soon.) It just makes me feel so guilty, which is ridiculous when I do a worthwhile job and she doesn't do anything except moan, and both my kids are fine and undoubtedly better off because I work. She hits a nerve with me, the same one Mum used to about working motherhood, but at least Mum is of a different generation. HND is just smug.

Anyway, she's been doing some work on her house, always is because he earns so much money as an estate agent and she has nothing to do but spend it on some ghastly new gadget (she's so smug about her brand new Mercedes estate car . . . how can we possibly compete when we have a J Reg Vauxhall?). So of course they are building a conservatory on to the back of their house, and it has to be the size of the Millennium Dome as well as hideous, and they never asked my permission, but of course I can't say anything because Clare is Lola's best friend. So I just smile politely at her daily, and utter platitudes, which give nothing away, through gritted teeth. Her builders have made the most incredible mess, all the plants in my garden are covered in dust, and now the wall is practically falling down and there are cracks in *our* back wall, but when I casually mentioned this on the doorstep this morning (in the politest possible terms of course), she didn't apologize, as you or I would, which would of course have made it all right. She said her builders were impeccable and that the cracks must have come from natural subsidence, and that perhaps it was time we got the builders in ourselves. I was so shocked by her attitude I was speechless and I've been seething all day, but I can't mention it in case Lola hears, and now I've been up all night worrying about Frankie, and I'm on call tomorrow, so let's hope that no one rings with an attempted suicide or schizophrenic breakdown because I'm not sure I could summon up either the energy or the sympathy . . .

What a moan this e-mail is becoming. Must be the 'time of life'. My periods have begun to go haywire – 21 days one month, 36 the next, and I seem to have permanent PMT – that's what Matthew says anyway. During countless years of marriage he's always called me Honeybun and it's never bothered me. I've always liked it in fact, it's affectionate. Now, when he calls me that just before I'm about to have a period, I could smash his teeth in. In fact that's how I know I'm about to have one and he (understandably) can't understand why it makes me so cross. The slightest thing makes me cry now. It's that raw feeling you have when you've just had a baby, but now I cry over everything and anything: toast burning, Matthew just being Matthew, and minor skirmishes with other motorists turn me into a wailing banshee . . . I looked up the symptoms for the menopause the other day for a patient: insomnia, anxiety and low self-esteem. That's me. I wake up at 3 a.m. and lie there worrying about how inadequate I am, whether or not I've left the oven on, or really important things like Lola needing a new pencil case. I used to feel so confident about things. What happened? I run through conversations with patients and realize what I should have said. I think nothing of prescribing HRT for sobbing women in my surgery, but just put the whole idea on hold when it comes to taking it myself. God how I wish you were here so that I could moan to you in person. Perhaps I'll be able to sleep now. Knowing you're awake really helps.

Love you and miss you S xxxxxxxxx

Sunday, 24th June

Dear Diary,

I kissed him!!!!!! It was WEIRD. Kind of nice but WEIRD, like I didn't know what to do. We stood there with our lips together, and then he put his tongue in my mouth and it felt all slimy and tickly, and our teeth clacked together and I giggled, and then he got all embarrassed and I blushed and said sorry and we tried again. If kissing is this difficult then full sex must be excruciating. How does anybody manage to do it at all? Then someone put the lights back on and we sort of flew apart. I went over to Saskia and Ruby and pretended I'd been with them all along, but they knew what had happened. My face went all hot and red. Then Saskia goes, 'Bitch' under her breath so that no one else could hear it and stormed off. When I asked Ruby what was the matter she goes, 'You kissed him before she did.' But she said she didn't fancy him! She made a huge thing about it, went on and on about how ugly he was, and how could I like him when he had such a big nose. It was so unfair of her. She can be such a bitch sometimes. I think she was just jealous

28

because it was her party and she didn't want anybody else getting all the attention.

The party sort of went downhill from then on. Toby ignored me for the rest of the evening and so did Saskia. I tried to make it up with her, but she wouldn't talk to me, and then her dad kicked everybody out at eleven and went ballistic when he found that someone had been smoking a joint. Saskia swore she knew nothing about it, but I know for a fact that Toby brought it with him, so she does too. He's been growing grass in the loft under some lamps, and his Mum only found out because she had someone come in to fix the roof. When she told him that he had to get rid of them he goes, 'MUM! But they're nearly ready!' and she laughed so much she let him keep them! If Saskia's dad knew that he'd probably send the police round. I helped him clear up a bit, but then Ruby, Fran, Nat, Hayley and Serena went up to Saskia's room to get the beds sorted for the sleepover, so I went too. Can't imagine Dad ever getting THAT cross about finding a joint.

I cuddled up next to Ruby and Serena, and decided that if Saskia was going to get that cross about something that wasn't my fault, I'd just ignore her too, but it wasn't long before she started having a go. Goes on about how I think I'm special, so up myself because I kissed a boy, but that's how *she* is, and when I accused her of the same thing she burst into tears and accused

me of being mean, and then Fran had to intervene and try and calm things down between us,
and then I burst into tears and ran down to the
loo with Ruby, and Saskia's mum woke up and
told us to stop being so silly and to go back to
bed. Honestly, friendship can be so hard. I try
to be a good friend to Saskia, but sometimes
she just makes that impossible. If I'd known this
would happen, I'd never have kissed him in the
first place. It wasn't that good anyway . . . kind
of nice . . . but definitely not all it's cracked up
to be. Bet she'd have done it if he'd chosen her
and not considered me, when she KNEW that I
fancied him.

Mum looked shattered when I got back on
Sunday morning, more tired than I was, and
that's saying something because I only got
about three hours' sleep. Saskia woke up early
and insisted that we moved our sleeping bags
downstairs so that we could watch a video,
and she was actually nice to me again. Mum
just wouldn't leave me alone though. She kept
trying to talk to me and asked me really
stupid things like 'How was the party?' and
'How many people were there?' She's so nosy,
it was like she could almost tell that something had happened, but I wasn't about to tell
her what. Then Saskia's Dad rang her about
finding that joint, and there was this rather
tense silence. I could hear her and Dad
talking about it in the kitchen, wondering

what to do. When they finally plucked up the courage to ask me about it over supper, I wanted to joke about it and say 'Everybody does it', because that's what teenagers are supposed to say, but I didn't think they'd see the irony of that. So I told them the truth, that I'd had one puff once and practically died, that it was boring, only saddos smoked and that I wasn't interested in it. There was this worried silence as they looked at each other and wondered whether to believe me. Honestly, they'd save themselves a lot of aggro if they did.

Dear Diary,

Wednesday. Saskia's been a complete bitch to me the whole of Monday and Tuesday and I can't understand what I've done. Honestly, is kissing Toby like SUCH a big deal?? We have to talk about her party the whole time, even though it's now history. All she ever thinks about is herself. I know that we all have to put ourselves first, that you have to learn how to love yourself before you can love anyone else, but that's like really hard when you haven't got tits or a pretty face or lovely long legs like she has. I've definitely decided to get a boob job if they haven't grown by the time I'm sixteen. I'm so flat-chested I look younger than some of the Year 7s. I wouldn't mind a nose job either. It's ginormous. Why does my nose have to be bigger than my tits? But Saskia really like takes the loving yourself theory a little too seriously. She finds it genetically, totally impossible to even think about something from another person's point of view. She spends more money on clothes each week than Mum does on Sainsbury's, AND she goes shopping with her mum, which is just sad. Every week she comes into school with like a whole new look and, frankly, half the time she just looks totally stupid, like she can't quite decide how she wants to look, but if she spends enough money on it nobody will notice: Fran was trying to stand up for Saskia's dad, about how like of course he was going to go mad about dope when he thinks it's dangerous, but she just said that was stupid. She's so self-obsessed that even friendship is difficult for her, she doesn't know how to be a good friend. My only truly great friend is Ruby. She's the only one I really trust to give me good advice and not to betray me. And maybe Fran.

Dear Diary,

Sunday morning. God how I hate Sunday mornings when I'm here alone without Ruby or anyone staying the night. Dad went absolutely mad last night because I got home at 11.30 instead of 11. What does half an hour matter when I got the last bus home anyway? He's practically grounded me for the rest of my life because of half an hour. Honestly, he really does need to get some sort of proper perspective on life if he's really gonna live it. He didn't ask why I was late back, or whether I had had a good time, just laid into me about the time. Time! What is time anyway but a relative construct? Time he took a look at his life and thought about what really matters to him. He actually sat there through supper last night and talked the whole time about how they're constantly digging up the roads in London, and that sometimes they even tarmac it over and then dig it up again. Well maybe they made a mistake. Are roadworks really THAT interesting?????

Dear Diary,

Thursday.

Either Mum is really really stressed or she's turned into an inconsiderate, unsympathetic person, which is not how you're supposed to be when you're a doctor. I told her that I was worried that there might be something wrong with me because my tits are minuscule, and that I wanted to see a breast doctor, and that it wasn't natural at my age and maybe I needed to take hormones or something, but she just laughed and said I had a lovely figure and that they would grow when they were ready. Ready? I could be dead before they're ready. When I asked her again if I could see a doctor she got cross, said that she knew I was fine because she WAS a doctor, and that if I thought this bit was difficult just wait until you get pregnant and they swell up like water melons. Fine, but I don't see why she had to get cross with me.

From: Sue James
Sent: Saturday 14 July 08.27
To: Angela James
Subject: AAARGH! HELP!

Ange, Darling

Something terrible/wonderful has happened and I don't know whether to be ashamed of my negligence or ecstatic at my good fortune. I'm nearly four months pregnant . . . and that's why I haven't been in touch this past fortnight . . . as you can imagine it's been something of a shock. I knew I'd put on a bit of weight and my periods have been irregular for ages, but I just thought that was the beginning of the Change. Then last week I began to feel that twitching in the belly, that sense of something alive inside, and did a pregnancy test. I still can't quite believe it, I don't know whether to laugh or cry – cry because I of all people ought to know better and what sort of an example is that to set a fourteen-year-old girl (although of course I haven't told Frankie that this was a careless,

36

contraceptive-less mistake). You're only supposed to be fertile for about ten minutes a month at my age, but then, as Frankie said rather knowledgeably, 'That's enough – all it takes is one tiny little sperm . . .' I'm just beginning to feel less tired, now that Frank and Lola are older, and just the thought of going through all that again makes me feel like stuffing my head into a paper bag, but the prospect of another chuch to cuddle and love and watch grow up is SO thrilling. Plus the fact that I can still get pregnant makes me feel less like a dried up old hag and strangely sexy.

Lola's the only other person who seems pleased. Frankie muttered something about how she was surprised either of us still did it any more and then went into a major strop, and Matthew's behaving like a jilted lover one minute and an angry teenager the next. His first reaction when I told him I was pregnant was 'It isn't mine, it can't be mine' because he persists with this notion that we never have sex at all (when in fact it's just not as much as he would like). Of course it's his child. I've never slept with anyone else. The thought of even trying is either terrifying or simply disgusting, but he won't believe me. He's gone into a major sulk and

I'm worried. It's OK for him to flirt out-rageously with Frankie's friends – you should see him, Ange, it's excruciating, he goes all sort of giggly and perches on the edge of the sofa, cracking jokes. No wonder they always disappear so quickly to her bedroom. If I'm embarrassed, imagine how she must feel? And here I am pregnant, and feeling slightly vulnerable anyway, and all we do is row about my imagined infidelities. He hasn't said anything nice about the prospect of having a new baby, just stomps about, complaining that the house is in a mess or that there's nothing to eat. Gotta go, he's up now and screaming at Frankie about some-thing. Seeing Mum tomorrow to break the news to her. I'll report back S xxxxxxx

Sunday July 15th

 E   R   I   R
D   A   D   A   Y

I can't believe how childish Mum and Dad are
being. Mum's pregnant, at 43! Doesn't she
know anything about contraception at all?????
WHAT does she tell all those poor victims that
wait for hours to see her at the surgery? I'm the
one that's supposed to be at risk of getting
pregnant not her, and of course she can't have
an abortion now because it's too late. How
could she leave it that long when she can get
the morning after pill without having to confess
to anybody? How could she be so selfish and
not think about what I or Lola think? We've
only got three bedrooms and I'm not sharing.
She's the one who used to say that she couldn't
understand how a teenager could be six months
pregnant and not know it. But look at her! Her
stomach's so fat that no one's going to notice
for at least nine months anyway, if they ever do!
  I thought babies were supposed to make
people happy but they've done nothing but row
since it happened. Dad was really horrible
yesterday. He came crashing into my bedroom

39

and woke me up really early on a Saturday morning and started shouting at me, said I'd left the kitchen in a mess and used up all the milk the night before so there wasn't any left for him, when I hadn't, and there's a shop over the road. Why can't he just go out and buy some? Why does he have to wake me up for THAT! I was fast asleep, having this amazing dream that I fought to stay in, doing a super-market run round Top Shop, only it was smaller than it really is but I could stuff as much as I wanted into a large paper bag before a whistle went, and there was this really amazing slinky black dress that I really wanted but I couldn't reach it because Dad was shouting FRANKIE! WAKE UP! Honestly what a moron. For one awful moment I thought it was a school day. When I dropped back to sleep the dress had gone and so had the whistle and I had nothing at all. And then he goes all heavy about my going out last night, said I should stay home . . . AND DO WHAT?? Watch *Match of the Day* with him?? NO THANK YOU. They were rowing so much last night that I needed to go out, just to get away from them. I know Mum's been pretty stupid, but he could be just a bit nicer to her, she is pregnant after all. He called her a 'scheming cow' which was unfair, and she goes, 'FUCK YOU' at him several times before he goes back, 'I WISH YOU WOULD', and neither of them seemed to care that Lola was sitting at the top of the stairs, crying as she listened to every single word. It's really upsetting, hearing them argue, because we're not used to it. If they were always shouting at each other we'd be used to it, but they didn't used to, and now they seem unable to even be in the same room as one another without shouting. It's like they might get divorced or something. When she screamed 'I HATE YOU' at Dad and then slammed the sitting room door, I sat down beside Lola and gave her a big hug. Said she could use some of my pink nail varnish and that I'd help her put it on if she liked.

Only ten more days to the end of school and it's not soon enough. I'm so tired and school's really boring. If it weren't for Ruby, Nat, Fran, Serena, Hayley and even Saskia (even though she still blanks me), there'd be no point in going at all. I wake up tired – I'm sure people lived longer when they didn't have to go to school. I daydream through most of the morning's lessons, and then only really wake up around lunchtime when I finally get to have something to eat (they should let us eat in class, we get sooooo hungry and we'd learn more I'm sure). It's only when I get a chance to sit down and talk about something really inter-esting, like Fran's birthday, which is the next opportunity for a party, and what she could do for it, and whether or not I should dye my hair

purple, that my brain starts working at all.
Saskia says I'd look like a tart, but then she
would. Serena says that it might clash with
some of my clothes, which is sensible, but I
REALLY want to know what I'd look like with
a stronger hair colour. My hair is so boring,
mousy, not really a colour at all, when Fran has
this lovely thick long jet black hair. Ruby thinks
I should highlight it and go blonder, but that
really would be tarty and Mum'd probably go
spare. But if my hair was a stronger colour,
then maybe it would make my tits seem bigger.
Maybe I'll dye my hair in the summer holidays.
Six weeks with nothing much to do but lie
around in bed in the mornings, shop and watch
TV, bound to be able to squeeze it in between
appointments. Can't wait. Mind you, there's
Italy to get through with Mum and Dad in this
state and I'm not looking forward to that. If
they keep on rowing like this while we're staying
with the Jacksons I think I'll just die of
embarrassment. It's going to be bad enough
having to be nice to Edward, who's a stuck-up
little prick, well he was anyway when he was
younger. Do you know he used to clean out his
ears every night with those little cotton buddie
jobs. EVERY NIGHT! What a weirdo! Is that
sad or what? And when I asked him why, he
said it was to stop him getting ear infections
when it seems to me that just sticking one of
those things into your ear is bound to give you

cancer. Haven't seen him for at least two years, so maybe he's matured a bit. He must be 14 now too. Anyway I plan to work full-time on my tan and get Mum to buy me a sarong.

From: Sue James
Sent: Saturday 21 July, 05.13
To: Angela James
Subject: What the hell is going on?

Ange Darling, Dearest Ange,

What a week! Is my entire world collapsing, or does it just seem that way because once again it's the middle of the night and once again I can't sleep? Matthew came home last night in full leathers on a second-hand Harley Davidson. What a statement! He knows that's the one thing that I've always said I couldn't stand. We agreed when we had Frankie that he would give up bikes because it was just too dangerous, and it was bad enough worrying about him when he was ten minutes late before we had children, because of my history, without that extra anxiety and vulnerability that motherhood brings. I can't help it. The fact that William died on a motorbike still haunts me. It was so devastating to lose someone like that at 17, my first love, and I still shiver

44

sometimes when I see bikes burning up the road much too fast. He knows all that, God how he knows all that. I have to leave the room sometimes when I just see kids riding motorbikes on the telly. So he chooses this week to go out and buy a motorbike without even asking me, when I'm pregnant with a child he says he doesn't want. Talk about saying Fuck You in the way that's going to hurt me most! I'm livid. And how did he pay for it? I'm so angry I can barely look at him, let alone speak to him. I can't believe he could be that selfish, that hurtful. This is more than just a middle-aged man having a mid-life crisis – this is vindictive provocation and I don't know what to do. What should I do, Ange??

He says we're too old to go through all that again with a new baby. He says two children is enough, three irresponsible. He says he'd find it hard to love it and be a good father, and that he doesn't want to be responsible for fucking up a child's life. Then, when he's really angry, he retreats into this delusion that the baby isn't his, which is just ridiculous. I can't believe how selfish and unsupportive he is being. What does he think it's like for me? I worry too about all that: how I'll cope with all those broken nights, Frank and Lola, and keep up the job at the same time. Of course it isn't ideal at our age, but it's happened, and the grownup thing to do is just accept it, because there isn't anything else that we can do about it anyway. I suppose he'll come round to the idea eventually. I hope so, because at the moment I simply haven't got the energy to argue with him any more, he's being far more childish than Frank and Lola.

It looks as if I've found a really good woman though, to help out, which is something. Frankie is old enough to take care of herself, and Lola is as well probably, but I feel that there needs to be someone else around after school. She's about 50, with children and grandchildren herself, and she's going to come in three afternoons a week and make them something to eat, tidy up and do the ironing. Her name's Iris, isn't that a pretty name? I've never known anyone else called Iris, except Murdoch of course, although I never actually met her, just felt I knew her. So that's one shining light in a gloomy week. And not to have to do the ironing at all will be bliss. I can work and just about be a good mum, but when I stare at the ironing I just freeze and feel sick. It feels so pointless that's all, even though I know we have to make some effort not to look scruffy, and then when it comes to Frank's clothes I just want to cry sometimes. You iron them, put them in her room and then find them all creased and scrunched up when they haven't even been worn because she can't even be bothered to put them away neatly. She sort of burrows through her chest of drawers like a mole, scattering clothes behind her. I think I'd do anything rather than iron. Even nit combing is positively exciting, which brings me neatly on to Her Next Door.

Both Lola and Clare have got nits, in fact there probably isn't a child in the school, or in the whole of the UK that hasn't got nits, but that's not the point. The point is that you have to accept that nits are a perennial problem and that you at least have to try to deal with them. But no according to HND. Clare of course couldn't possibly have nits. Oh No! Those nasty little head lice are able to spot that Clare is of course a clean, well-bred, tidy little girl and a cut above everybody else, so they of course leave her alone. Better not touch that one they say, or that mother'll get out the blow torch. Every few days I smother Lola's hair in conditioner and religiously go through with a nit comb, but no matter how much I comb or go through her hair afterwards when it's dry to remove the eggs, like some monkey defleaing its child, there always seem to be one or two of the little bastards floating around the sinkful of water each week. You have this delight to come with those boys, dear sister, unless nits haven't made it over there yet of course. When Clare came over after school on Tuesday I noticed her scratching at her head and gently looked through her hair. She was completely infested, poor thing, it must be awful for her. She's probably been reinfecting Lola because they practically live in each other's hair, but when I tactfully told her mother she went into complete denial, said I must be imagining it, that she'd taken her to the doctor about an ear infection only last week and he hadn't said anything. When I said that was perhaps because he was looking into her ear and not her hair she just stormed off in a huff. Honestly, the woman's perfectly happy to get me to examine every tiny spot in case it's melanoma or meningitis, but when it comes to the common or garden nit she just doesn't want to know. I've a good mind to go through that child's hair myself. With a mother THAT stupid what other choice do I have? Make Lola wear a shower cap whenever she sees her? I'm really fond of that child, and I can't quite believe that she can be so sane and sensible with such a fussy and reactionary mother. When she's smoking cigarettes and dope at 15 she'll go into denial about that as well – 'Oh, Clare couldn't possibly . . .' Oh yeah???

It's been raining for about a fortnight so all of the flowers, as well as all of the dust, have been washed off my plants. My roses have been completely battered. GOD this weather, bet it's baking there . . . But that ugly, bloody conservatory of hers is still there. It seems to sing 'I'm richer than you are' whenever I go into the back garden, and I'm beginning to have fantasies about blowing it up. Matthew says that I'm becoming obsessed with her, that I'M the one with the failed aspirational problem. 'YOU WANT ONE SECRETLY DON'T YOU?' he says, or rather shouts, and then more hurtfully, 'There's a rather large part of you that wishes you were more bourgeois, just like her.' How could he think that? I wouldn't mind the money, I envy her the time and the fact that she can go to the gym three times a week, and that she goes out for lunch with friends, even probably squeezes in a nap before collecting Clare from school, but the three-piece suite and the blown glass ornaments I can do without . . . Although I wouldn't mind her clutter free shelves. (Where does she keep all that 'Stuff' we have to live with when there are children?) She hardly has any books at all and when I said that I wanted to take Clare and Lola to a Picasso exhibition she said, 'What's that?' There's far more class in culture than materialism, but I do rather hanker for a set of matching cutlery, and I'm desperate to re-cover the living room sofa and chairs – with some nicer material, they could be matching without looking naff couldn't they? I'm not secretly bourgeois am I??? Really? Be honest . . .

Matthew . . . Matthew . . . He's fast asleep but I'm so angry with him that just lying down beside him is impossible. Perhaps that's why I can't sleep. We've both retreated into a stony silence, not quite talking to each other through the children yet.

I'm doing the rounds with all the latest high-tech antenatal testing this week. A colleague at the practice has put me through fast track so maybe that will take the whole thing out of both our hands. The baby could be Down's with a hole in the heart and then . . . well who knows . . . I'm going to go now and do something really useful like clean the oven, so that I can feel some sense of domestic achievement . . . Not much point in going back to bed . . . I won't sleep. At least this way I can take my mind off everything with a little scrubbing. Love to those fab nephs of mine. If they were here I could at least look after them for you and let you have a lie in . . . more fun than the oven. Sorry to hear that the new rose paint in the living room has come out darker than you expected. It'll look fine once the furniture's back and there's pictures on the wall, as well as bogeys from the boys! Promise. Mum seemed fine last Sunday, almost indifferent to the idea of another grandchild when what she really wants is to see you. She's made some good friends there and the staff are really nice, so I don't think she's being tied to a chair, beaten and fed rats' tails, but you never really know with those homes. I just wish it was nearer London, it's a hell of a schlep just getting there.

E-mails are great, particularly since neither of us seems to be getting any sleep, AND they're dead cheap, but I miss the sound of your voice. We need to chat. If things don't get any better over the next few days I might just give you a ring for some stabilizing sanity. Masses of love from your big sister who misses you . . .

Dear Diary,

It's Friday 27th and that's it, no more school, goodbye Year 9 and hello Summer!! We finished school at 12 and went to Starbucks for lunch, well a smoothie which I tried and failed to make last for about an hour by sipping it. Couldn't afford any food. I've spent all my allowance, but it's only a few days and then August's money'll be there. I want to get a new bikini for Italy. Mum won't buy me one, stingy bitch, says last year's one still fits.

The best news this week is Dad's new bike. It's SOOOO COOOOL!!! Red and silver with those neat boxes on the back, and it makes this really deep sexy rumble when he leaves on it for work. I'd love one. I asked Dad if I could have a bike for my eighteenth, but he said only if Mum agreed. She knew someone who got smashed up on a bike when she was young so she's a bit paranoid about them. So I asked if he'd take me on the back, and he said he'd think about it, but that if he did, and got me a helmet, I absolutely mustn't tell Mum, she'd go nuts. Which means he will!! I know he's only trying to be extra nice to me because of Mum. When he picked me up from Serena's house on Saturday night we had a talk about things in the car. He asked me how I felt about the prospect of a new baby. I just shrugged my shoulders – how can I know what I feel about it until the baby's actually there? No need to ask how he feels about the baby, we all know that. And then he says, 'I love your Mum you know', like we're in some sort of schmaltzy movie with the windscreen wipers going at full speed and the rain pouring down, and I looked out of the window at the night, pavements all black and shiny from the rain and I said, 'Well why are you being so horrible to her then,' under my breath. I meant to only think it, but it just came out, and then he got really cross and started shouting at ME! He was gripping the steering wheel, and then I thought, 'Oh no, here's where we drive into a lamp post and die.' He only stopped going on at me when I reminded him that I wasn't the one having the baby, although with this sort of pressure at home who'd blame me if I did? He said he was sorry, so I thought I'd get it in then about the bike, and he said he'd think about it, provided I didn't tell Mum. Just our secret. But then, when I asked him whether they were going to split up, he just stared ahead at the road and pretended not to hear.

From: Sue James
Sent: Sunday 5 August 10.42
To: Angela James
Subject: crying an ocean, don't talk to me
about rivers

Dearest,

It was so good to talk last night, to hear your
voice and you're right. There is nothing I can
do but try and stay strong for Frank and
Lola. What else can I do? If he wants to go,
let him go and work things out. Maybe if he's
on his own for a while he'll see sense, that
there is nothing else out there worth having
outside of us . . . At least I hope that's the
case . . . I don't think there's anybody else.
I've thought about what you said, Ange, and I
know you're right, it's what men his age 'do',
but I've asked him three times, told him that I
want the truth and he categorically denies it.
He's staying at Mike's and muttering about
renting a flat round the corner so that he can
be near the kids and help out, but he hasn't
shown his face since Thursday, hasn't even
phoned. I cried buckets after we talked last

55

night. It was hearing your voice, wishing you were here to hug me and tell me that everything is going to be just fine and dandy. I just felt so sorry for myself, which is pathetic really when I spend most days talking to people who are far worse off in life than I am, but Lola was asleep and Frank out at a party, so I just threw myself at the sofa and wailed. Who does he think he is, walzing off from his responsibilities like some sort of teenage boy? What about me? Never mind the kids, although that ought to be important enough, but what about me??? Don't all these years together count for anything?

It must be the hormones making me this tearful. I woke up this morning feeling drained but lucid – maybe it is better this way. If he's going through a mid-life crisis then I ought to be grateful that he's doing it elsewhere, because that's one less thing to cope with, but it's the selfishness of his behaviour that really gets me. He seems to think HE'S the only one that matters, the only one with any problems. I'm the one who's pregnant and working, and left to explain everything to the kids. Lola's missing him already, and I tell her that he just needs a little time on his own that's all, and Frank just looks at me knowingly and then gets on the phone to her friends. Maybe the news that all the tests were clear is what pushed him over the edge? Maybe he hoped that I'd lose it anyway? And then what about money? I'm still seething over the motor-bike. He's taken out a bank loan to pay for it, but what about all the other things we could do with? The roof's been leaking for years, and the car just about scrapes through its MOT every year, but that doesn't matter, Oh no, Matthew has to have his toy. When we rowed about the money he accused me of being tight-arsed, said if I really wanted a new car we'd have got one and that I hate cars anyway, which is true. But if he's moving out, how are we going to manage? We need his income. Bastard!

I can't quite believe that he's serious about leaving. I really do think that he's just angry and feeling trapped, but who knows how long he's going to wallow in this, so I've got to get tough about it. What stinks is that I'm the one left literally holding the baby, yet he expects me to be oh so understanding of what HE'S going through . . . he moans on about how stressed he is at work, how he's been overlooked as a partner yet again, how he just wishes the world would stop for a while so that he could chill out, that there's more to life than this – WELL THERE ISN'T, NOT WHEN YOU'RE OUR AGE. Honestly, he's so inward looking that I could kick him (actually I did, just before he finally left on Thusday), instead of which I'm the one who has to be mature and remind myself that he's probably depressed . . . I've got Iris though which is something, so I must make sure she's happy enough to stay. I'll up her hourly rate if she's good, and if I have to take time off work before the baby comes, then so be it. Life's too short . . . I'll cash in some of the equity on the house and increase the mortgage. I'm having a baby at 43 and I'm glad. I'M THRILLED!

We go to Tuscany on Friday to stay with Tim and Julie in a villa they've rented. Matt isn't coming, which is probably a good thing as we'd probably find it hard not to row in front of them and that would ruin their holiday, but it's tough on the kids, particularly Lola. I'll try and write before we go. If not, masses of love and don't worry, PLEASE DON'T WORRY, and don't tell Mum about it next time you call – Matthew on the run I mean, she knows about the baby S xx

11th August. Saturday. ITALY

Dear Diary,

Julie Jackson is a really good name, it just sort of rolls off the tongue, I think I might use it as a stage name. And she's really nice. It's a relief really to be with a normal mother, now that Mum's in such a state. Mind you, I'm not sure when Mum has ever not been in a state really. She works too hard. Worries too much. Maybe this baby'll slow her down a bit.

The house is really cool, the insides all modern and spacious and there's this INCRED-IBLE pool. It's black and huge, and when you're swimming in it you can't see the edge, it sort of disappears into the hills. Mum goes on and on about the view. Every time she swims (with her head above the water, honestly, so embarrassing, it's like a sort of doggy paddle and she puts her hair up into a bun so it won't get wet) she talks INCESSANTLY about the view, how beautiful it is, how green it is considering it's so hot, how she'd love to go for a walk perhaps when it's cooler. If she wore goggles and swam properly with her head UNDER the water, she wouldn't be able to talk and then we'd all get some peace.

I'm not at all brown yet. Mum keeps handing me the sun tan cream and I put a little bit on, but surely it STOPS you from getting brown, you have to go a little red before it goes brown. Still it's only the second day and most of yesterday we were flying, and Mum had an argument with the hire car man and then we got lost. She missed the right exit off the motorway and we were practically in Rome before we could turn round. I'm sharing with Lola which I HATE! She talks all the time as she goes to sleep, then she gets up (waking me up) in her sleep. Mum says it's because she's so excited just because she's in the same room as me, because she's that much younger, and please would I make an effort to be kind to her, because she's bound to be missing Dad, and she doesn't really understand what's going on . . . well, what's to understand? Dad's left – and what about me? Am I too old to be missing him? Edward's kind of OK though, less geeky than I remembered him. No sign of those cotton buds in the bathroom, so maybe he's wised up.

Monday

My nose is bright red. It burned because it's so big that the sun can't get to the rest of my face without taking a detour, and suns don't do that. So my cheeks are white and my nose is bright red and it's sore, and I can't bear for anybody to see me like this. Mum's slapped lots of cream on it and given me a cap to wear to keep the sun off my face, so I'm working on the rest of my body – with suncream of course. My bikini bra is much too big, so I'm scared that everyone can see down and I keep having to check all the time that my nipples aren't showing. Edward never says a word. Just sort of stares at me over his book from his sun lounger. Creepy.

Tuesday

We went to a market today. Mum went into overdrive because of the fruit and veg there, and guess who had to lug it all back to the car in this heat – me of course, although the cool Julie (she's so trendy compared to my frumpy mother) did make Edward help me carry the basket, so I didn't have to do it alone. There was this awful silence as we dragged this weight up to the car. Neither of us knew what to say until he dropped his end and the watermelon perched on the top rolled down the hill and wedged itself between the legs of a chair at a café and we both burst out laughing. What was really amazing was that it was still whole. Edward ran down to get it and he looked quite sweet really. When we got back to the others, Mum had bought Lola a beaded purse and necklace, and insisted on paying for everyone's drinks and ice creams, but she didn't buy me anything. There were loads of things I liked, there was even a really pretty sarong, but she just said it was too expensive and walked away. Thanks Mum.

Thursday

The tan's coming along nicely, there's a real line now at the edge of my bikini and my non-existent tits look really white when I squeeze my arms against them. Even my nose is calming down a bit. I'm trying to work on my back today, which means I am making progress with my book, which always makes Mum happy. 'I love to see you reading,' is one of her most frequent phrases, when she's not on about the view. She says she can feel the baby moving around inside her which is sweet. Lola's so excited that she's going to have a little sister and she's already named her 'Tiny' because Mum's answer is always 'tiny' when Lola asks her how big she is.

Edward's being a bit more talkative. We stared a marathon game of Monopoly last night and he's very competitive about it. He's also very kind to Lola. He spent about three hours in the pool with her this morning, trying to teach her how to use a pair of goggles and snorkel. It was hilarious because the goggles kept steaming up because she would breathe through her nose instead of her mouth and the snorkel. Don't fancy him though.

Friday

Dad rang after supper last night. Said he missed us, but I doubt that. If he loves us as much as he says, why has he left?

Saturday

Monopoly game still going strong with Edward definitely winning property-wise. He's got Pall Mall and Mayfair, plus all the reds and stations, but no cash to buy any houses yet, which will start cranking up the rent. Mum's also doing well. I've got Oxford Street which is great because that's where Top Shop is, and Lola doesn't really care provided she gets to do the bank. I think Edward cheats though. I haven't spotted him actually doing it yet, but there's a shifty look in his eye. I really miss Ruby and Fran. I wish I had someone to talk to, someone to have a laugh with. Wouldn't it be just great if we could all be here for a holiday on our own.

Sunday

It's pouring with rain so Mum and Julie dragged us all off to look at pictures. Tim was allowed to stay behind because he hates going to galleries and he wants to finish his 600-page book on the Napoleonic wars (what a book to take on holiday!), but we have to go because 'it's good for us'. It's so unfair. We sat in the back of the car for at least 200 hours getting to Siena and Lola felt carsick, and then the pictures all looked the same to me – how many pictures of Jesus on the cross do you actually need? Give me Tate Modern any day, much more exciting – but the shop was good. Lola and I bought a present for Dad there (although I'm not sure he deserves one), a tie with motorbikes on, and Mum bought me this really lovely set of coloured pencils that real artists use, not your kids' stuff, and I'm going to keep them really clean and sharpened and NOT LET LOLA TOUCH THEM.

Carried on with Monopoly after supper cooked by Tim – risotto with grated Parmesan, followed by home-made panna cotte – delicious. I'm out, landed on Pall Mall with no money, so it's just Mum against Edward now. Poor him.

Monday

I can't believe it's the second week already. Julie said that I should rub some aftersun on to my legs because they were looking a bit red and dry. She let me use some of this really lovely French cream that looks incredibly expensive and smells of roses. Said I could hang on to it because she had another tube. I love it . . . SOOOO much classier than that boring old Nivea that Mum uses. Honestly, she really doesn't look after herself at all, which is kind of strange for a doctor.

Tuesday

Edward won Monopoly SURPRISE
SURPRISE. I know he cheated, he must have
done, but he made Mum laugh and look happy
for once AND he succeeded in getting Lola to
use the goggles and snorkel properly this
morning. She was so pleased with herself that
Mum had to practically drag her out of the
pool at lunchtime. I wish I *DID* fancy him.
He's really nice, a bit like an old-fashioned
gentleman, except that he doesn't say much.
You know what's really strange about life?? The
fact that anything could happen at any
moment, and you're either not prepared for it
or you could miss it completely. The love of my
life could be walking down the lane outside
this villa at this very moment and I'd never
meet him. We could have a car crash on our
way to the airport on Friday and be permanently disabled, but avoid injury altogether if
we'd set off just ten minutes earlier. How on
earth can you know? How can you really keep
yourself safe, or make sure that the really good
things happen, without a crystal ball. I tried to
talk to Mum about it today by the pool but she

just laughed. 'We're not going to have a car crash darling, I'm a brilliant driver,' she said. Whenever I try and talk to her about something serious her response is to laugh. Why is this so funny????

Wednesday

The days are beginning to roll into one and I'M BORED . . . SO BORED. I've finished my book and I can't find anything else I want to read and I'm desperate to talk to someone, ANYONE. Edward's conversation revolves around Monopoly and skateboarding . . . he goes up and down the slope at the front of the house most of the day, when he's not in the pool or staring at me from a sun lounger. Perve. When Mum's not telling me how much Dad loves me, she's on about the view. Tim still has his nose stuck in his book on the Napoleonic wars and even Lola's silent, which is saying something, because she is face down in the pool most of the time, hoovering up leaves. If it weren't for the Divine Julie, who seems to quite like me, I think I'd go mad. She painted my nails for me this afternoon. It looked really good, like a professional had done it. She showed me how to push back the cuticles so that you get a bit more nail to paint, and gave me a nail file so that I could shape them. Why doesn't Mum EVER bother with her nails? I'm longing to talk to Ruby and Fran. Even Saskia would do, but of course I can't even text them from here because Mum refused to put my phone on to roaming. Cow.

Thursday

Only one more full day to go. I love it here, the luxury, the pool, the sunshine, the ice creams, but I can't wait to go home.

From: Sue James
Sent: Sunday 26 August 14.22
To: Angela James
Subject: WOW!

Ange, darling,

What wonderful news! I can't believe it, both of them starting to walk on the same day! If the geneticists in the Nature v Nurture debate knew that about this set of twins they'd probably wet themselves. They'd be there monitoring every developmental milestone to see how much is innate. They didn't say exactly the same word when they first started to talk did they?? And hold off on the pets things, they're much too young to really notice. Wait until they've been begging you for at least three years and then say well maybe . . . and then DON'T GET A HAMSTER – THEY'RE BORING, THEY SLEEP THROUGH THE DAY AND YOU'RE LEFT FEELING SORRY FOR THIS POOR LITTLE NEGLECTED RAT AND GET

IT OUT TO PLAY AFTER THE KIDS HAVE GONE TO BED, AND THEN WHEN IT GETS ILL YOU HAVE TO TAKE IT TO THE VET AND THAT COSTS A SMALL FORTUNE, ENOUGH TO BUY 50 MORE HAMSTERS (not that you'd want to). Yeah, get goldfish if you have to get anything, they're cool and soothing to watch, but here anyway, not sure if it's the same there, you have to get those water purifier things because the water is so full of chlorine that it kills them . . . honestly why is there so much that one has to know as a mother that you couldn't actually care less about . . .

We had a really good time. They found a wonderfully luxurious villa and the view was spectacular, Ange, and I can't remember the last holiday we had which was so restful. Perhaps Matthew's absence had something to do with it. He hates sunbathing and his idea of a holiday is a great deal of exercise and exhausting sightseeing, and I always spend my time trying to keep everyone happy. This time I just lay in a sun lounger and read THREE BOOKS (which is a record on holiday since having children), played Monopoly and cooked pasta. Julie took very good care of us and was a great help – she's such an old friend and had some valuable insights . . . Said I was a forceful personality, successful and secure. (I don't feel that way, how can one ever feel secure when all my money goes in Sainsbury's and on the children, and I never have a spare penny to put away for my pension. We're all going to end up as bag ladies roaming the street, isn't that every woman's secret fear?) She reckons that Matthew has always been less confident about his abilities, and the fact that he has never been made a partner of the group is a severe blow to him, and that one should never underestimate how damaging that is to a man's sense of self-esteem, that he has always felt like something of a failure and now that he's 45 he has to face up to that fact. Maybe she's right, but he IS a successful solicitor, he HAS work and is well liked and he earns a great deal more than I do, and he doesn't have the headache I live with trying to keep home and children healthy and happy as well as work. That's always been my lot, he goes out to work and then pitches in when he comes back again, whenever that might be . . . I know I have to be understanding but it is hard when I'm the one left behind, I'm the one that has to soothe Lola to sleep when she's crying and say nice things about him,

I'm the one who feels tired and pregnant and drained, and I'm the one that has to deal with poor, sick and depressed people in my office nearly every day of the week. Why DO I have to be understanding of his mid-life crisis as well??? I simply haven't got the time. I feel as if I'm constantly on the edge, running from work to home, to cooking dinner and emptying the washing machine. Sometimes when Lola asks me the simplest thing, like she just needs help with her homework, I feel so put upon, so tired, that I get angry with her which is so unfair and then I feel guilty. Perhaps this baby wasn't such a good idea. I could just about hold everything together before, but I'm in tears most of the time now (when I'm not shouting at the kids), and what choice do I have? OK, so I should have been more careful, but all he's done is leave me when I most need him . . . sorry, had to go and blow my nose . . . honestly, Ange, I must look a wreck, only I haven't got time to look in the mirror.

Matthew stayed here while we were away and has now moved back in with Mike. He's renting a room off him. He says he'll be round most evenings to see the kids, but I'm not sure that I'll believe that until it happens. Maybe I won't want him here at all . . . it's a bit Bluebeardish – we're here locked up in this castle and he's the only one that can get away.

Kids seem OK though. Lola's a bit tearful at times and Frankie just seems like normal Frankie – indifferent, obsessed with her friends. Do you know that she switched on her phone as soon as the plane landed and she had about 45 text messages? The phone also actually rang before we had even got off the plane. She talked all the way through customs!

Must go and take Lola to a party. Fuck! I haven't wrapped the present or bought a card. It'll have to be one of those postcards from Italy. Renaissance painting, how appropriate for a nine-year-old's birthday party!

Masses of love S xxxx

Tuesday

Dear Diary,

Honestly Saskia is such a BITCH. While I've been away she's been coming on strong with Ruby, invited her over for the weekend and did nothing but bitch about me. Ruby told me the whole thing last night. She said she felt really uncomfortable about it, but I know she's been stolen by her. Saskia has this power over people and I don't understand it. I don't understand why she finds me so threatening.

We sat up talking late into the night and then Mum woke me up at 8 to say that she was off to work and that we had to look after Lola until 3 when this new woman comes to iron and cook for us, which I said I'd do, but why does she have to wake me up? I tried to go back to sleep again, but Lola just thinks it's OK to come into my room when I'm supposed to be looking after her and go through all my stuff. I could have killed her today, but if I shout at her she gets upset and tells Mum, and then Mum gets upset and blames me and says I should try harder to be nice to Lola because it's really REALLY hard for her at the moment without

Dad, and then I feel guilty because I know, but it's hard for me too, particularly since Mum doesn't seem to notice what's going on in my life AT ALL. I had a screaming match with Saskia on the phone tonight and told her that she was a mean, calculating bitch with absolutely no dress sense, and then I slammed down the phone and ran up the stairs in tears but Mum didn't seem to even notice, just carried on looking at the telly and hugged Lola. I suppose I'm so grown up that I don't need hugging any more.

Dad came round just before supper and helped Lola with some homework. Asked me if I wanted to go to the cinema with him at the weekend. Depends on what the others are up to, I said. 'Ahhhh' he said with this rather knowing look on his face. What the hell is that supposed to mean?????

From: Sue James
Sent: Sunday 2 September 22.19
To: Angela James
Subject: Juggling

Ange,

God how the summer holidays drag on.
Frankie looked after Lola most of last week,
bless her. Her Next Door still on holiday
which is a relief – one less strain to have to
deal with because I'm not looking forward to
the conversation we're going to have to have
when she discovers through Clare that
Matthew has left. Both the children are so
bored, they need to go back to school and get
into a routine again. Usually I feel that these
last few days together are rather precious. In
the past I've taken a couple of days off work
and taken them somewhere fun for a last treat
before school starts, but this year I am so
tired, so overstretched, that I just can't wait
for Monday . . .
   Matthew's been round a bit, trying to
schmooze up to the kids and pretend that

everything's normal when of course it isn't. I'm so angry I have to leave the room whenever he's there. He tried to talk about it last night, but what is there to say?? Either he's here or he isn't. I'd rather sleep than talk late into the night about him, I know that sounds mean. So I said, 'Look, I'm shattered, take Lola out for the day tomorrow and let me rest . . . then maybe I'll think about discussing it . . .' He doesn't seem to realize that it's all the tiny things that make up family life that matter so much. The fact that he's not there to help Lola with her shoes in the morning (she still can't tie her laces and he has always done it for her), or give them their breakfast (not that Frank's up often before lunchtime), or help by unloading the dishwasher or taking the rubbish out before he goes to work . . . those are the things that make up family life and I'm the one that has to do them now that he's gone. I'm not sleeping well either, hormones are beginning to pick up strong so I lie there seething, tossing and turning like a washing machine in this empty bed. I'm beginning to really bulge now, a definite hard lump beneath the rolls of fat, and I need to go back to M&S again for a bigger bra. But it is so comforting to feel this baby

. . . I'm not ever really alone. We talked again this evening, before he went back round to Mike's . . . I said, that if he needed a motorbike fine, if he needed some space to himself fine, I could do with that too (but am never going to get it), but actually this baby is his baby too and it's going to need a father to acknowledge and love it when it comes into the world, and if he can't do that it's over . . . what more was there to say? He listened and nodded and cried a little and wanted me to hug him and reassure him that I was OK, so that he could go back to his rented bachelor room and not feel guilty, but after he left I just sobbed into the sofa . . .

Midwife reckons the baby is due early Jan which means I'll be as large as a house over Christmas. Know you can't come, but we'll talk on the day and I will endeavour to get those nephews of mine some presents posted before the cut-off date . . . must check out when that is.

Masses of love Sue xxxx

Wednesday 12th September

HELLO DIARY!

Only three days back at school and already I'm
SO BORED I could SCREAM! School is SO
boring. Don't they know that we only have an
attention span of 22 minutes? So what IS the
point of making us sit there for 50 long
minutes? They tell us off for talking, but we have
to talk just to stay awake. Dissecting cockroaches
would be more interesting and probably more
educational than anything I've learned since
Monday. I'm trying deliberately not to learn my
timetable off by heart because as soon as that
happens, the week becomes so predictable and
prescribed by routine that you wake up and
think 'Double Science today – yuk', and then
getting up becomes so much more of an effort
that you roll over and go back to sleep and get a
detention for being late. I've been moved up to
the top set in maths with Miss Smart (lucky for
her she's not called Miss Stupid). Mum hardly
registered the triumph. 'Really?' she said with
that sort of dreamy indifference she usually only
reserves for the news that Granny's phoned. And
I've got this really creepy form tutor called
Araminta Moulder (we have to call her Araminta

rather than Miss because she says we have to think of her as a 'chum', someone to talk to if we've got problems. Honestly hasn't she moved on from Enid Blyton, 'chum' is such a weirdo word). She likes to put her arm around you, like she knows you really well. What a pervert! What a psychopath! Wouldn't go anywhere near her even if I was desperate.

Saskia continues to be a complete pain in the arse. I was late down to our spot in the playground at break-time because the English teacher wanted to go over something with me, and I could see them huddled together talking about something, Saskia was making them laugh and then she sees me coming and they all blank me. She was bitching about me, I know it, having a real go, and the others are too weak to stand up to her, they're completely seduced by her when she's like that, except Ruby and maybe Fran. I got really upset about it, burst into tears and ran off, and Ruby came after me but the others didn't. Probably gave them more to bitch about – 'Honestly, Frankie's such a weirdo . . . gets upset over nothing . . .' I rang her up and told her I thought she'd been bitching about me but she just denied it, said I was being paranoid. Then I rang Ruby and she told me everything – that Saskia had said I was 'too up myself', that I was able to criticize everyone else but that when it came to them criticizing me I couldn't take it, how I'd been mean to Hayley about her hair which is what really hurts because all I said was that I liked it better long . . . I know she's just had it cut, but I like it long, so what's wrong with that?? I rang Saskia back and repeated all this back to her, and all she could say was perhaps I should think a bit more about how I affect others, rather than just how they affect me, and then put the phone down. Well I could say exactly the same about her. At least I don't still suck my thumb at 14. It really upset me, but all Mum could say was 'Could you get off the phone NOW because I need to call Julie. Haven't you got any homework to do?' So I stormed out of the room, slammed my bedroom door and kicked it hard. It took Mum more than an hour to come and find me, and then all she could do was poke her head round the door and ask me in a rather patronizing way whether I'd calmed down enough to come and eat supper, which was so disgusting I couldn't eat it. There's never anything decent to eat in this house. As far as she is concerned all that matters about school is the work. She doesn't understand that the work becomes more mind-numbing and about as pointless as knitting if I'm not getting on with my friends.

Dad's driving me nuts too. Keeps on suggesting that we 'do' things together, but he never used to 'do' much with us when he was at home, and he still hasn't taken me for a ride on his motorbike.

He took me and Lola out for lunch last Sunday – Mum was on call all day – and do you know, all he could do was complain about how awful he felt with a cold, and how he'd pulled a muscle on his leg jogging and couldn't run for a while and expected us to feel sympathy for HIM! Lola was nice about it but I couldn't take him seriously. I'm never allowed to be ill. With a doctor for a mother and a hypochondriac for a father I never get much of a look in. I have to have a temperature of at least 40 degrees and be unable to stand before they let me take a day off school. I don't see why we have to be nice to him when he's the one who's left us, and if he can just up and leave when the going gets tough, well, why shouldn't I? Ruby's the only one who really understands because her parents got divorced when she was much younger and she says you get used to it. I hope so.

Fran's got a boyfriend. Sean. He's quite fit but really short.

From: Sue James
Sent: Thursday 13 September 20.59
To: Angela James
Subject: Thanks for the reminders . . .

Ange darling, you're right. It's so easy to
forget how lucky we are in life. We have
riches beyond compare to most of the rest of
the world, and yet we always feel as if we
haven't got enough. Sometimes I wonder
whether any of us have moved on from
Frankie's stage of development. Like every
other teenager, she thinks she needs clothes
and material goods to be of any value at all –
but what example do we set when all anybody
seems to want to do is rush off to shopping
centres at the weekend and stuff their car
boots with all sorts of goods that they don't
really need? Why does she NEED a conservatory next door? Why does she NEED to have
a Mercedes estate rather than a perfectly ordinary car? Because she NEEDS to show the
world that she has value, just like Frankie
does. I wouldn't mind some new clothes
though! Nothing I have fits any more because
I've put on so much weight. I wish I could

86

believe that it was all baby and amniotic fluid when in fact it's chocolate and puddings. Mind you that's where we're really lucky, being able to have babies at all. I see so many women now in my surgery who are desperate to conceive, it takes over their whole way of life. They worry that they may have left it too late and I can't imagine what that must be like. Life without Frank and Lola is unthinkable, even though I moan on about my lot as a working mother – now a working single mother . . .

Iris is heaven, although Lola doesn't like her much. She always makes sure there's enough tea for me to have something to eat when I get home, and it's wonderful not having to live with the guilt of not having done the ironing hanging over me like some giant guillotine. Lola doesn't like her cooking, but Frankie says it's a great deal better than mine, and I say we're lucky to have her at all. 'Have we had a family meeting about this?' Lola asked in a rather bossy but endearing way when we all had supper together last night (Wednesday's my half day so I cook, much to Frank's annoyance). 'What's to discuss?' I replied. 'We need Iris to help out.' But as far as she was concerned she should have been involved in the entire selection process. Lola's reached that age when she's suddenly all-knowing, and throwing her weight around like she owns the place. I caught her reading the cereal packet when I got up this morning. She was dressed, shoes on (although not tied) with her hair neatly pulled back in a pony-tail and she'd helped herself to breakfast. 'Do you know how much sugar there is in this?' she said with horror, looking at me as if I was the worst mother in the world. 'It's the second listed ingredient which means there's a LOT! I think you should buy different cereal when you next go shopping and look at the packaging! Recycle, Reuse, Reduce. Those should be our 3Rs from now on.' Can you believe it!! What would working mothers do without pre-packaged food that they can just bung in the oven?

HND has tried to corner me on Matthew three times since the weekend alone. Clare's obviously told her, but she doesn't just come straight out with it and say, 'I hear Matthew's left, how awful, is there anything I can do to help?' She skirts round the issue with a sickly sweet. 'How ARE things Sue?', hoping that I'll confide in her, and then gets the hump because I don't. If she genuinely wanted to help I wouldn't mind, but she's just being nosy and clearly feeling smug because it's not her problem. At least I don't have to pluck the hairs out of my upper lip like she does. It's amazing how indiscreet Clare can be about her own mother – do you think Lola talks about my deepest secrets to her???

We're having a lovely balmy, sunny September. Other than that not much else to report – baby's growing and I'm beginning to feel very tired indeed, too tired to summon up enough energy to be lonely. Matthew's been round every evening, helping Frankie sort out her room and Lola with her spelling, which is a good thing and certainly more than he managed to do when he was living here, and the kids seem fine really, considering. Although Frank goes in for major door slam-ming teenage strops at the moment. Must be the hormones, she's at that age as they say. Her breasts are swelling and she's getting some fat on her bottom, so I guess we must be just moments away from her first period . . . I'll keep you posted . . . We'll have to celebrate THAT when it happens! Masses of love, must grab a bath before the news . . . S xxx

HELLO DIARY!

Sometimes I think that if I didn't have you to tell my problems to I'd go completely mental. Then Mum'd really have problems on her hands so I'd better stay sane. Honestly, they say that this is the best time of your life, but if this is as good as it gets then it's rubbish. Crap, complete crap. I feel as if I spend my whole life waiting, waiting for things to happen, waiting for breasts, waiting for lessons to be over, waiting for the weekend, for a boyfriend, for a future, for a life. From the moment I'm standing at the bus-stop, waiting again, I'm worried about the size of my nose and the fact that everybody is looking at it. When I'm not struggling to concentrate in lessons, my friends are giving me a hard time about what I said to so-and-so and how mean I am. And then, whenever I'm not with my friends, I spend the whole time worrying that they might not like me any more. I got caught carving my name on to the top of my desk this morning and had to sand it down again in detention, and Mum gave me money for a coursebook which I spent in Starbucks on the way to school and daren't tell her. Still, I haven't lost my bus pass yet, or my phone, and

I've been back at school for two weeks now so that's something. At home Mum's completely exhausted or distracted, and Dad either isn't there or he's poking his nose into my business, asking too many personal questions because he feels guilty about not being there to pour the Coco pops into the bowl in the morning. I'm already behind in my maths coursework and I wasn't concentrating in the lesson today so I'm not sure what we're supposed to do, and I've rung Saskia, Serena and Ruby and they're not sure either, at least that's what they SAID anyway. There's never anything to eat, my head hurts and I'm constantly tired. Sometimes I feel so angry that I just want to scream and kick the walls. Honestly, life's crap and what's more I'm on my own, completely on my own. I could grow horns and nobody'd notice. If they get divorced and we have to move house and change schools well that'll be everything ABSOLUTELY EVERYTHING FUCKED UP . . . I really, really REALLY don't want to have 2 houses and have to shunt my stuff from one to the other and have split holidays. Then I really might have to kill myself. Do you think they'd notice then? If I just had one thing to deal with I think I could cope with it, but everything stresses me out. Life is so much easier when you're Lola's age. All she worries about is what she's going to do for her birthday and she doesn't even worry about that much. In fact, what does she have to worry about? Mum fusses over her the whole time, she even bought her a present from the toy shop last weekend but she didn't buy anything for me. She just expects me to do things like help look after Lola and tie her shoelaces (surely she's old enough to be able to do that by now?) and clear the table, but she never ever says thank you. Talk to you later.

Dear Diary,

It's Friday 21st of September and I'm at home babysitting, while Fran, Ruby, Saskia, Serena, Nat and Hayley are all at the cinema with Sean, Fran's boyfriend, and some of his friends, because Mum is out on a call, Iris had to go home and Dad is nowhere to be found. He's not round the corner, or at work or answering his mobile, so I have to stay in. I suggested that Lola could go round to Clare's until she got back, but Mum wouldn't hear of it for some reason which is so unreasonable it's just not fair. I was all made up and everything. If this goes on much longer I am going to be the only one in the gang without a boyfriend because they'll all be going out with someone before me, and then nobody'll want to go out with me and I'll be called a lesbian or frigid in the play-ground and I'll be spending every Friday and Saturday night at home like some saddo . . . Sometimes I feel so much emotion inside that I don't know what to do with it. It sort of swells up from nowhere and if I didn't squash it down I might just explode and cover the walls with blood and guts. I couldn't get angry with Mum. She was so apologetic and it sounded like a possible case of meningitis with a five-year-old, so of course she had to go, but I did kick the wall in the hall so hard that there's a dent in it, and I did shout a message on to Dad's voice-mail after Mum had gone. If he'd been home, then I could have gone out. Lola's been really irritating as well. She just wouldn't go to bed, kept crying for Mum, and I had to lie down with her on her bed and read to her and then stay with her until she was asleep, which meant I didn't even get to watch *Friends*, and then Mum came in all tired and upset because she had to drive the mother and child to hospital because she was a single mother without a car, and what with it being Friday night, Mum didn't want them to have to wait too long for an ambulance in case it was meningitis. She slumped down on the sofa and began sobbing into her hands, and I didn't know what to do. I put my arms around her and just let her cry, but the sobbing was so deep and anguished . . . even I can't cry like that. Things must be really bad for her. For a moment I felt like I'm the mother and she's the daughter and that was kind of scary.

From: Sue James
Sent: Saturday, 22 September 09.13
To: Angela James
Subject: I can't believe this is happening . . .

Ange Darling,

Matthew seems to have disappeared off the face of this earth and we have one of those typical family weekends which involves driving about 100 miles around London. If I'd bought one of those Linguaphone tape sets in French or Spanish, and played them religiously every time we had to drive the children somewhere in the car, sitting in jams and waiting outside houses for parties to finish, we'd all be absolutely fluent by now. Lola has her swimming lesson this morning and then a party in one of those ghastly soft play places in FINCHLEY (can you believe it – it would probably be easier to get her to outer Mongolia) and Frankie wants to go to a party tonight in Notting Hill and needs picking up at 11. I wanted her back at 10, but she insists this is a special birthday party, so I've caved in. In between all that I need to get to Sainsbury's and stick about three hundred loads into the washing machine so that Iris has something to iron next week. That's the real downer about single motherhood – having to do absolutely everything – drive everywhere, respond to every need, and smile through gritted teeth pretending I don't mind. I can cope, because I have to, but my main logistical problem is how to get Frankie back home when Lola will be in bed asleep. Book a babysitter or wrap her up in a duvet on the back seat and take her with me? She says she can stay the night with Hayley, but that feels like I'm just copping out . . . Do you think Matthew's all right? He doesn't seem to be anywhere. Do you think he could have smashed himself up on that ludicrous bike? I think I'll give it until lunchtime before I start phoning round hospitals.

✉

From: Sue James
Sent: Saturday, 22 September 15.54
To: Angela James
Subject: Re: I can't believe this is
    happening . . .

Lovely that you were logged on. When it's
this quick it is almost like having a conversation. You're right, I should either let her
stay with Hayley or book her a taxi back. I
think I prefer the Hayley option. What if the
taxi driver is a paedophile rapist?? But don't
worry, I'm not being overly hard on her.
When I was 14 I had to do much more than
she does. We did all our own clothes washing
by hand – do you remember? She is being
surprisingly supportive (moans about things a
lot, but does do what I ask), happy to stay
home last night with Lola when I had to rush
out on a call, and she seems to be quite cool
and grown up about the whole thing, much
cooler than me, but then she's not pregnant (I
hope). She has all the usual teenage moods
and grumpiness, picks fights over the silliest
things, like the fact that Iris has put creases
into her jeans, and she did manage to call me

a mean old bitch the other night which was particularly hurtful since I slipped her an extra twenty last weekend when she went to Top Shop (again) with her friends. But basically she seems fine. Yes good idea, I'll investigate online shopping this week. They can deliver while Iris is here . . . Masses of love S xxxx

Sunday 23rd September

Dear Diary,

Dad was supposed to be here tonight to help me with my essay on *Romeo and Juliet*. I understand the story, like the story even, it's kind of about teenagers, and Juliet was my age 'Rancid Miss Roberts' told us on Friday, but I don't understand the language and I have to explain a speech which reads like Ancient Greek to me. He never showed, so I haven't done it. I asked Mum if she'd help me and she said she would, but then Lola needed nit combing and I talked on the phone to Serena for about an hour and a half about absolutely nothing at all – I couldn't remember a single thing that we'd talked about the moment I put the phone down. Dad finally came in around 10 when I was almost asleep in the bath. They had this massive, mega-row in the kitchen. Mum just let rip at him, shouting and swearing about how selfish he was, how he thought it was OK to disappear without telling anyone where he was going, how he could just swan in here whenever he felt like it . . . and what about the kids, she goes, what about their needs, couldn't he for once, JUST ONCE (she shouted) put their needs first? At that point he went ballistic and told her that he always put their (our) needs first, and that he'd told her that he was going away for the weekend and that she was such a stupid cow she'd simply forgotten, and that if she ever stopped to consider his needs for just one moment, maybe he wouldn't have needed to leave or go away at all, at which point Mum burst into tears and he goes on shouting at her, shouting and shouting, so angry, so full of hatred. I lay in the bath and listened to all this and it was as if I wasn't there. Tears just came from nowhere and rolled down my face into the bathwater. It felt as if they were tearing at my own flesh as they tore each other apart, and I felt so alone suddenly, so distant and irrelevant, lying in an almost cold bath, listening to them rowing, terrified to get out in case they heard me, but also wanting to scream and cry at them both myself to make them stop. Then Mum kicked him out. She told him to go, so he did, without even coming in to see me, or Lola asleep in her bed upstairs. So then it really was as if I wasn't there. I lay there in the bath until it went completely cold and cried some more. Mum heard me get out of the bath. She sat down on the loo seat and pulled me on to her lap and rubbed my back like she used to do when I was a kid. She smiled weakly at me and said it was time I went to bed. She laughed when I asked her where Dad had been. 'I completely forgot to ask . . . Probably off with some bright young thing who doesn't want babies,' she goes. 'I don't know how he can suddenly come over all selfish, now of all times . . . he's so selfish, so preoccupied with his own little problems, so critical of me, everything I do isn't right . . . sometimes I think he doesn't really love me any more,' she said, as if she thought I might have the answer. But I don't. I don't want to hear how awful he is from her. How can I help her understand what's going on in her marriage when I've only ever snogged one boy and that didn't go very well? They're just my Mum and Dad. I don't want to know about their 'relationship'.

Dear Diary,

It's Wednesday and the house has been pretty calm since their mega row on Sunday. Dad hasn't been over and he hasn't phoned and I miss him. I miss hugging him last thing at night. He's also completely forgotten his promise to help me with my English homework and if I don't hand it in tomorrow I'll get a detention. Mum came in late and did a good arse-licking job on Iris – I'm soooooo sorry I'm late, group practice meeting went on for ever, here's an extra £20 – and then turned on me! Can you believe it! I'm sitting there watching the TV, not hurting nobody, minding my own business and she starts having a go, told me to take my feet off the table, had I remembered to empty the rubbish bin in my room and scoop the dirty washing off the floor, and why was Lola still up? Why hadn't I helped her with her spelling? And then she turned off the TV just as it was getting to the good part and told me to go and have a bath! How would she like it if I did that to her when she was in the middle of watching something! I'm fourteen now, I don't need to be TOLD to have a bath like I was six or something. I decide when I want a bath. She's out all evening and then she comes in throwing her weight around like that, like some mental retard, and there's no point arguing with her about it because she never listens, really listens when she's in that sort of a mood. I have to scream at her just to make myself heard sometimes, and then she doesn't actually HEAR what I'm saying. So I locked myself in the bathroom and used up all of her best bath stuff and now I smell really nice. I wish Dad was here though, to kiss me goodnight. Talk to you tomorrow.

From: Sue James
Sent: Wednesday, 26 September 23.13
To: Angela James
Subject: Frankie

Ange,

What a shitty, godforsaken, crap-filled day
I've had!!! A waiting room of patients,
including several of my least favourite who
seem to think I ought to be able to wave a
magic wand over them and make them
instantly better when I can't do anything for
them. Their future lies in their hands – give
up smoking, eating crap, fat food and go for a
walk every once in a while rather than
blaming me, then you might feel better is
what I'd like to be able to say bossily, but of
course can't. Matthew rang in my lunch hour
and continues to lay the blame at my feet. I'm
the one who stops him from feeling free
apparently, well what is 'freedom' for Christ
sake when you're 45 with a professional job
to do and two children and another on the
way? Does he think I have it any easier, any

freer? What does he want to do, travel the world like some adolescent and find himself? So lunch was indigestible and upsetting, followed by calls, one particularly upsetting one, won't go into that now, and then we had a group practice meeting which went on and on because none of the others have kids or homes worth going to, where they had the gall to have a go at me for not returning my patient files when there are stacks of them in their own rooms. So I stayed on and put them all back. What do we pay receptionists for if isn't to file as well . . .

Then home to chaos. Frankie watching some ghastly, gruesome hospital drama surrounded by crisp packets and sweet wrappings with a box of juice overturned on the floor, Lola running around NOT in her pyjamas at 9.30 and Iris looking glum because I was late and couldn't get through to her on the phone because it was permanently engaged (Frankie talking to Ruby/Serena/Saskia/Fran etc . . . probably nine-way calling at £100 a minute), and she's also probably had to contend with an unhelpful stroppy teenager all evening (we just can't lost Iris, how would we cope then?), and then, when I turned off the telly, Frankie just went berserk, screaming and shouting that she hated me with such anger in her face that

I know it's true, she really does hate me. There are people out there who really have it tough, real poverty. This child I saw today was malnourished, Ange, that was why he was ill, and when I had a look round their kitchen there was next to nothing in it. If Frankie knew just how lucky she was then maybe she'd appreciate me more and how much I do for her. She just ranted on, calling me every obscene name under the sun, accused me of never listening to her, and dumping down my responsibilities as a mother on to her. She's 14 Ange! She's not a baby any more, she's bigger than me. In two years' time she can leave school and earn her own living. She accuses me of never listening, but what about her? I have to call her about ten times before she comes down for supper (yet when I call 'Phone' she's there in a matter of seconds) and if she listened to what I said, I wouldn't have to nag her all the time about doing things, because she'd hear me in the first place. Do you think I've spoilt her? Is this all my fault? I know it's been difficult without Matthew and me pregnant, but we have a good life, she doesn't want for anything, she's LUCKY, only she doesn't know it.

Then to cap it all, in the middle of all this, Her Next Door chooses 9.40 p.m. – when

Lola's not in bed (Clare of course is), the house is in a mess, Frankie's screaming obscenities and I haven't even got my coat off – to have a little chat about the teacher, who she maintains can't spell the word 'toiletries', and seems to be picking on Clare, and had I noticed anything funny going on with this new teacher and Lola?? Well, have I had the time to notice? We're almost at half term and I still don't even know the woman's name. Is she even female? So I invited her in and offered her a cup of tea while Frankie sulked in the bath and Lola took herself to bed and I listened, just like I do at the Surgery, to her litany of complaints about the school, which seemed to me to be petty and indicative of a woman who doesn't have enough to do, and then my eyes fell upon the maple worktop where the phone stands by the fridge, and saw to my horror that Frankie had inscribed her initials with black biro into the corner. That worktop cost over £1,000 little more than a year ago! AAARGHHHH!! Well, I hope you have a better day, as you get up on the other side of the world. I'm off to bed! Night Night. S xxxxx

Dear Diary,

The trouble with Mum is that she thinks she's
the only one with problems. I don't know
whether its pregnancy which is making her so
self-centred, but it's all 'I've had such a bad
day/ I'm so tried/ I'm having to cope with all
of this alone without Matthew.' Well, what
about me? I don't have long, tiring, boring,
difficult days obviously and I'm just fine
without Dad, living with one grumpy old bag
for a parent and having to do all the work. She
asked me to take out the rubbish on my way
to school this morning. How was I supposed
to carry my school bag, which weighs about as
much as she does, as well? When I was
younger, Lola's age, she was just Mum and I
just loved her. Now I'm older she's just irritating. She thinks that having a neat, clean,
tidy house really matters and is miserable
about the fact that she can't have that. I think
that being true to yourself is much more
important. She thinks that wars and poverty
are inevitable and laughs when I argue with
her and accuse her of being complacent and
middle-aged, because how can one ever just
accept these two evils when they are so clearly
man-made? She gets really, really worried

about the smallest things and never seems to have any fun. I mean who are her friends exactly?? I am never, ever going to be like that when I'm older. I'm going to keep on having fun and BE FUN with my own children. It's so depressing just seeing her so depressed. Sometimes she looks so old and tired and that makes me feel happy because I don't look like that, but then I feel bad about thinking such a bad thought and sad because she is still my Mum and I love her, sometimes, when she's being nice and mumsy. Sometimes there are even times when I know that I really, really don't love her at all, when I hate her so badly I could hit her, and that makes me feel like an even badder person, because I ought to love her always. She is still my Mum.

Ruby's mum is fun. They have candle-lit dinners with interesting people dropping by, cool people who work in films and the music business because she's in PR and she has good dress sense. They TALK about things over dinner, important things, and they LAUGH. Serena's mum lets her stay out until 11 on a Saturday night, while Mum and I argue nearly every Saturday over whether it's 9 or 10. If I can stay out until 9, why can't it be 10? I never go to bed that early. Fran's mum is a shrink and spends most of her time chain-smoking at the kitchen table, which means that Fran will probably never smoke but be even more fucked up than the rest of us. At least she listens. She sits there and talks to us about things in an adult way, and I never hear her telling Fran to do things. We sit and discuss who is the most insecure and why. Ruby asked her to analyse her dreams last weekend. We all went back there to spend the night because Hayley's mum wouldn't have us all, and we had such a laugh interpreting what they all mean. Snakes are supposed to be willies apparently. Then Ruby asked Fran's mum to give us a definition of a psychopath, so that she could know when she came across one, and then we all fell about laughing when her mum listed the symptoms and Hayley said, 'That sounds like you, Ruby.' We can't ever laugh like that here. In fact Mum's in such a state that I'm not even sure that I really want any of my friends to come back here. I'm worried about what she might say. She's bound to shout at me in front of them, or make them feel unwelcome, AND there's never anything decent to eat here. Sometimes, when she's being really sweet to me, like the other night when all three of us curled up on the sofa in front of *Little Women*, eating our way through an entire box of Quality Street which she had bought on the way home, I feel like she's Mum again, but most of the time she's just irritating, either because she's sucking up to Iris and laughing in that fake way, or because she's having a go at me, in which case the only thing to do is escape to my room and put on the music really loud, so that I can have a good dance and I can't hear HER. Honestly, if I didn't have my friends to talk to, and you to talk to about my friends, I'd be pretty psycho now. Do you know that I found a rotting cucumber at the back of the fridge today? It had 'Best before September 4' on the label. That was weeks ago! Honestly doesn't anybody EVER clean out the fridge?

Monday, 1st October. I can't believe it's only Monday! *Four whole days until the weekend!*

Dear Diary,

I can't believe it. Do you know that in both breaks today all anybody could talk about was their boyfriends? I was SO BORED. Serena couldn't seem to say anything other than 'Should I dump him?' or 'I don't know whether or not I should dump him', and Fran kept going on about how good-looking and fit Sean was. I just sat there in between them, listening to this endlessly banal conversation, feeling stupid because I haven't got a boyfriend and can't contribute. Sean's gang eyed us up all lunchtime from the other side of the play-ground. They were probably saying the same things about us. Toby pretends I don't even exist, but I don't care really. He's had his hair cut too short and now all you can see are these enormous sticky out ears. Saskia wants us to bunk off early from school on Wednesday and go to the Common. It's double RS. What psycho timetabled that! What is the point of RS anyway? When I asked Mrs Friend all she could say was that most people in the world have

some faith and it is important to understand
their rituals and beliefs. Well they're all
complete IDIOTS aren't they, believing all that
rubbish.

BOYS I QUITE LIKE/LIKE/FANCY???

Toby – NO! Snogged already. Will – Spotty.
    Short. BO and Halitosis. Not even on the
list until he gets himself sorted.
Leo – OK . . . bit up himself though. Wears
    too much Lynx.
Sean – NO! Fran's boyfriend.
Mark – Quite sweet but his clothes sense is
    really sad and too much hair gel.
Simon – YES YES YES! Good looking but
    Saskia fancies him too.
Edward – At least the others don't know him,
    so I can pretend he's cool.

Dear Diary,

Tuesday. Saskia still wants us to bunk off to the
Common tomorrow, says the boys are planning
to meet near the lake. Feels risky, so many of us
disappearing. Ruby's not keen, says we'll get
caught and get detentions and that it isn't
worth it, just for an extra hour. She's right, but
it's still only Tuesday and the weekend feels like
a year away. The trouble with school is that they
cram all this information into your head, and by
the end of the day, you're so tired and you feel
as if there isn't any room left for anything more.
I have to write a two-page essay on a white
door for English – can you believe that!! I've
run out of things to say after just two sentences
– it's white and well, er . . . it's a door.
   Dad came round tonight for the first time
since their mega row. He was wearing this really
weird T-shirt, that said 'Cool Dude' across it,
and trainers! He never wears trainers unless he's
jogging so why now? Is he trying to look
younger or something? If so it doesn't work, he
just looks sad. He bought some flowers for
Mum, which made her smile, and a large
chocolate cake for us to share. Lola clung to
him like a limpet and wouldn't get off his lap.
I'd have liked to have done that too, but he

didn't offer, and then Ruby rang and we talked for ages about Saskia's plan and whether or not we were going. I want to; she's scared. Dad put Lola to bed and then asked if I wanted help with that essay on *Romeo and Juliet*. I said thanks but I'd done it, it was due in last week. Actually I copied off Serena at break-time, finished it off in detention and got a terrible mark for it.

Dear Diary,

Wednesday and I went. I've never done that before. Hope Mum never reads this. I'll have to find a good hiding place. The most thrilling thing was planning our escape and running at top speed out of the gates to the end of the road. It gave me this exhilarating sense of freedom, busting out of timetabled routine, and it was a lovely sunny day on the common, so we went hyper and ran around screaming, and then Serena picked up some conkers and we threw them up at the trees to try and dislodge some more. It was fun when we were just girls together, but then we met up with some of the boys and Fran and Serena went all silent and giggly and flirty which REALLY irritated me because I don't see why they have to be so two-faced about it, just be yourself. They passed round a joint and I had a bit. It made me cough a lot, but then I felt all lightheaded and dizzy and it was kind of nice not to be thinking of anything. Then, when the boys left, Serena and Fran started on about 'Should I dump him?/ Do you fancy him?/ It'd be better to dump him before he dumps me, wouldn't it?' And then they started texting the very boys they were talking about dumping, and since I had no one to text because all my friends were there, I went home. Mum already home and cooking worst thing. She seems to think that the way to get us to eat more vegetables is to fry hundreds of them up together in an indigestible stir fry. So I eat a Kit Kat and a Mars bar from the larder without her noticing it, just to keep me going, and then as I'm trying to eat the stuff she calls dinner, she starts having a go about Granny, how we have to all go and see her on Sunday because we might not get much of a chance once the baby's here. Dad's offered to drive us up and take us out for lunch and won't that be fun to be all together. Can't wait. Honestly, she hates Granny. She's just making us all come along so that she can feel less guilty about having dumped her in a stinking old people's home 100 miles away. It takes ALL DAY to get there, in a smelly car with Dad cursing every other motorist on the road. That's one whole day out of the two a week that are free to call my own. I don't see why I have to go, she's not my mother, and when am I supposed to do my homework? I asked her if she could think of anything I could write down about a white door, but she just looked blankly at me for a few seconds and then said, 'What a ridiculous assignment,' and walked out of the room. Thanks Mum.

From: Sue James
Sent: Sunday 7 October 22.41
To: Angela James
Subject: Mum

Dearest,

All four of us went up to North Butting today. Matthew bounded in through the front door wearing a slashed T-shirt, combat trousers and sneakers – brand-new clothes meant for a 22-year-old, at which point I sort of knew that something is seriously wrong. I just felt so sorry for him. I may be enormous and totally devoid of all dress sense according to Frank, but he looked ridiculous and Frankie just laughed at him. It was his idea though, that we should all go up and see Mum, which is amazing and the first sign of the ice thawing . . . I told him that I hadn't seen her since the beginning of the summer, and that when we had our weekly conversation on the phone last Friday, she sounded pretty low. Driving that distance alone, when I'm only just over the six-month mark and

118

already the size of Anglesey (can't think why Lola still insists on addressing my stomach as 'Tiny'), felt frightening. Funny how pregnancy makes you that much more wary of any potential danger, yet if danger were to be staring me in the face I know I could summon up the strength to move mountains. Matt said we should all go, and booked lunch in this amazing French restaurant. Mum was thrilled to be taken out. She twinkled as she sat there and wolfed down every morsel on her plate (it was delicious), drank half a bottle of wine, and then racked up the guilt by complaining about the food at North Butting. She KNOWS that there is no alternative, that she needs round the clock care, and that if she falls any more that could really be the end of her, but still she digs in the knife, knowing how to hurt and make me feel bad. She's always been adept at that. When we talked about her in the car on the way home, Frankie uttered her one and only considerate sentence of the entire day which was, 'I think you need therapy Mum.'

'Nothing I'd like better,' I replied. 'Only I haven't the time.'

We hardly argued at all and everyone tried to be on their best behaviour, except Frankie of course, who made a point of not trying, and sulked all the way there in the back of the car with her Walkman headphones on and refused to play ball with Granny. She reminds me of Mum actually when she's in that sort of mood, you never know quite what she'll say next. She's SO recalcitrant at the moment she makes me want to scream . . . typical teenage narcissism, nobody else in the world matters except her, and then Matthew comes on far too strong with the 'Don't you talk to your father like that' attitude, because he feels guilty about being away, which winds Frankie up even more because he's not there. 'I'll talk to you any way I want,' she snarled at him at one point on the way home. She was being particularly abhorrent, but he needs to go easy on her. You don't have to have a degree in psychology to see that he was arguing with her so that he didn't have to argue with me. Anyway, Mum seemed fine really, but she does want to see you and the boys 'before I kick the bucket' as she so charmingly puts it, and I promised I'd talk to you and see if we could fix on some date next year that she could look forward to. I know, I know. She's laying on the guilt thick and fast because she hasn't actually got anything else to do (although she has made a lovely tapestry cushion cover with an owl on it – you might get it for Christmas), and because she knows that there isn't much more that either of us can do. Anyway, let me know what you think . . . perhaps you could make it here in the spring. I should still be off work then with 'Tiny' so we could have some fun together.

The leaves are beginning to turn a golden brown and already there are fireworks going off every night, bangers in dustbins and underneath cars. Nothing much else to report other than that I'm getting to the 'not being able to see my feet' stage. Went swimming with Lola yesterday and couldn't match my feet with the leg holes in the costume. Lola had to guide me in. Clare's been given a designer dressing gown costing £200 by her loving mother because it's Saturday I suppose, and, as Clare told me rather knowingly last night, 'It is getting much colder' as she refused my lasagne but helped herself to heaps of chocolate ice cream for pudding. So now Lola wants one and can't understand why I won't buy her one too, and thinks I'm a stingy cow for saying that I wouldn't even spend that kind of money on a dressing gown for myself when I've stopped growing, well almost. They've both got nits again so shoved them in the bath after supper, smothered them with DDT and spent about six hours combing out the eggs in front of *Blind Date*.

Getting used to being home alone . . . there's more to do for the kids, but there's also Iris (Lola's beginning to warm to her), and it means I don't have to think about Matthew at all. I can eat pasta and cheese with the kids and then haul myself up the stairs to bed with Lola at half past eight and not feel guilty about not having the energy to listen to his day, like a good wife should, because he isn't here. Not having to worry about sex is blissful too, when I feel about as erotic as a lump of lard . . . the combination of pregnancy and middle age is SO unsexy. I caught sight of myself in the mirror as I was going to bed the other night. My face was covered with anti-wrinkle cream, I wore a tent-like, stripy prison night shirt and it was only 9 o'clock!! All that was missing were the curlers. And then there's Frank, oozing sexuality through every pore, alert, youthful, vibrant, she runs up the stairs two at a time. Mind you I did have a rather wonderful frisson yesterday in the car wash. Matthew usually does that and now I know why. There is something deeply sexy about sitting inside your car while a host of young, black rough trade soap your body without saying a word, just staring in this rather blank and mysterious way through the bubbles . . . ooooh it still gives me the shivers. The car is going to be a lot cleaner from now on!

Must go to bed – correction – must drag Frankie away from the TV and make *her* go to bed. Who knows, we might even get to have a conversation rather than an argument about Matthew and today. Let me know what you think about Mum, and when you might next be able to come. Sorry to do this, but I have an ulterior motive, I long to see you too . . . much love S xxx

Dear Diary,

It's Thursday 11th October and I have today, officially, become a woman. I got my period in Geography and had to ask to be excused. The teacher didn't want to let me go at first, you're not supposed to go to the loo in the middle of lessons, but then Ruby who was sitting next to me spilled the beans. 'She's got her period Miss. Can I go with her?' she said at the top of her voice. Thanks Rubes.

It's kind of manky getting it at school. I didn't have any pads on me or any spare knickers of course, and Ruby had to lend me one of hers and explain how to put them in the bins rather than down the loo, which most of the cretins in this school don't seem to know, or else they think it's funny, which is REALLY PATHETIC AND IMMATURE because the loos are so disgusting when they're blocked that you don't want to go in at all and have to hold your nose when you do. I didn't have any pains or anything, but it did feel kind of weird walking around with this great wadge between my legs. I mean, how do you run for the bus exactly without it falling out? Everyone was really nice about it at break-time. We've all started our periods

124

now except for Saskia and Hayley, and Saskia's really pissed about not getting hers before me. I could tell because she was completely silent, while everyone else told when they first started. I thought that you bled bucket loads but apparently not. Ruby says it's normal to just have stains at first and it has this really sweet smell, the blood. I felt quite light-headed on the way home, like I had this secret that nobody else knew about and I felt suddenly much more grown up.

Mum wasn't there when I got home and I wasn't about to tell Iris and Lola. Then when Mum did finally come home she was so stressed out and tearful, because she'd had another mega row with Dad on her mobile as she was driving home through the pouring rain and had smashed into the back of a car and had to wait for ages for the police to come because the other driver was so furious that swapping names and addresses wasn't good enough . . . so I left it, didn't tell her, didn't wanna bother her with it really. Wasn't sure though how long the bleeding would last and whether I had to wear pads at night as well, so I rang Ruby.

From: Sue James
Sent: Sunday 14 October 08.51
To: Angela James
Subject: Re: Mum

Don't give me a hard time about this, please Ange. I actually don't think it's so unreasonable to ask for some sort of date out of you, so that Mum has something to look forward to. If you have to pull out or change your plans then so be it. She may not even remember by that stage, who knows what might happen by next year? She seems to me to be steadily ageing and decaying anyway. Do you think you might be able to make it over for the funeral? Sorry Darling, I know you feel guilty about living so far away from her, but think how guilty I feel when I'm the only one here and still I don't have the time to go and see her or be nice to her. PLEASE ANGE . . . I'm shattered, hormonally in orbit. Lola's practically a teenager, criticizes everything daily from the way my shoes aren't polished to the fact that we never ever have what Clare has next door, which drives me completely round the bend, and Frankie is so pre-menstrual that

I think she just might explode if she doesn't get her period soon . . . I'm permanently in tears and irritable, everything and everyone drives me mad, the house is a complete tip and I just long for a day to myself when I can sort everything out . . . Imagine having whole school days to fiddle at home like HND, I think I could be the vision of contented pregnancy if I did. As it is I crave just an hour to myself, I crave fun before I forget what that means AND I smashed the car up this week. It's so worthless that it's probably a write off anyway . . . So I really don't need this from you too. PLEASE, ANGE, PLEASE GIVE ME A BREAK AND JUST GIVE ME A DATE, ANY OLD FUCKING DATE WILL DO . . .

Gotta go, promised Lola pancakes before Matthew picks her up to take her swimming. Frankie asleep with half a dozen girls on the sitting-room floor after a night of back-to-back videos, so Lola can't watch Sunday morning telly and is FURIOUS. Sue x

✉

From: Sue James
Sent: Sunday 14 October 21.51
To: Angela James
Subject: Re: Mum

Sorry Sorry Sorry, I'm sorry too . . . I hate
scrapping with you, always did. Even when
we were kids I was always scared that something would happen to you when we fought,
that you'd die or something and that I'd never
forgive myself. Perhaps that was just secret
sibling rivalry wish fulfilment! Easter fab –
I'll call Mum tomorrow, and yes, good idea,
I'll get some of those photos you sent printed
up and send them on to her. Love the one of
all four of you on the beach. I've made it my
screen saver.

I'm calmer now because Lola's been out all
day with Matthew and I fiddled a little in
the kitchen and then went back to bed for
most of the rest of the day with the Sunday
papers. Frankie's walked round in a zombie-
like state after her sleepover, but managed to
load up the dishwasher and put it on which
is a miracle, before she crawled into bed
beside me which was rather sweet. She

128

looks like she did as a baby when she's asleep, her cheeks sort of puff up and it was lovely just being us two together all cosy. She hasn't got into bed with me like that for years, not since she was about ten when she went through that excruciating stage of not being able to go to sleep, and we used to snuggle down together in her bed and I told her stories in the dark, soothing stories. Funny how even though she's bigger, almost a woman, she still so much a child. When she woke up I made us hot chocolate and toast, brought a tray back to bed and we read the papers together. It was such a relief just not doing anything else, and then she asked me rather sweetly if I was frightened about the pain of giving birth, so we talked a bit about that, and I tried to reassure her that it's not all that bad when of course it's worse than having red hot needles shoved through your eyeballs . . .

Then Matthew came back with Lola and made us all some cheese on toast and we actually had quite a nice time together. I think it has something to do with the fact that I am so tired that I just can't be bothered to argue with him any more, whatever he wants goes at the moment, so he feels in control and rather paternalistic. He's offered to take charge of the car and find a good nearly new one this week, which is a complete weight off my mind. Frankie wants a purple one, Lola wants pink, Matthew said he'd do his best to make them both happy (which means it'll be yellow). I also asked him if there was any chance that he could pick up Lola from a party on Thursday and take her shopping for some new school shoes at the weekend (the only pair of size 13s in black or brown in the whole of London that I managed to track down during the last week of the summer holidays have fallen to pieces – so much for cheap, off-the-peg shoes) and miraculously he agreed to do both before he slipped off to his oh so precious freedom. I hate him not being here, it's like there's this massive aspect of the house that is missing, but then, when he is here, I wonder whether I hate him being here more. He's still just as irritating as he ever was, and as soon as he walks in through the door every single aspect of his personality that I find most irritating seems to resurface in less than ten minutes, and I feel like I have to leave the room. I know you still think he's having an affair, and you may be right, but I'm so tired at the moment I haven't got the energy to fight with him, or to try and trick him or track whoever she is down, so it's just a relief to shut the door on him.

Masses of love Sue xxx

Dear Diary,

It's Thursday 18th October and nearly the end
of another boring week. Araminta Moulder
cornered me in the corridor and said I'd been
late six times this term, and I owed the maths
teacher three lots of homework, and was everything all right at home. Prying bitch. Lesbian
saddo. She always wants to know about stuff,
like the moment I'm not talking to someone she
wants to know why, she wants us to sit down
together and sort it out, but she's soooooo
creepy and maybe we wanna be able to sort
things out for ourselves. Told her everything was
fine and that I'd catch up with the maths over
the weekend. Saskia got caught texting Fran in
the middle of a really boring history lesson and
has had her mobile confiscated until half term
which has sent her psycho – 'What if I'm lost
and need to call my mum? What if some weirdo
tries to come on to me and I need to call the
police? What if I SEE a murder and need to tell
somebody?' She can't stop talking about it and
she has a point. I mean what is the point of
giving kids mobiles to keep them safe if the
teachers take them away? Fran's dumped Sean,
and now, instead of talking the whole time
about whether she should dump him, she talks

about whether or not she's made a mistake, and should she get back together with him? 'He's so fit,' she says, but he just looks like a wimp to me who thinks he's better looking than he is – but when I told her that once, she didn't talk to me for days, so I daren't say that again.

The highlight of today was definitely on our way home from school when I dared Ruby to nick as many packets of sugar as she could from Burger King. She managed to stuff two fistfuls into her bag before she ran out on to the pavement, and then we got so hyper on all that sugar that we couldn't stop laughing, and then she dared me to jaywalk across the road with my eyes shut and my arms stretched out in front. I gave her my bag, listened out for cars, and then crossed without looking. It was kind of scary but it was a quiet road with not much traffic. She did it too, and then when Fran did it a car had to brake suddenly and we all ran off up the street laughing.

I'm thinking of getting my hair cut, shorter, in a bob, and sort of shaped to make it look thicker. I feel I need to do something to make the most of myself. Saskia has such long legs and a perfect figure – BITCH – and enough money to buy whatever she likes. If I had what she has maybe I'd feel happier about myself. I'd like my hair to stick out but I'm not sure how you do that. Mum says she'll pay. She's thinking of going shopping at the weekend to get stuff for the baby. I might go with her and get it done then. I mean all shopping's fun isn't it, even if it's for baby stuff? And who knows, there may even be something that I can wangle for me.

From: Sue James
Sent: Saturday 20 October 22.39
To: Angela James
Subject: Baby gear

Had such a lovely day with Lola today, she is so excited about this baby, she's cleared a corner of her bedroom for Tiny to sleep in (in what though is my worry), talks all the time of how she's going to feed it with a bottle and sing it lullabies and look after it while I'm at work (which is a rather worrying thought) and she churns out regular works of art for the walls for Tiny to look at in his or her corner. I'm beginning to feel quite energetic really, all things considered. It's those hormones sizzling around and my skin feels fantastic with all that oestrogen. Perhaps HRT really is a good idea. We had such fun picking out baby things together. You can get such groovy stuff for babies now, really lovely Babygros, rather than the boring old pink, blue or white plain ones which were around when Frank was tiny. We bought a furry snuggle sack in fake leopard skin to go inside a buggy because it will be January when Tiny's born and I'm contemplating getting one of those three-wheel buggy things rather than a Maclaren. What do you think? What did you use with the twins? Don't know what to do about a cot yet either, they're so expensive that I'm wondering whether I ought to see if I can borrow one, but the trouble is I'm so off the baby circuit that I don't know anyone with small children any more. Lola of course wanted to get mobiles and teddy bears and baby toys, but I held her back and told her that Christmas was the time for all that. I know it's stupid, Ange, pathetic really, but just touching all that stuff made me feel really cosy again. I'm planning to really snuggle down with this miracle baby, with or without Matthew.

Frankie was a complete pain in the arse today. (God I feel like it's such a betrayal to even say this about one's own child, even to you.) She wasn't remotely interested in the baby stuff, snarled when I tried to involve her and made it quite clear that she resented every minute of being with us and was only blessing us with her presence because the next step was a hairdresser's appointment, for her. She followed us round the store texting her friends, sent a tower of nappies flying because she wasn't looking where she was going and didn't seem to care, and then accused me of being mean when I refused to buy her a T-shirt with I SWALLOW written across the chest. (Honestly, what is a T-shirt like that doing in the children's department, even if it is the teens section??) I could have killed her. She was of course the height of politeness to the woman who was cutting her hair (at least that's something to be proud of I suppose) and she looked fantastic with her hair shorter, really grown up and stylish, and I'm thrilled because it means that she can't spend hours fiddling with her hair and fretting over how it looks every morning before school when she ought to be eating breakfast, but the moment we got back to the car (with heaps of shopping, which she refused to help carry because she had to text every single one of her friends and tell them that she had just had her hair cut) and she looked at herself in every wing mirror, she went into a major strop and said that she hated it! I used every ounce of my remaining energy trying to reassure her, because it does look really good, but she wouldn't believe me, said she wished she'd never had it done and burst into tears.

The awful thing was that I didn't feel in

the least bit sympathetic, because she'd been so awful to be with for most of the morning. I hugged her of course, told her there was no point in crying, to which she just wailed 'THERE IS!' and cried even more, but I just felt cross with her, and then guilty for not being a loving enough mother, and of course she picks up on that and said, 'You don't even care, do you, that I've just ruined my whole life?' and 'You've always loved Lola more,' which isn't true, it never was true. I love them both so much that it hurts sometimes, but what children don't realize is that when they are monstrous, they are harder to love at that moment, but that doesn't mean you don't love them, if you know what I mean. Anyway, then Lola burst into tears and I burst into tears, and we stood there hugging each other in the car park, and then Frankie started to laugh and said that maybe her hair wasn't that bad anyway, and that perhaps with a clip to one side it would look better, and then Lola really made her laugh by saying that if she has a spot she could pull the long side down a bit over her cheek and nobody would see it. So I took them both out for a slap-up lunch, said we'd go classy, provided Frankie didn't text anybody even once.

She perked up once she had some fillet steak and pommes frites and a 5000-calorie chocolate milkshake. She couldn't resist banging on about how you should never eat protein and carbohydrates together though, 'I mean EVERYBODY knows you shouldn't have meat and carbs together because it just makes you fat', but she ate it all the same. Every meal we have some sort of comment or lecture about the food on her plate – she refuses toast because it's 'dripping with butter', meat revolts her because all she can see is the fat which somehow jumps straight on to her bottom. She's not anorexic, she loves food too much and I don't think she's puking it up, but she does look at the food on her plate sometimes as if it were an enemy rather than a friend, which worries me a little. I chat on in a sort of doctorly way about nutrition and the need for some fat in order to be able to menstruate, but most of that either goes over her head or irritates her. 'I wish you didn't know so much Mum' she once said when I listed the iron content of various red meats. I know I'm not the best example as a mother. It's hard to eat just one biscuit and not the whole packet, and half the weight I've put on this pregnancy has been because of comfort eating, but since I can't drink there

139

has to be SOMETHING to reassure me with Matthew gone. I'm bound to be diabetic by the time I'm 50, which is irresponsible, BUT honestly, how can protein and carbs be bad for you when most of the best food in the world involves the two? Smoked salmon and cream cheese bagels, spaghetti Bolognese, bangers and mash . . .

The waiter looked a bit like Leonardo Di Caprio and flirted with her, which helped, and she only went to the loo three times to check on her hair, and we talked a bit, the three of us, about Matthew, or at least I talked about how much he loved them both and that he just needed some time to himself. They listened and looked a little glum, which made me want to cry all over again. I tried to coax stuff about school out of Frankie – how was the coursework going? what was her form tutor like? that sort of thing, but it was like getting blood out of a stone. I wonder sometimes whether it's the right place for her . . . I THINK she's learning and happy there, but how can I really know? It won't be long before I have to go through that whole transfer thing with Lola . . . what a ghastly thought . . . Bedtime. Have a good day. Masses of love Sue xxxxx

Sunday Night

Dear Diary,

I REALLY HATE MY HAIRCUT UGHHH-HHHH! I wish I'd never had it done and I wish that someone, anyone, of my friends, even Saskia, was here to tell me what they really think before I have to face the whole world at school tomorrow. They're all gonna laugh at me, on the bus, in the playground, I just know it. Why does everybody have to be away this weekend? Why couldn't someone have taken me with them, taken me away from this dump? Staying in with Mum and Lola on a Saturday night was just the pits. There was nothing good on the telly and Mum spent about an hour on the phone with Julie (perhaps she'd like to adopt me since she hasn't already got a daughter and Mum's about to have three) so Mum wasn't much use, as a mother that is. I mean it would have been quite nice to have her help me with something important like the hundred maths homeworks I owe Miss Smart, instead of just gossiping like that about Fuck All. I sat there listening until Lola screamed from the bathroom because she had shampoo in her eyes and Mum asked me if I could help Lola rinse her hair. Do you know they talked for at least ten minutes about the vast quantities of rubbish we seem to produce, with Mum wittering on about how we recycle our newspapers and bottles, we never go shopping, and yet still we seem to have mountains more black bin bags outside our house than anybody else in the street – God! Can you believe it? I'm SOOOOOO BORED I COULD SCREAM . . . And I've run out of credit on my phone so I can't even text anyone. When everyone's away like this or busy, I feel as if I'm the only person left alive on the planet, so after I got Lola out of the bath I went up to my bedroom and put Capital radio on full blast and customized a few T-shirts by cutting jagged slashes down the front.

We spent so long in the baby department yesterday that Mum came close to actually having it. She's GIGANTIC. She makes a whale look small. It must be really weird being that big and she's put on tons of weight around the top of her arms and the fat sort of wobbles . . . EUGHHH! When she walks she waddles like a duck which is soooo embarrassing and when she climbs stairs she wheezes. I mean how can a doctor be that unfit?? She can't drive the new car. She keeps scrunchign the gears and when she tried to park in a multistorey car park yesterday it was so excruciatingly embarrassing I just wanted to die. There were three cars waiting patiently behind us while she went backwards and forwards, gear scrunching, stalling and even clipping a post with the bumper ('Don't tell dad' she goes, 'how much is it worth?'), trying to get into a space which was wider than Top Shop, and when I asked her if I could get out (so that I could hide) she just shouted at me to shut up so that she could concentrate. Charming. When she finally managed to park the thing about three hours later she had come in so close to the car next door that she couldn't open her door wide enough to manoeuvre the stomach out and had to climb over to my side and get out that way.

I don't know whether it's pregnancy that makes her louder or just middle age, but she has this awful thing of chatting with sales assistants as if they were her best friends (probably because she's only got one friend in the whole world) in this loud way. It's like she thinks she's the only one in the shop and she chats on and on, asking unanswerable questions, like is this buggy waterproof? Is this mattress filled with natural fibres and flameproof? She even had the nerve to try and barter with one of the sales assistants. This is a department store Mum, not an Arab market. So I kept my distance, pretended I wasn't with her. And then she goes all soppy over the Babygros just because they're small. What's the big deal about that? Babies are small, so they need small clothes. What a saddo! She spent so much money on stuff that she can't possibly need yet that I didn't dare ask her for anything for me. I really want an eyelash curler, but Mum just laughed when I asked her if I could have one. What's so funny about that?

Why does she have to be having a baby NOW? Why didn't she get him to use a condom for fuck's sake. If she wasn't pregnant, Dad'd still be here. I think even *Match of the Day* and the sound of them rowing is better than the deathly silence there is here after Mum and Lola have gone to bed.

I can't believe I didn't mention the car! It's a 2-year-old Ford Focus, black with greyish seats and I'm planning to keep it really clean. All food consumption is banned and I'll be at the car wash at least once a week. It feels really good just sitting in it, and driving round London is almost a pleasure. I can't believe that we waited this long to invest in a new car, given that I'm in it most of the week, on call, driving the kids round, Sainsbury's. My only worry is that the seat doesn't go back any further. It's already at full stretch and my rotund belly only just gets in behind the steering wheel. What happens in a month's time if I can't even get in the bloody thing to drive it? That's what happens when a non-pregnant man buys a car. (I know . . . I know . . . I handed over the entire job to him, but I think he should have at least rung me and asked me if I wanted to come along and test drive the thing. Take care of it

Matthew, but at least consult me.) Still, it's got a radio and CD player and a heater that really works, so the girls are thrilled! No more blankets in the bleak midwinter . . . . HND typically patronizing about it, was out there the moment Matthew brought it round and called it 'Sweet'. Matthew wants to take Lola away next weekend. Frank steadfastly refuses to go. He was wearing an extra-ordinarily expensive looking purple silk shirt when he came with the car, not the sort of crisp white or stripey style he usually buys at all, which was a little ominous.

Absolutely no point sending over any of your baby stuff, but lovely thought, and yes Mum loved the photos. She's very perky at the moment on the phone. S xxx

Dear Diary,

Everyone SAID they liked my haircut except for
Saskia, which means she's probably jealous. I put
SAID because you never know what they might
be really saying about it behind my back. They're
all so two-faced, I can't trust any of them, except
perhaps Ruby. I think it's so sick, so immature,
you ought to say what you mean and mean what
you say. I suppose it's not that bad, my haircut.
I'm gonna get some gel tomorrow and see if I
can make it stick out at the side with the
hairdryer. Mum commented today on my breasts,
said she thought they were growing, which is
progress I suppose, except that one of them
seems to be bigger than the other which is still so
dormant it's probably dead. What happens if I
only get one breast? When I asked Mum this
question she just laughed and said, 'How many
one-breasted women do you see walking the
streets?' Well how would I know when you can
buy false ones? Maybe half the world's women
only have one breast and nobody realizes????

Dear Diary,

Mum is driving me more mad than ever because Dad isn't here. I get asked to do EVERYTHING, just because Dad isn't here to do it. She's decided that we all have to have specific jobs, now that she's so fat she can barely walk up the stairs. I have to unload the dishwasher BEFORE I go to school, when it's hard enough work just getting there on time in the first place AND I have to take all the rubbish out. All Lola has to do is tidy up her toys. When I pointed out that this was really unfair, Mum just said that when she was 14 she and Auntie Angela used to have to wash and dry up every night and do all their own clothes washing by hand. Well, what's the point in us doing all of that when we have dishwashers and washing machines now? She should be pleased that we don't have to do all that crap, that we can have a better childhood and spend more time on our school work. I get shouted at because Dad isn't here for her to shout at. I'm the one that has to be more grown-up around here, just because Dad isn't grown-up enough to stay. I hate it and I hate Dad for leaving. He's taking Lola away next weekend, but I'm not going to go because it means not being with my friends for two weekends, and we're going shopping on Saturday afternoon, and he's cross about that. Well, too bad. He should find something that I want to do if he wants to see me, like take me and my friends to Thorpe Park. Now that would be fun. Isn't that what divorcing dads are supposed to do?

Dear Diary,

Araminta Moulder asked to see me at break-time, which was really annoying because not being with my friends means they get the chance to bitch about me. She says I'm still behind with my maths homework, but it's not true. I know I handed at least one in and smart-arse must have lost it. She kept stroking me on the back as if she knew me really well, like she was my Mum or something. How dare she? She really is some sort of Lesbian Psycho, and she thinks she's so cool, like she's young or something. 'Come and talk to me when you need a friend,' she said in this really creepy way. UGGHH! She'd have to be the last person on earth I'd go to if I had problems, but I just said, 'Yes Miss . . . Sorry Araminta.'

When I got back to the others on the bench they were planning another break out, but for the whole afternoon this time. So long as it's on double RS day I'm up for it. Told them about Miss Moulder and Ruby reckons she fancies me. How sick is that???

Dear Diary,

Shopping wasn't much fun today because none
of us had any money, and Fran and Saskia
wanted to go to Covent Garden while the rest
of us wanted to stay in Oxford Street, and we
couldn't decide what to do. It was so wet,
pouring with rain and in the end we danced
around in the rain instead and kicked through
puddles. Then we couldn't decide what to do
next, whose house to go to or whether to go to
the cinema. I went home with Ruby and we
had a hot bubble bath and talked about boys.
The trouble is there's no one that I fancy at
school. They're all either creeps or short, and
the taller ones are sixth form and much too old.
Mr Thompson's all right. Except he's a teacher
and that's against the law. Mum says she'll take
me for a bra fitting after school on Wednesday
because she's got a half day and she needs a
bigger one. I wanna go, except that's the day
that we're planning on taking the whole afternoon off. She offered to give me the money if I
wanted to go and buy one with my friends,
which could be fun, but it would also be nice to
do something with Mum and NOT with Lola
for a change. She's on call tomorrow so we
can't do it then. Ruby came back to stay and

the three of us watched *The Shining*. Mum got so scared that she buried her head in my lap and said the baby was jumping around inside her. She's sweet when she's scared. She's also much nicer to be with when she isn't with Lola. Lola rang and said she was homesick and that she had to go riding in the rain and hated it. How could she be homesick when she was with Dad, when half her genes come from his willy and when she complains all the time about how much she misses him when she is at home? Pathetic.

Dear Diary,

Wednesday. Mum said this morning that she had to work late because one of the other doctors was off sick, so we couldn't go for the bra fitting. She gave me some money in case I wanted to go anyway with Ruby, but actually it would have been quite nice to have gone with Mum. She said we'd go at the weekend if I didn't get one today, but if she had met me after school I'd have had a perfect excuse not to bunk off with the others and give the sicko Miss Moulder another chance to sexually assault me in the corridor because I've missed school. Instead of which I sort of felt I had to go with them. We went to the Common, and then it started to rain, and then Saskia goes how we ought to go to my house because Mum's at work and she'll be back late. When I said why can't it be your house, your Mum's at work too, she goes that my house is nearer and it's raining, so I said yes because I didn't want to seem mean by saying no, but actually we all know that Saskia's mum'd probably ground her for a year if she found so much as a smudge on the carpet. We had a laugh on the bus – decided it was National Smiling Day and went up to everyone we passed and said 'Happy

National Smiling Day', which made them all smile even though it was raining, but then, when we got home and Toby, Jack and that spotty freak Will arrived, I wondered why I'd agreed to any of this in the first place. They went through the cupboard and ate all the biscuits. Toby had a look through Dad's drink cupboard, and I had to shout at him to leave it alone, and Jack knocked one of Mum's plants off the windowsill and smashed the pot. If Mum'd been there it wouldn't have bothered me. She could've dealt with it, but because she wasn't I felt responsible, and also we weren't supposed to be there at all so I got really stressed out. 'Chill out,' Toby kept saying. 'Frigid cow needs a good jacking off,' said the sicko Will. 'Why don't you give her one,' he added as they raced upstairs to my bedroom, laughing, and left me to clear up the mess.

Ruby and Fran stayed with me to help, but Saskia, Hayley and Nat ran up after the boys like some sex addicts. We sat round the kitchen table eating our way through a large packet of crisps, talking about piercings. Ruby wants to get a double ear piercing, but her Mum says one hole in any ear is enough, and I want to get my belly button pierced, but Mum won't hear of it, says it's mutilation and it'll get infected and pusy when actually it just looks good when you're wearing hip trousers and a small top, and I'll keep it clean. Fran's mum'll let her do whatever she wants. It's my body not Mum's, it's up to me what I do with it, but neither me or Ruby can face the row if we do anything about it. It's hard to hide a belly button ring when the whole point is showing it. At least we haven't got a mum like Saskia's. She won't let her do anything. She freaks completely when she wears clothes other than the ones her mother puts out for her. Can you believe that? A mother who tells you what to wear when you're fourteen? I mean, I know my mum's strict, but she's not that bad really, not half as overprotective as Saskia's mum.

When we finally got up to my bedroom, there was crap music playing, mud on my carpet and Toby was prancing around with a pair of my knickers on his head, smoking a joint. I really really wanted them all to get out of my room and go, but I couldn't say so, and now I feel really weak and pathetic for not being able to stand up to them. So I coughed on a joint and felt a bit better about it all, and then Toby starts trying to come on to me, and although I suppose I ought to feel flattered that he still fancies me, actually I just felt sick at the thought of kissing him, so I didn't, and then he got cross with me for not kissing him when I never wanted to in the first place. He let me roll a joint though, which was kind of fun. I don't think I did very well, it sort of came unstuck. By the time Iris came home with Lola

I didn't really care about anything any more, and it was all worth it, just for the look on her face when she found ten people giggling in front of *Blue Peter*. We've invented a new game – sofa surfing. The boys sit in a line on the sofa and then you run and throw yourself across them and they surf you over the top. Quite fun, particularly when you're stoned. Iris didn't know what to make of it. 'Are you all staying for tea?' she goes rather nervously, which just made us all laugh even more.

Dear Diary,

Thursday. Mum didn't mention the mess, so she either didn't notice that her favourite pot had been broken and that the sofa legs are rather wobbly, or she doesn't mind. She picked up Lola from school at lunchtime today, so that she could take her with her to the hospital when she went for a check-up about the baby. Why didn't she take me as well? I'd have liked to have seen my new baby sister in the womb, and I too would have liked an afternoon off school and hot chocolate and cakes at a patis-serie. She didn't manage the bra fitting, but she could take Lola to the hospital with her. I know it's childish to say 'It's not fair' but it just isn't. They came home so happy, and I just felt left out. They brought me a chocolate éclair, and a picture of the baby which we've stuck up on the fridge with a magnet, but it's not the same thing.

From: Sue James
Sent: Sunday 4 November 08.22
To: Angela James
Subject: Are you OK?

Ange darling, are you OK??? Haven't heard
from you at all in two weeks, that's all. I
know I haven't been in touch either, but I'm
just such a worrier at the moment and I had
this extraordinary and rather terrifying dream
about you which has kept me awake half the
night. I dreamt that you and the twins were
in a rocket that was orbiting the earth, and
you couldn't get back down, and I was
standing on the roof of this very tall building
waving at you, with the wind and the rain
lashing around me and making the building
shake, and I was calling your name and
crying. I woke up crying. I never normally
remember my dreams, but with this pregnancy for some reason they've all been so
vivid. I think now Matt's not here I miss you
more. It's like I'm completely alone, with
Mum in a home, you in a rocket somewhere,
and Matthew roaring round London on a
Harley Davidson.

I took Lola with me to Antenatal on Thursday because I knew they'd give me an ultrasound at 30 weeks and I wanted her to feel part of the process. Frankie's too old really to get jealous, but Lola might. She says she's really into the idea, but once it's born and I'm preoccupied and exhausted and breastfeeding, things could easily change, particularly with Matthew not here. Had to pay a call this week on a family where a four-year-old pushed his six-month-old baby sister down the stairs. She was OK, but she could easily not have been. We saw the baby yawn inside which was amazing, even for me, and then she sucked her thumb. Lola kissed my tummy as I stood up to get dressed, and said, 'See you after Christmas, Tiny,' which was sweet. Hospital policy is not to tell the mother the sex of the baby (high Moslem community and don't want too many aborted girls), but the registrar said he'd tell me if he could see anything obvious, but the damn umbilical cord was smack in front of the genitals, so it's probably a girl, possibly a boy and hopefully not a hermaph-rodite . . . I'll just have to wait and see . . .

Frankie's latest antics are putting family relations under even more strain. She had a whole load of friends over after school last week, which is fine, I've said her friends are always welcome because her friendships matter, and I remember how horrible Mum was to mine. She never liked any of them, and when they were allowed they were confined to my room and frowned at whenever they so much as went to the loo. It was so embarrassing bringing them home that it was almost better to stay out, and I don't want Frankie to feel that way. Was Mum like that with your friends too?? I can't remember them much. There was Amy of course, but who else? Were you ever in a gang? Anyway, they managed to smash a beautiful pot that I lugged back from Italy more than ten years ago AND they've practically destroyed the sofa. Must have been jumping on it or something. Teenagers behave like children, but they have the body size of adults, so they can't help but cause a mess. I'm livid but daren't say anything, because I can't bear the thought of another row with her. It's so exhausting. Iris reckons they were 'taking drugs' (which I suppose means dope), and obviously felt threatened by such a large crowd. While she isn't on the point of leaving, she is not going to be able to put up with this every week, so I felt I had to raise the issue gently with Frankie, who of course flatly denied that there was any smoking going on and said that Iris was lying or mistaken. Saskia smokes cigarettes she says, which fills me with absolute gloom, so it must have been that – but I found a roach in the living room bin, and there was definitely a whiff of cannabis resin about the place when I got home.

The whole dope thing is really difficult. We smoked, and Matthew still likes the odd joint after the kids have gone to bed. Those kids probably had no idea that there was at least half an ounce in the box in the sitting room. But when it comes to my own kids, I really really hate the thought of them doing it at all. They're too young, the dope they smoke is stronger they say, and it isn't good for them. That's not hypocritical is it, just because we did it? I mean they are much younger than we were (I had my first spliff at medical school), and when she's 18 she can do what she likes with her own body, but until that time I am responsible for her. I don't think that's an unreasonable stand do you? When I mentioned this incident to Matthew, he had the nerve to blame me. He said I shouldn't be working so hard, and that maybe if I wasn't pregnant at this 'ludicrous' age I'd have the time to notice that Frankie needed more support. OUTRAGEOUS!!!! I said that if anyone was to blame it was him, for walking out the door, for failing to be there at those bizarre moments when teenagers need to talk about something, for failing to be there to help with the homework, and failing categorically to support his eldest daughter while I'm pregnant with his third child. How DARE he accuse me of not being there for her, when he's the one who's pissed off! I'm so angry with him I can't even speak to him at the moment.

Please just hit the reply button and ping back an 'I'm OK and not in a rocket' response. Love you. S xxx

Dear Diary,

Sunday. Mum's in a suspicious mood. As she
drove me to Ruby's yesterday, she came on strong
with the lecture about how bad dope is for you
these days, when I know that Dad has stacks of it
in a box upstairs, which has somehow mysteri-
ously disappeared now that he's gone. He can
leave half his clothes and his tennis racket behind
(as well as us), but when it comes to the drugs
they go with him everywhere he goes, along with
his complete boxed set of Bob Dylan. What a
dreary singer. He came round this afternoon and
started having a go about my friends and dope.
What a hypocrite. Does he think I'm a complete
cretin or what? When I accused him of being a
dope head and a lawyer (which is pretty fucking
stupid since it is illegal) he went crazy! Psycho!
He was so angry and frightening I went and
locked myself in the bathroom until Mum asked
him to leave. Why should I even listen to him, let
alone waste my valuable free time arguing with
him, when he's just a hypocrite? Rang Ruby and
she was really supportive. She said that most
parents were completely irrational at the best of
times, and it was best to give them space to chill
out until they cooled down.

From: Sue James
Sent: Sunday 4 November 22.13
To: Angela James
Subject: Re: Are you OK?

Glad you're fine and not in a rocket high above the Earth. Computers are a complete pain in the arse when they break down. How did we get to be so dependent on them so quickly? Yes you're right. I will go now with a big pair of scissors and shred all of his remaining clothes. I'm also thinking of changing the lock on the door. Frankie had a row with him this evening and I was entirely on her side. How can he be so stupid as to think that coming on strong with the authoritarian 'I'm your father and I forbid you to take any drugs until you're 21' will work when she obviously resents him so much for leaving. Lola pines for him, Frankie just seems to loathe him, but then again, perhaps that's where I've been fooling myself. Perhaps he really is stupid. He's an idiot for leaving me anyway because they are of course queuing up at the door to take his place. Lola was playing at Clare's for most of the afternoon, and came back just as Matthew roared off on his bike, and then burst inconsolably into tears. She wailed 'Daddy, my Daddy,' just like Bobbie does in *The Railway Children*. HND hovered on the doorstep nosily, asked if everything was OK (when it clearly wasn't), and then went into great detail about how they wanted to take Lola to see *Swan Lake* at Covent Garden because dickhead husband had a box, and could she come, and would that be nice, when all I wanted to do was slam the door shut, like you do after a screaming row, and hug my lovely daughter. So now I add insensitivity to the woman's list of character flaws. I said, 'I'm sure she'd love to come,' with a smile, and then slammed the door shut in her face instead. S xx

Dear Diary,

Guy Fawkes Day, but Mum's forgotten to buy sparklers. We ALWAYS have sparklers. Lola's not too old for them, even if I am. Sometimes I wish I was someone else. Someone with an easier life. Someone who didn't have to go to school. Someone with lots of money to buy stuff, like Saskia. Someone with nicer hair, a prettier nose, proper tits and longer legs (like Saskia). Someone with loyal friends they can trust, that don't bitch about you the moment your back is turned, and a really nice boyfriend. I look at Mum sometimes and pray to a God I don't believe in that I won't end up short and fat like her. I caught sight of myself walking in a shop window today, and I looked just like Mum, which is so so scary. Please make me tall and thin like Dad, with a small arse.

It's kind of depressing being 14. You're not a grown-up and you're not a kid any more either. You're sort of stuck in no-man's-land and nobody seems to notice you. There you are, a person, and they say things like, 'Haven't you grown/blossomed/my what a young lady now,' but they don't really see you for who you are. They can't really see the real you, although I'm not really sure who that is any more. They look

at you kind of weirdly as if you were somehow
different, but actually I'm still Frankie, just
bigger that's all, but when they look at me that
way I just feel more insecure, like who am I
really? It's depressing at school – I mean what
on earth is the point of algebra? – and it's
depressing at home, unless there's something
really good on the TV and Mum's been shopping for chocolate. We sat in the cloakroom at
break today, it's too cold to be outside any
more, and Saskia smoked a cigarette. I had a
puff on it and didn't cough much. In fact, it
was quite nice, sort of soothing, something to
do. I said I felt false sometimes, like I was
different people with different people, and that I
wasn't sure who I really was inside. Fran goes
'That's because your parents are fighting, it's
bound to make you feel more insecure, I mean
don't they love you enough to stay together?'
Do you think she's right? Her Mum is a thera-
pist, so maybe she is, maybe Mum and Dad
should go and see her? They're so selfish they
haven't even considered going to Relate.

Toby, Jack and Will thought they were being
really cool smoking a joint in the darkroom at
lunchtime, but I just thought they were stupid.
If they got caught they'd probably get
suspended or expelled, but if you get caught
smoking or bunking off, the worst thing they
could probably do is ring your parents, and
mine are never here to answer the phone

anyway. I could easily pretend to be Mum. If Iris answered she'd just write the message down and that's easily chucked away. I suppose I ought to get on with my maths homework, since there's nothing good on TV, but what is the point of algebra, exactly???

Dear Diary,

Thursday, which means that tomorrow is Friday which is GREAT!!!! Friday is the best day of the week because the next day is Saturday and I can sleep late. It's Serena's birthday tomorrow, so we're all going over to her house and her Mum is going to cook her favourite dinner. I bought Serena a box of Quality Street for her birthday present, and a little beaded purse on my way home, and a packet of cigarettes. I've only got ten pounds left of this month's allowance, and it's weeks until the first of December, AND I haven't bought anyone's Christmas present yet . . . Why DO they have to sell cigarettes just in tens, I only wanted one. I sat on the bench at the end of our road and smoked it before I came home, and it sort of calmed me down and gave me enough energy to face Iris, Lola and Mum. Do you know what Iris cooked for tea? Toad in the Hole. I've never tasted anything so delicious in my whole life. I gave her a huge kiss, which made her giggle, but she wouldn't let me eat Mum's portion, mean cow. She's all right really. It's nice to have someone there when I get home. I'm trying out a new signature, which one of these do you think is the best?

169

frankie

FRANKIE Frankie Frankie.

frankie

Frankie,

Dear Diary,

Saturday afternoon on the day after Serena's birthday, I think it's the 10th. It was well good her dinner (unlike Mum's cooking). Her Mum let us drink some champagne and it made me really giggly. Dad's just bawled me out because he SAYS that I agreed to go to the new James Bond movie with him last night when I never did, he never said that at all. Why would I want to do that with him, and miss a dinner party with my friends? He must be mental. So then he goes on about how I never listen, and how self-obsessed and selfish I am, that I only do what suits me, when most of the week I don't get to choose what I want to do – I HAVE TO GO TO SCHOOL, I HAVE TO GO TO MATHS LESSONS AND I CAN'T EVEN GO OUT OF THE BUILDING AT LUNCH-TIME, so why shouldn't I do what I want in the few hours when I do get to have some choice over what to do with my life, why is that so selfish? And I suppose he isn't selfish at all for leaving Mum when she's pregnant. I know she's a fat, unattractive pain in the arse at times, but she's not that bad, and he married her after all, he must have seen something in her once and he should stick by her. How are

171

Lola and I to develop any sense of moral values or trust in sexual relationships when he behaves like that?? It's pathetic. Then he said that he thought I spent too much time with my friends, and how like Ruby I was becoming, too into having a good time and not studying enough. Well, what does he know?? And aren't you supposed to have a good time when you're young? I said I'd go to see James Bond with him tomorrow if he liked, but he just walked off in a huff and said he was busy. Now how pathetic is that? And exactly who is the child in this situation???

From: Sue James
Sent: Monday 12 November 06.24
To: Angela James
Subject: hello – can't sleep again

I'm so large now that I can barely move.
Getting into bed takes the weight off my feet
(varicose veins are disgusting, never had those
before) but then within ten minutes my sides
are sore and I can't sleep on my back any
more because Tiny's pressing on my spine,
and actually it'd probably be more comfortable standing up. So I sort of doze and dream
extraordinary dreams, propped up against a
mountain of pillows, listening to the radio. In
a way Matthew not being here makes all this
bit easier. He'd probably be sleeping on the
sofa anyway if he was here, cursing me for
ruining his working life. Knowing that I don't
have to worry about him as well, and having
the whole bed to myself, means that actually
the nights are quite restful.
   Managed to get out through the front door
without having to turn sideways to get to a fireworks party last night (actually Saturday
night, we're already into Monday but since I

haven't slept I feel as if this has been one long, hungover day). I had a really good time. Lola out with Matthew, Frank didn't want to come, so I went on my own which felt really weird, arriving alone and then leaving when I wanted to, without having to consult/wait for Matthew . . . Although the worrying thing is that I can't actually remember leaving, or indeed how I got home. Haven't done that since before we were married. Quite liberating really. It was full of doctors from the practice, chain-smoking and getting pissed like so many do. Fell into a really interesting conversation with the sister of someone at the practice who is an art dealer, and she was telling me all this amazing stuff about forgeries and art theft and how she once found a Picasso in a junk shop, and I just began knocking back the red wine – had a glass, my first since pregnancy confirmed, and it felt so warming I had another and then another. I think, (although I'm not entirely sure about this) that I may have been flirting with this doctor from another practice, because Mary rang me up in the morning to check that I was OK and question me on 'Max', which was utterly pointless because I can't remember much at all after about 10.30. I don't think I've been drugged or date raped or anything, so I guess I am . . . 'OK' that is! I know I shouldn't have – foetal alcohol syndrome unlikely in my case, but it isn't good for babies – but boy do I feel better because of it!

Talked to Mum at length yesterday afternoon. She's taken up oil painting and loves it! She even sounded quite happy, so I delivered the bad news that I was unlikely to get up to see her again before Christmas, given my size and work commitments, and she took it quite well considering. She's coming here for Christmas. Matthew's agreed to go and collect her on Christmas Eve. So it should be a jolly scene here – me the size of Wales and on the point of delivering Number 3; Mum complaining that she's cold here, badly fed there, and bored stiff with the company of elderly lunatics; Matthew trying to reassert his position as father of the house at this deeply family time; Frankie sulking because she has to be apart from her friends for two whole days AND go to Church on Christmas morning because of Mum; and Lola complaining that the house is too hot because we've had to turn the heating up for Mum. And then of course Matthew and I never row at Christmas because it's such a stress-free time!! I can't wait! The Christmas lights are up everywhere already and the shops are full of baubles and crackers, the afternoons are gloomy, windy and dark, I'm getting letters home from school reminding me about the Christmas Craft fair, Christmas hat day, and can I help with the rehearsals for the Nativity play, and I haven't even begun to think about Lola's birthday at the end of this month, let alone Christmas. Aaargh!!! I expect HND already has all her Christmas presents wrapped and labelled and hidden away neatly in the loft. Cow!

Lola can't decide what she wants to do for her birthday so I've given her two choices – either she has some friends over for a special supper plus sleepover, or we take some of her friends out to the cinema plus pizza MINUS the sleepover. This may sound completely illogical but I sort of think we're either 'in' or we're 'out' . . . mad really. She's not wild about either idea because of course what she's most concerned about is what will impress her friends, and most particularly Clare next door, but what I'm keen to avoid at all costs is the party scenario, which of course demands maximum effort on my part when I can't move. Tried to talk to Matthew last night about her present – i.e. do we give one together from Mummy and Daddy, or does he want to start separate presents. He just looked sad when I said that, as if my even considering separate presents was symptomatic of something deeper, that I was beginning to accept his absence as long-term. He's clearly really ambivalent about the whole thing, but if he wants me to beg him to come back he can just forget it. He's left and he has to come back because HE wants to.

The house is so quiet at this time of day. Lola's begun to sleep longer in the mornings and when she does get up she's happy to dress herself and watch telly, so I really ought to be savouring this peace before the baby comes. I think I'll go and make myself some tea and toast and take it back to bed.

Love you heaps, and thrilling news about Spike's new job – what's he going to be doing? Same as before or branching out into a different form of banking? I never did understand money much, other than how to spend it.

Sxxxxxxxxxxxxxxxxxxxxxxxxxxxxxxxxxxxxxxx
xxxxxxxxxxxxxxxxxx

Dear Diary,

I sit down every evening on that bench on my way home from school and smoke a cigarette. I even look forward to it sometimes, it's like my chill time, time to calm down and think about things. Last night I even snuck out there for a smoke when Mum and Dad were rowing. They think they're keeping it all from us, but just shutting the door to the kitchen isn't really enough to stop us from hearing them if they're going to shout at each other. Lola looked white and frightened, so I helped her into her pyjamas, read her a story, and told her I'd be back in ten minutes. It was fucking cold on that bench, but at least it was peaceful and I like watching the way the smoke makes shapes in the cold night air. When I got back, Dad had gone again and I cleaned my teeth before Mum could smell anything. She was snuggled up next to Lola and stroking her hair so that she could go to sleep. 'Love You' she called out from the pillows of her bed. 'Could you turn off all the lights before you go to bed darling?' Course Mum, yes of course.

Dear Diary,

Saturday 17th November. I'm in bed and I can't really be bothered to get up. It's rainy and horrible outside and Mum and Lola have gone shopping. Mum came in and asked me if I wanted to go too, but I can't be arsed. They're doing Christmas shopping and choosing party stuff for her birthday next weekend – she's having a treasure hunt and a sleepover. I thought about going too, but I haven't got any money, and Mum's just gonna get stressed and I'd rather not be there to take it when she does. I said I'd design the treasure hunt with Mum, and that'd be my sort of present to Lola because I'm broke. Mum said she'd see if she could find me something for her today, and sort of sneak it in when she wasn't looking, which is nice of her since I'm supposed to buy her a birthday present from my allowance. Now the house is really quiet and I kind of like it, having it to myself, but I also sort of wish I'd gone with them too. I thought about ringing Dad to see what he was doing today, but he hasn't rung me since Wednesday and he's probably busy, so I rang Ruby instead and she's going to come over later. I made myself a breakfast tray full of things to eat and took *Hello!* and an ashtray back to bed. Mum'll be out long enough for me to get rid of the smell.

From: Sue James
Sent: Sunday 18 November 08.12
To: Angela James
Subject: Re: Hi

Darling Ange,

Lovely to get such a long E from you with so much news. Life with the babes must be getting easier now that you're getting more sleep. I can't say whether 2 is too young for Nursery without really knowing them . . . (wish I did). Some kids thrive, others are more clingy, but if you feel they're ready for it, and you've got a place in a good school next year, I'd go for it. They'll grow up even faster over the next few months, and they'll have each other, and there's no question that toddlers need other kids around them in order to learn. I would think that was parti-cularly true of twins in order to stop them from becoming too co-dependent. The hardest thing about being a mum is pushing our kids to take on bigger things without us, because it means losing another bit of them forever, but if it's what they need we have to do it, and then think of all that lovely free time every morning, time for yourself.

Plans are heavily underway for Lola's ninth next weekend. (Thanks for the present, it arrived yesterday and has been stashed away.) We're going to have a treasure hunt, not just in the house but also up the street, with three teams, one led by me, another by Frankie and the third by Matthew. If it's raining we're revising plans and hoping to use Clare's next door instead. Then we're having a dinner-plus-video followed by a sleepover and pancake breakfast. Went shopping yesterday and got some things for Stan and Ollie for Christmas which I'll post in the week, and managed to stop myself from buying things for Matthew's nephews and nieces. Honestly, WHY SHOULD I NOW?? Bought Mum some paints, brushes and a canvas to keep her busy with her new hobby, and Lola lusted over a doll in the toy department, so I snuck that in without her looking, for Frankie to give her for her birthday, but God knows what we're going to give her. Decided in the end that I had to give her something from both Mummy and Daddy, even though it pains me, and that if Matthew decides to buy her something from him, well, that's just a bonus. Why is it that women always have to be good in these sorts of situations??? Lola's made a list as long as her arm for her birthday which includes a mobile phone, walkie-talkie so she can over and out with Clare next door, a dolls' house and a karaoke machine, as well as numerous Sylvanian sets and about twenty-five different plastic games and useless toys that they've been advertising heavily on the television. As far as the phone is concerned, over my dead body, but the walkie-talkie is a nice idea, and what do you think about the karaoke machine? I think both of the girls might have fun with that, and I want them to have fun. There's not enough laughter in this house at the moment and it worries me.

Got home shattered yesterday afternoon from all that shopping to find darling Ruby staggering around the kitchen in some six-inch heels. They were both overdressed, with short skirts, too much make-up and tousled hair, but they were giggling away and having so much fun. These were real 'fuck me' shoes . . . eeeugh . . . and they'd cost her £25, which is a hell of a lot of money to spend on something when you're fourteen, and for something that you can't actually walk in. I was surprised by how shocked and sad I felt, seeing them both looking so tarty and sexual.

I wanted to tell them to change into some-thing more comfortable, that they looked sexier and happier when they felt relaxed, but how can you really understand that at that age? AND it would only cause a row. So I giggled with them, and remembered how I'd once bought a pair of shoes with 4-inch leopard-skin heels that were a complete mistake. I never wore them anywhere, but I loved looking at them when I was alone in my room. They were so grown-up and glamorous.

She's just my little girl, she'll probably always be just my little girl . . . God knows how we'll cope when there are boyfriends and periods, do you think we'll go into menstrual synch??? The house is completely quiet at this time of the morning and its blissful, but I wish you were here to have breakfast with . . . Roll on springtime. Masses of love
S xxxxxx

Dear Diary,

Ruby and I spent all of yesterday trapped
indoors, so when Mum went to bed with Lola
at about 9 (honestly why doesn't the woman get
a life!) we suddenly got this urge from nowhere
to do something crazy, like if we didn't actually
get out of the house I just might have to smash
something. There was nothing on the telly and
we were all dressed up, so we closed the front
door quietly and sneaked out. Ruby could
hardly walk in her new shoes and my frilly
flamenco skirt was so tight around the waist it
hurt, but we held on to each other and jumped
on to a bus that might take us somewhere,
anywhere, away from here. There was this
incredible, exhilarating sort of whoosh as the
bus took off into the night, like we were really
living for a change, living on the edge, and
Ruby and I squeezed our hands together tight,
just to hold on to the fact that we were really
doing this and to stop ourselves from
screaming. Just the fact that we were doing
something quite so daring made all the colours
of the shopfronts and street lights seem stronger
and brighter.

Ruby wanted to stay on the bus until the
terminal and see where it ended, and then get

on a bus back home, but I wanted to walk through Soho and take our dare one stage further. I mean how dangerous is it really out there on the streets at night? I pulled her off the bus and we hobbled through the dark streets, trying not to look scared. The shop windows had red and black lacy underwear hanging in the windows and giant vibrators, which made us screech with laughter. Then Ruby spotted this woman standing in a doorway smoking a cigarette and asked me if I thought she was a prostitute. How am I supposed to know, when I've never seen a prostitute before. She just looked like a woman to me, with these amazing black plastic boots that went over knees to her thighs, and a little too much make-up. Ruby dared me to go over and ask her, but I said I couldn't. We found this really cool café full of really grown-up-looking people drinking coffees and smoking, so we went in there for a hot chocolate. There was this really amazing-looking guy there, dark skinned with black hair and green eyes. I couldn't take my eyes off him, and then, when he looked over at me and winked, I blushed so badly I couldn't bring myself to look at him again. 'If our mums could see us now,' I whispered to Ruby as I lit a ciga-rette and tapped it nervously on the ashtray. 'They'd never believe it . . .' We texted Fran and Serena and gave them three guesses as to where we were, but they didn't get it. When

Ruby said, 'He's getting up to go' through a closed mouth I couldn't believe it. He walked past my chair and brushed his finger across my cheek on his way to the door!!!!!!! Can you believe it?? I just wanted to die from embarrassment because Ruby shrieked, and the boys he was with laughed, and I just didn't know what to do. I mean he's at least 20, more probably, but he was soooooooo gorgeous I just went to jelly!!! Ruby wanted to leave and follow them, but that didn't feel safe somehow, and what would I say? So we stayed another 20 minutes and I smoked three more cigarettes because we couldn't afford another drink, and then we took the bus home. Ruby walked to the bus stop in her tights, wishing she'd never bought those shoes. 'I could've bought some new jeans with that money, and I need mascara,' she moaned, but all I could think about was HIM . . . I wonder what his name is . . . I think I'm in love . . .

187

Dear Diary,

Monday. We told the others about what happened on Saturday night, and of course they didn't believe us. Then they started talking about how maybe all of us should go down there next Saturday night, only I can't go because it's Lola's birthday, FUCK IT! Ruby says she'll tell me if he's there, and that it'll look cooler my NOT being there, but she's just trying to make me feel better, AND Saskia is bound to go straight for him, because she's SUCH a bitch and out to get me back because of Toby. Honestly, she still goes on about it, when she's welcome to him.

I can't stop thinking about him. Maybe he ACTUALLY likes me. Maybe he followed me home and knows where I live. Maybe he's planning a party for me at this very moment at his penthouse flat with a balcony overlooking the Thames. I'd love to live in a penthouse with a doorman and a glass lift. I bet he works in TV, or maybe in the music industry. He probably goes to that café every morning for a latte and croissant. He's too good-looking to do anything less interesting. Every time I think of how he brushed his finger against my cheek it feels as if he's doing it again, as if he's there and I go all hot and embarrassed. I wish I knew his name. How am I going to get out of helping with Lola's party?

Dear Diary,

Tuesday. Asked Mum this morning if I could
stay the night with Ruby, AFTER Lola's
treasure hunt, so there'd be more room here and
they could sleep in my room and use my duvet.
She looked a bit disappointed and said she'd
think about it, so I threw a major strop on my
way out of the door about how I'm always
expected to help, and how much fun was it
going to be for me to watch *Bambi* with a bunch
of nine-year-olds, and I'd have thought she'd be
pleased to have me out of the way. By the time
she came home from work she'd changed her
mind, 'although you will help me with the
treasure hunt though won't you darling?'
   'Course Mum, course.'
   YESSSSSS . . . The guilt trip worked!
   Now I'm worried about what I'm going to
wear. I've pulled out everything from my
cupboard and nothing's quite right, so I rang
Ruby and told her I was staying the night with
her and she said she'd lend me her off-the-
shoulder top. Do you think that might be a bit
too sexy?? Maybe it'd be better to be cooler,
just jeans and a T? I think maybe he works in
advertising.

190

Dear Diary,

Wednesday. I can't stop thinking of how it will be on Saturday. I'll walk in and he'll be sitting at the same table, except with his back to me this time, and not notice me, and then he'll turn and . . . Or . . . they invite us over to their table and we can't take our eyes off each other, and then we go outside into the cold night air and kiss . . . I've never known anyone I wanted to kiss like that before, but when he kisses me I can feel his arms around me, holding me . . . I think he must be a music promoter. Maybe he's really really rich, with a heated swimming pool, and a jacuzzi in his bathroom.

Dear Diary,

Thursday. Only two more days and I can't wait.
Got a detention in French today for not
listening and not handing in my homework, but
how can I be expected to listen when I'm
thinking about HIM. Anyway, that's what detentions are for, doing your homework, there's
nothing else to do. I think I'm gonna wear my
short skirt and cowboy boots. I had this amazing
dream about him last night, it was kind of
sexual I suppose, but really weird as well. We
were on this beach and it was really really hot
and he was stroking my arm and my leg, and
then I woke up to Mum shouting in my ear to
get up and that it was already eight o'clock, and
I could have killed her for pulling me out of this
delicious dream before anything at all had
happened.

Dear Diary,

Saturday and Mum's in a complete state about Lola's birthday. She never takes this much trouble over my birthday. So what's the big deal about this one, it's just a treasure hunt and a sleepover for fuck's sake, what's so stressful about that?? You'd think this was the most important birthday anybody has ever had in the whole wide world from the way she's behaving. Lola was completely, totally and utterly happy. Loved her presents, loved having Dad there for lunch, and is completely and totally overexcited about a treasure hunt at 6 in the dark with torches, so why get so stressed? Even Dad's being helpful and nice, for him. Mum and I worked out the clues together last night after Lola had gone to bed and had a good laugh together. We made hot chocolates and argued in a nice way about what her friends could under-stand from the clues. I thought she was making it too easy for them, they're nine now, they need it to be hard. 'You spoil her,' I told her. 'Maybe that's because she isn't going to be the baby for much longer,' Mum said. I guess it will be harder for Lola once the baby comes. I've had years of being an older sister, it won't change things much. When I asked her about

193

Dad and what was going to happen, she said she wished she knew what was going through Dad's mind, and that if this really was the end of their marriage she'd do everything she could to keep things happy and the same, which was nice to hear from her because it kind of worries me, the future without Dad here and the baby coming. She talked to me like I was a grown-up, instead of pretending that everything was going to be all right and how this was just a bad patch – but this morning she's gone mental. It's as if she's trying to prove to Dad that she can cope without him when she so clearly can't. She can't seem to laugh at anything – she's shouting at Dad and me and being so bossy I just want to hide in my room. I don't think she realizes how much she shouts at everybody all the time and how that puts everyone in a bad mood. She's in a complete state now about the clues – says they're in a muddle, so I'd better go. Talk to you later.

Dear Diary,

Sunday. He never showed up. I can't believe it. We got there at about 9 o'clock and sat at a big table in the window. Saskia has gone out of her way to dress up. She looked fantastic, but kind of overdressed for a café, and when I told her that she just snaps back that I look like I'm going to some fancy-dress party, and all I'm missing is the cowboy hat, and that maybe I'm getting a little too thin and had I been starving myself this week because of HIM, and Fran had to intervene and tell us to shut up. SHE'S SUCH A BITCH! We sat there until about 10.30, sharing three Coca-Colas and smoking my cigarettes, and then the others got bored and wanted to go, but I kept on begging with them to stay just another five minutes. I felt sure he'd walk through that door, but he didn't. Prick.

So we left and wandered up through Soho, sort of in the direction of home, but I felt so gutted I couldn't really care less where we went. Saskia laughed and teased me about being dumped, so I deliberately hung out at the back and Ruby put her arms around me and told me not to freak out and react back. We followed them through the streets, not sure where we were going, and then we passed this warehouse with really loud

195

music thumping through the walls, and two tall black guys standing by the door.

Fran asked them if this was a party, and whether we could go in for a bit, and when they said that it was a club and that girls were allowed in free before 11 o'clock we couldn't believe it. 'Now you're talking,' Saskia goes, rubbing her hands together. She didn't think twice about going in. I was a bit nervous, I didn't really feel like this, I just wanted to go back to Ruby's and talk about why HE never showed, but Fran said we couldn't leave Saskia in there on her own, that it might not be safe, so we followed her in. It was amazing, this huge dark basement with a few flashing lights and a fluorescent pink bar. Saskia just marched straight up to it and sat on a stool, like she was always in here and knew what to do, so we followed.

'First drinks on the house for girls. You lot are eighteen aren't you?' the man goes, behind the bar.

'Course we are,' lied Saskia.

I was so glad it was dark in there. I'm sure my cheeks were deep red with embarrassment. It's one thing lying about your age to get into the cinema cheap as a child (well they owe us, don't they, for all the full adult tickets I've had to pay for, lying my way into a 15), but lying about your age to buy alcohol feels like a whole new thing when I've only ever sipped a bit of champagne before. Saskia asked for a Bacardi

Breezer, which tasted OK, so we all had one. It made me feel really lightheaded, I forgot completely that I'd been stood up. (As Fran pointed out, we never really even had a date in the first place. I mean how was he to know that I'd even be there?) We danced a bit, but there sort of weren't enough people there to make you feel like you could dance without being noticed, so we mainly just sat round a table and watched what everyone else was doing. What a place, everyone eyeing each other up. It was so tense and just about the most exciting thing I've ever done. The others wanna go back there next week, but the drinks are at least a fiver each, so you'd have to make the free one last all night or club together for a couple of extras to share.

It was well after midnight when we got back to Ruby's on the night bus. We crept in, so as not to wake her mum, but she got up anyway, must have been listening out for us, and hit the roof with 'What sort of time do you call this?' and 'Where have you been?'

'We got lost,' goes Ruby.

'Lost?'

'Yeah, we got on the wrong bus and ended up in Clapham. We were talking so much that we didn't even notice.' Nice one Ruby.

From: Sue James
Sent: Sunday 25 November 18.04
To: Angela James
Subject: Birthdays

Ange Darling,

You know what the REAL advantage of twins is? Only one birthday party, a double whammy. Every year on this day I could bask in the knowledge that there were exactly 364 days until the next party. Actually, we all had a really good time, and thanks for the hooded sweatshirt. She loved it and has been wearing it today. (Frankie eyed it up too, bound to be a fight over that one when she nicks it and stretches it next weekend.) The treasure hunt was fun, Frank and I got the level just right. It took them ages to find the ones in the street, mainly because they were all arguing over who was in charge of the torches, but they were really triumphant when they finally found the prize (in the wendy house). They all felt like winners, which is unusual I suppose for children. Matthew even managed to be funny,

198

although I didn't laugh because the joke was at my expense, but the kids enjoyed it. He said my gang needed to be given a handicap because of my size and kept that up as a running gag throughout the party, but then, when it came to singing 'Happy Birthday', he put his arm around my shoulder and asked Lola and her friends to sing 'For she's a jolly good fellow' to me for organizing her party, baking a cake (a rare achievement in this house – it was absolutely disgusting) and giving birth to such a lovely girl 10 years ago. I always cry when it comes to singing 'Happy Birthday' to my kids, find it hard to get the words out at all, but at this point, in this state, I sobbed. I really don't know how to handle him at the moment, Ange, it's like he hates me one minute and then loves me the next.

He managed to leave well before the sleep-over though. Nine kids lined up in the sitting room on mattresses in front of the telly. I'm not sure how I'll ever get those mattresses back up the stairs. God how I hate the disability of pregnancy. They really ought to give us badges, so that pregnant women can park on double yellow lines in front of shops. (I've used my 'doctor visiting' sign occasionally, when I've been really desperate, naughty I know but you've gotta have at least one perk to this job.) Frankie says she'll help me, but she's unbelievably tired today. I sent her to bed this afternoon – sleepovers just kill kids and their parents the next day. I hope they've gone out of fashion by the time your boys hit 8. Inevitably one child got homesick and had to phone home. One didn't like anything I offered for dinner, said she NEVER ate vegetables, and ended up going to bed having eaten nothing but pudding. Two others fell out over who was sleeping next to whom, and one infuriated me by asking what was in the party bag before the party was over (such manners, I was tempted to say 'What party bag?') THEN she asked me three times for a new plaster for a finger that didn't look at all sore (talk about attention seeking). Clare burst into tears because she only got one meringue instead of two with her ice cream for pudding (I know, stupid me for not counting them out before hand and making sure everyone got exactly the same, but grow up, kid, it's just a meringue). Seeing other people's little 'neurotic treasures' does at least make me feel proud of the fact that Lola eats and rarely complains. I got about four hours' sleep. They were giggling and fighting until about midnight and then I lay awake half the night, worrying that they were going to asphyxiate themselves because there were so many of them in such a small room. I went down once to check that they were all still breathing, and then I lay awake wondering if they'd all die of the cold if I opened a window. Pathetic isn't it, as if I haven't got enough to worry about. Anyway, Lola was happy, so that's the main thing – so long as the kiddies are happy. Now all I've got is a house in a tip, with Iris coming tomorrow, so I need to clean up before she sees the state we're in and immediately hands in her notice, plus it's time to shovel food into Frank and Lola and get them all into bed, and mustn't forget the nit combing, after last night's head-to-head encounters there's bound to be an orgy of activity in Lola's hair . . .

Masses of love from a very tired house S xxx

Dear Diary,

Thursday 29th November

Honestly, Mum's beginning to get so old now that she's lost the plot. What exactly IS the point of tidying up when things only get messy again? She goes on and on about tidying up the place for Iris, when Iris is paid to tidy up and clean! She was shouting at me tonight about the state of the kitchen, and then got the mop out to wash the floor. I mean, why bother? It didn't look any better after she'd washed it than it did before. What we need is a new floor, not a clean floor, those tiles are disgusting. I wish she'd just get off my back and either do it herself or shut up. And why is it all my fault? Why should I keep the kitchen clean? I found a note on the kitchen table yesterday, when I got back from school, asking me to strip Lola's bed and stick it in the washing machine, and money to take her to the fish and chip shop for tea. She expects me to do so much now, I could put 'Mother stand-in' down on my CV. I've got enough to deal with just with Maths homework, Araminta Moulder who's asked to see me at lunchtime tomorrow (I've had five detentions since half term, no doubt she wants to probe into my private life to explain why and then snog me), and I've got a cash flow crisis with only weeks to go until Christmas, let alone the fact that I still haven't got a boyfriend now that HE failed to show up. I want to go back to the café on Saturday night, but the others say that's boring, they want to go back to that club.

BOYS TO CONSIDER NOW THAT HE IS NO LONGER AN OPTION:

	PROS	CONS
Toby	Likes me. Good for Dope.	Not good at kissing.
Will	Nothing worth mentioning.	Spotty, bad breath, rude.
Tom	Good dress sense, plays guitar.	Plump, don't fancy.
Sean	Fun to be with, fit.	Fran's ex, leave well alone.
Simon	Mum works in TV, v.v. fit.	Saskia fancies him.

From: Sue James
Sent: Sunday 2 December 07.15
To: Angela James
Subject: Hi

Dearest one,

It's so dark out there now at 6 in the morning that it feels as if it's the middle of the night. I'm sleeping so badly that I get a really cosy feeling when I hear the first bus tearing up the empty high street, because it means the day has begun and the night is over. I lie in bed most mornings, thinking of you and the boys having tea in the sunshine on the other side of the world, and it really does feel as if you must be on a different planet, not my world here at all.

HND took Lola to *Swan Lake* last night at Covent Garden, and I have to say I was jealous. We had such a row over her clothes and what to wear that by the time they knocked on the door to collect her I couldn't have cared less if she'd been naked. Nothing was right, her really groovy dress wasn't smart enough, her skirt wasn't chic enough, her hair wouldn't go the right way into the scrunchie. Basically, I think she wanted a nice billowing velvet dress with a large ribbon that ties at the back, smocking or embroidery on the chest and black patent leather shoes like Clare, but we've never gone in for that sort of thing. I couldn't wait to see the back of her, but within an hour I was missing her. Frankie's at Ruby's AGAIN for a sleepover (I sometimes wonder whether she prefers her house to home at the moment, and it's probably all my fault, I'm not much fun to be with, I can see that), so I was here all alone on a Saturday night. Me and my bump in front of some mindless television. Nobody to cook for, nobody to put to bed, nobody to shout at or clear up after, and even though the peace was/is blissful, this house feels like a ghost house. Evidence of them lies all around – Frankie's dirty trainers by the front door, Lola's pyjamas on my bed (she's spending the night next door), and her entire Sylvanian collection is lying in a heap on the sitting-room floor. I suppose I ought to tidy it up for her. My children's things lie on every surface, in every drawer, on every wall – hairbands, socks, pictures, toys, make-up and deodorant (who ever uses that disgusting stuff over the age of 20? And they probably cause breast cancer) –

but these are lifeless objects without them around and I miss my kids. I miss them badly. Matthew ought to be here with me now, he ought to be here so that I can curl up in bed in his arms and reminisce. What are partners for if it is not for moments like this, those 6 in the morning moments when you lie in bed and remember something about a conversation or a place you've visited together, or something the children said or did when they were much younger? He should have been here last night with me. We could have shared a bottle of wine and a conversation, or laughed at the shopping channel. Without either of them here we could even have gone out for dinner without having to pay for a babysitter. I feel so alone, Ange. It's that mid-life thing of everything feeling like it's falling away – Matthew leaving, youth and vitality gone, Frankie about to leave home. This baby may be all I have to keep me company in the years to come . . .

Still, it'll be Christmas soon. There are trees up and fairy lights and the supermarket shelves are stacked with crackers and boxes of choco-lates, and already I've bought more stuff for my children than they could possibly need. I can't imagine what Christmas can be like over there, without that contrast between bright glit-tery lights and the darkness of night. Lola's nativity is next week (she's Mary and I'm so proud of her!), so that'll make me laugh until I cry, and then Frankie's carol concert is the week after. Do the schools in Oz do this too? Do they sing carols in shorts and T-shirts instead of scarves and bobble hats? Busy time at work though, everyone gets ill because it's so stressful.

The dawn's coming up now and it looks as if it's going to be a beautifully crisp winter's day. The sky is bright blue. I'm going to jump in a hot bath now and soak away the aches and pains of pregnancy, but I'll log on this evening and see if you're there. Much love, Sis xxx

Dear Diary,

Sunday

If you subscribe to the notion that you could be dead tomorrow (which is SO true) AND you're broke, then you've gotta go for it. I get these sudden urges to do something CRAZY . . . like scream at the top of my voice, or jump into a fountain, or hold up the traffic on a busy road while the others walk very slowly across to the other side. We were in Top Shop, trying on silly hats and jewellery, and Saskia dared me to nick something. If it'd been anybody else I'd have told them to fuck off, but because it was Saskia I said I'd do it, but only if she did too, and that I betted I could nick something that was worth more than she did. Serena and Hayley went off with Saskia, and Ruby and Fran came with me. It was really, really crowded, lots of people Christmas shopping, and it was raining hard so there were loads of people there just passing the time until it stopped. So if ever there was a time to try it without getting caught this was it. Saskia stayed on the accessories floor, where it must be quite easy to slip something into your pocket because it's all so small. We wanted a bigger challenge and went down to the basement and looked through all the racks for the most expensive things to take into the changing rooms. We tried it all on – no point nicking something that doesn't fit, and Ruby checked for the white security tags and Fran goes how this is really stupid and I'll get caught. When actually, just shut it, Fran, if I do it's because of you and your big mouth. She gets so scared of doing things, anything, when all I wanted to do was stuff this top and amazing pair of trousers that I could never have afforded into my bag and run.

It was amazing how easy it was. No one seemed to notice us at all, and I even bought a pair of earrings – Mum's Christmas present – before we left the shop, just to make it look more normal. We met up with the others in Starbucks round the corner and fell giggling into each other's arms. Saskia managed a beaded necklace she doesn't like and a pair of tights – total retail price of £29.99, while I got away with trousers worth £45 that fit and a top for £20. Saskia tried to be nice, but I could see she was furious with me for winning and accused me of cheating by going down to the basement. So I bought her a Diet Coke to try to make her sweet, but she just grumped at me, didn't even say thank you.

I wore my new clothes to the club and felt really cool, almost cool enough to dance, but there was this guy who was looking at me in this rather creepy way from the corner and tried to buy me a drink, so I didn't really want to be separated from the others. Fran and Serena sat on either side of me the whole time. I said I'd never talk to them again if they left my side for a moment. What a pervert, he looked as old as Dad. Still, it kind of makes you feel good, knowing that SOMEONE has noticed you, even if they're a creepy, dirty old man.

From: Sue James
Sent: Sunday 2 December 21.52
To: Angela James
Subject: Re: Hi

Sorry darling, didn't want to worry you. I'm fine, it was just one of those middle of the night, early morning moments. You know how vulnerable you can feel when you're very pregnant, you can't run away from danger any more, and I know it's pathetic and not very feminist, but actually I could really do with Matthew being here to protect me a bit more.

The kids are back now so I'm happy, so happy to have them around that they could ask me for anything they wanted and I'd probably say yes. Frank's in a very good mood and has bought herself a fabulous pair of trousers from Top Shop. I'm almost jealous, except that I know they'd look ridiculous on me, and Lola has spent most of the day singing the theme tune for the Swan. The ballet was clearly a big hit. They had dinner in the floral hall, sat in a box and ate their way through a large tin of Quality Street for pudding, and Lola says she saw one of the

Blue Peter presenters in the stalls below with a child about her age, so she is blissfully happy and spent most of today writing it up for her school diary and painting a thank-you card for HND. Also, they came home in a black cab. 'Why don't we EVER do anything fun like that Mum? We never EVER go to see the ballet in taxis,' she said in a rather horrid voice this morning. Well, maybe that's because it costs a week's salary, and anyway, everyone has different things to offer, I explained, trying to be reasonable. We do lots of other sorts of things that Clare doesn't do with her Mum and Dad.

'Like what?' she replied sternly.

'Like go to exhibitions.'

She didn't think that was much competition, judging by the look on her face. Still, she hummed away through the bath and in bed, so perhaps she's musical. Maybe I've been missing a huge trick by not hot-housing her with piano or cello lessons from the age of 2. She could've got a music scholarship to a really good school. Do you think it's too late to start? Baby kicking away like mad, and I've got chronic indigestion most of the time, but not long now. I can't wait to see this little person and not be pregnant any more.

Sounds like a terrific lunch party, hard to

imagine barbies in the garden and worrying about smothering enough suncream on the kids when it's dark, gloomy and cold here. I know it's a worry, but don't let it get to you. All you can do is slap the stuff on whenever you remember – and don't forget the hat; sunstroke is no fun at all. We worry and worry about their health, but in the end we can all only do so much, and your boys are a million times healthier than most of the poor kids I see on call. Child health is driven much more by economic background than anything else. They look pasty and grey, mainly from a diet of junk food, and when they're over-weight even their fat looks unhealthy, all sort of watery, with 'bingo wings', as Frankie calls them, hanging from their arms. Not substantial, nourishing fat like mine at all. You're a good mum, you look after your kids, so relax, they're fine.

Must go to bed, might even sleep for a few hours now that both Frank and Lola are home. Night Night. S x

Dear Diary,

Wednesday. Fran bought me this amazing book with all this amazing stuff in it about star signs. I'm a Gemini, the 'butterfly of the zodiac', constantly moving on from one thing to the next and easily bored, which must be why I can't stand maths. It's the sign of the twins, which means I'm constantly flitting from one thrill to the next, trying to do what two people do in one life. Apparently I'm sophisticated, sociable, intellectually curious (about everything except maths) and a great communicator, so that's nice to know. My opposite sign is Sagittarius, which is Dad's sign, which is probably why I'm not getting on with him at the moment. My ideal partner in love and for marriage is either Aries, Leo (I think gorgeous Simon might be a Leo), Libra (Toby – oh dear), Sagittarius (how can that be when it's my opposite, and I'm supposed to fight with them?) and Aquarius. So, first question whenever I meet anybody from now on is 'When's your birthday?' I think I'm going to become a vegetarian. Gemini's don't like harming living things.

Dear Diary,

Friday. SIMON IS A LEO!!!! I'm thinking of asking him out at the Christmas Carol Concert the week after next. Do you think I dare?? Ruby thinks I should, she says I may never know if he likes me if I don't ask, but the thing is, if he says no, that's another dream dashed and Saskia will know and just use it against me.

Miss Moulder gave me a letter to take home to Mum so I opened it. She says I've missed several RS lessons and am getting behind with my homework assignments, which is just so not true, so I tore it up and chucked it in the bin. I'm home tonight because nobody's doing anything, so I suppose I ought to get on with some homework, but tomorrow we're going to sleepover at Ruby's. Her mum's having a dinner party, so there might be someone interesting there like Brad Pitt, or a film director who wants to put me in a movie. Lola says *Top of the Pops* is on now, so I'm going to go and see who's number one. Talk to you later.

From: Sue James
Sent: Wednesday 12 December 19.28
To: Angela James
Subject: Christmas Shopping

Ange Darling,

Had the day off and just about got the whole
thing done. I decided that I'd go for broke
today because the weekends are now so hectic
in the shops, and this could be my last free
day before parturition, let alone Xmas. It feels
close, birth that is. I keep getting urges to do
mad and utterly pointless things like wash
down the venetion blinds in the bathroom, or
the shelves in the sitting room. I just shopped
– picked up something, thought that'll do for
so and so (rather than I wonder if they'd like
this) and bunged it in the basket. Frankie
wants a token for Top Shop, so that's easy,
and Lola wants the Sylvanian Canal boat,
which I've done mail order. So the only thing
left to do is a few more stocking fillers for the
girls and a Secret Santa present for someone
at work (it has to be something for less than

216

£5 which is HARD). Then there's the food, but I think I'm going to dump that one on Matthew. I got him a rather beautiful dark blue cashmere jumper from Selfridges (nice of me, wasn't it?). I wonder what he's going to give me – divorce proceedings?

We all went to Lola's nativity play last night. Matthew and I were on complete 'no speaks' (he's furious with me because I said that Lola couldn't spend the weekend with him – I really couldn't face the thought of another Saturday night on my own), so we sat on either side of Frankie, who was so bored by what was on the stage, and probably so fed up with both of her parents behaving like children, that she spent the whole time texting her friends. How do they manage to do that so quickly? I spend so long trying to get the right letter on to the panel that I usually give up. I can see that it's fun, and cheaper, but honestly, it's much easier just to phone. Maybe I need to buy a new phone and learn how to do it. Anyway, the play was fantastic, and of course I cried buckets. All the kids move me, but there was something particularly moving about Lola as Mary. Her headgear kept slipping over her eyes, and she managed to drop the baby Jesus twice, and then swung him round by his legs as she walked across the stage. Not the way to treat the Son of God at all! One of the girls from the reception class spent the whole time waving at her Mummy and Daddy from the front of the stage. A little boy from Year 3 fell off the platform in the middle of 'O Little Town of Bethlehem', and the child who was holding up the star kept getting tired, and it would slowly lower over Joseph, and then he'd shove it high above his head again – it's hard work holding your arms up like that for longer than a few minutes. It was classic stuff. God how I love a good nativity play! It's the best show of the year – you've got some treats ahead of you with those boys. I bet they make them into Wise Men.

I always used to think that the nativity play was a pretty pointless piece of propaganda from the Church, given that what Christmas really means for kids is presents, but when you have children, the whole story seems to take on greater significance. It's about the miracle of life, not just the Miracle Birth. The child is King and all children are special. It's not really about the birth of one special baby at all, and when I see and hear children singing about that miracle it just breaks my heart, and that was before I was menopausal and pregnant with a miracle third child – imagine how the mascara ran down the cheeks. I had to go to the cloakroom and wash my face while Matthew went to collect Lola. Frankie just thought I was nuts, and said the play was crap, but then, when she saw her sister, she gave her the biggest hug and said, 'Well done, Lola,' which must mean something. She may come across as the recalcitrant teenager, but actually she cares deeply about her sister. I said I'd help her with science homework, since that's the only subject I can remember anything about, so I'd better go, but love you loads and talk to you soon. Sue xxxxxxxx

From: Sue James
Sent: Thursday 13 December 01.38
To: Angela James
Subject: Re: Christmas Shopping

I know, I never know what to do about
Christmas cards either! They've started
flooding in through the door – have you
noticed how there's always one that you can't
actually read who it's from? You turn it every
which way, but still the signature is illegible.
Got the annual one yesterday from Leticia
Hugh-Johnson with the photograph of her
three kids and their horse. (Last year it was
just the dog – must be going up in the world.)
I've never met these children, I haven't seen
her since university and yet still, year in year
out, I get these cards, and every year her children are bigger, the card gets thicker and the
message always reads 'Another year gone . . .
hope all is well with you and yours, and that
our paths might cross in 1998/1999/2000/2001/
. . . etc.' Why does she bother?? I never send
her a card. I'm not sure I'd know where to
send it, even if I ever got it together. Every
year I think shall I send cards. Sometimes I

even buy a pack, thinking I should, and then I go through my address book and there are only about three people I want to send one to anyway, so I think, well, why bother. I always send one to Aunt Maud, because she really appreciates it, and I never see her, but as for my real friends – imagine writing 'Dear Julie, Happy Christmas, lots of love . . .' No, it's too ridiculous when I speak to her all the time on the phone. I bet HND sent about 300 at the end of November. But you are in Australia, and there must be lots of people you would like to see or talk to or keep in touch with and can't, so, yes, but please not one with a photo of the boys! It's exploitation and it's smug.

I've spent this evening wrapping presents in front of News 24. I think I'm just going to give up sleeping completely and start polishing the silver.

Sxxxxxxxxxxxxxxxxxxxxxxxxxxxxxxxxxxxxxxxx
xxxxxxxxxxxxxxxxxxxxxxxxxxxxxxxxxxxxxxxxxxxx
xxxxxxxxxxxxxxxxxxxxxxxxxxxxxxxxxxxxxxxxxxxx
xxxxxxxxxxxxxxxxxxxxxxxxxxxxxxxxxxxxxxxxxxxx
xxxxxxxxxxx

Dear Diary,

Tuesday. Mum went into hospital this morning. She said the baby gave her this massive kick while she was making a cup of tea, and there was this pool of water all over the kitchen floor, which she was trying to clear up between contractions. Disgusting. She kept getting these pains, but wouldn't let me call Dad, and said not to worry, so I called him on my mobile on the way to school. She said she'd go into hospital when the contractions got really strong. She said it takes ages to have a baby, and that she might still not have it tomorrow, so I should pack some stuff and stay with Ruby tonight, and she'd arrange for Lola to stay at Clare's. She said she was OK, but she looked white and sweaty and she didn't look all right at all. It was kind of frightening, seeing her in pain like that, without Dad there, and the baby's not supposed to be here until well after Christmas, about three weeks, so it's early. I hope they're both all right.

She said she was really sorry that she wouldn't be able to make it to the carol concert tonight, and I said that it didn't matter, but then when it came to it and I stood there singing about Christmas, when everyone is supposed to be so happy as families together, and nobody at all from my family was in the audience, not even Granny, I started to cry. I sang but the tears ran down my face, even though I kept wiping them away. It was like my whole family had just fallen apart, really scary. I mean, people can die in childbirth. I ran to the cloakrooms as soon as it was over, to wash my face, and Miss Moulder followed me there. I think she must have seen me crying. I told her that I was just worried about my Mum that's all, that she was having a baby, and she tried to cheer me up by saying how lovely it was going to be, having a baby brother or sister for Christmas, but I don't know about that. They may just ruin it. I'm in bed now at Ruby's and I'm glad I remembered to bring you with me to talk to because Ruby's bored with hearing me go on about my wretched parents, and I don't want to bother her Mum. I forgot my pyjamas and toothbrush, but Ruby's Mum is being really nice to me and has given me a brand new pair as an early Christmas present – they're pink and fluffy and really cosy – and Dad rang to say that everything was OK, but Mum hadn't had the baby yet and that he would ring me in the morning. I wish people didn't have to give birth to babies. I wish it didn't hurt them so much. I wish the stork did bring them after all.

Dear Diary,

Wednesday 19th December. MUM'S HAD A
BOY! Which means another Sagittarius in the
family. Dad rang as I was having breakfast and
sounded really happy, said that Mum was
absolutely fine and so was the baby, just a little
small, and did I want to skip school today so
that I could go and see them. DID I??!! I went
through Ruby's wardrobe after she'd gone to
school, for something different to wear, and
then walked back home to meet him there. Lola
was so excited she was jumping up and down.
Not about missing school but about having a
brother. 'I'm going to call him Jasper,' she said
authoritatively.
    'No son of mine is ever going to be called
Jasper, it's a wimp's name,' Dad said,
pretending to be cross. 'It's Basil.'
    'BASIL!' Lola was outraged.
    'Only joking, but it's not bad, I think I like it.
We'll tell Mum. But first we've got to pick up
some chocolate croissants for breakfast. Your
mother's half starved in there.' He picked Lola up
in the air and swung her round, and it was like
having the old Dad back again. He was so happy.
    We bought lots of food for Mum and a large
bunch of flowers. She was lying in a bed by the

window. She looked really pale and tired with greasy hair, but she was alive. The baby lay beside her, wrapped up in a white hospital blanket, fast asleep, and Mum said he looked just like Dad but I couldn't see it. I thought he just looked like a baby. Lola bent down close to his little cheek and kissed him and wanted to hold him, but I just wanted to hug Mum. I wanted her to hug me. Lola said he looked just like baby Jesus, and Mum and Dad laughed, and Dad said, 'My, he does have a promising life ahead of him,' and they all laughed again, but I couldn't see what was funny. I stood there and watched them all, and it was like I wasn't a part of it, I couldn't feel anything. I wasn't happy like they were, like I was supposed to be, just numb. Why didn't I feel happy? What's wrong with me?

Lola held the baby first and Dad took a picture of them. She beamed at the camera. So proud. I sat down on the bed beside Mum. I wanted to get in beside her, but the bed was too narrow and I'm now so big that it just wasn't possible, so I put my arms around her neck and told her that I'd missed her, and when was she coming home? She said hopefully tomorrow. The paediatrician had to check out the baby because he was a little small, and then she could come home. I hope it is tomorrow. It's not the same here without her. She's never away like this. Dad's here, but for how long???

It's the last day of school tomorrow and it's half-day, so we're planning to go down to Oxford Street. Dad's given me £20!!! There's an amazing slinky party dress in Hennes, but it's more than that, so I'll see how much money I've got left in my bank account if it looks really great on.

Dad took us to the Italian restaurant on the high street. He chose the most expensive bottle in the place, seeing as it's his birthday tomorrow (I've completely forgotten to get him a present), and he let me have a glass. 'If Basil had been born tomorrow, he'd have been born on my birthday,' he said dreamily. Funny how he seems to have completely forgotten that the baby isn't actually supposed to be his at all.

Dear Diary,

It is Thursday the 20th December. Which means it's only 5 DAYS UNTIL CHRISTMAS DAY!!!!!!!!! We did Secret Santa in Starbucks, and I got the sweetest little fluffy dog. Saskia bought it. She said I could give it to the baby for Christmas if I didn't like it, but I do, I love it. He's so soft and he smells nice. I'm not too old to sleep with a soft toy, am I??

The strapless dress looked really good on. For some reason it made my tits look bigger. Still haven't had another period though, which is a bit odd. I thought you were supposed to have one a month. It was £40! Amazingly, Saskia offered to lend me the money. She is being sooooo nice, I can't understand why. She said it looked really good on me because I had nice arms, and that it'd never look that good on her, and I should buy it. Dad loved the dress too, and said he'd give me the money to pay back Saskia, so that's good, but then he starts having a go at me about clearing up. Said the place was a complete tip, and that we needed to make it nice for Mum and the baby to come home to. Well, why is that my fault? Maybe if he'd been here a bit more in the last few months, it'd be tidier? Anyway, I thought about storming off and throwing a wobbler, but he had just given me £40, so I said I'd tidy up the living room while he and Lola did the kitchen.

Mum still not home, but hopefully it'll be tomorrow. She HAS to be home for Christmas. Dad and Lola shopped for food and nappies while I was in Hennes, and they bought a Christmas tree on their way home from the hospital. I thought we should wait for Mum to come home, so that we could decorate it together. We've always done it together, but Dad said it would be a nice cosy thing for Mum and the baby to come home to, and we could make letters that said 'Welcome Home' in foil to hang off the tree. It looked really good when we'd finished with it – white fairy lights, red balls and silver letters – and then we sat and ate some pizza out of the box and just looked at it. 'All it needs now is presents,' said Dad as he produced a large bag full of baby toys and some wrapping paper. We wrapped them together and sang silly songs and laughed, and it really was like having Dad back again.

I think he's going to be called Tom. Tom or Max. I think I like Max better, or maybe Tom. Not sure.

Dear Diary,

Friday. Mum came home today. Lola and Dad put lots of balloons on the gate and then went to get her. I was still in bed when they left, but by the time I got up, there they all were – Mum, Dad, Lola and Tom. Mum looked much better. She loved the tree and the decorations and I cut her three pieces of fruit cake with her coffee. She says they starve you in hospital. I spent most of the day running up and down the stairs with mugs of tea, we had so many visitors. Why do they need to drink so much tea? Clare and her mum came round to see the baby and give Mum this really cool Babygro and matching furry snuggle sack for the pram. Those things cost a fortune. Mum wasn't nearly grateful enough for it. Mum let Clare hold the baby, until Lola got jealous and ran off crying. Honestly, what a baby, and of course Mum didn't tell her off for being such a selfish brat. She's sooooooo spoilt my sister. Can't even let her best friend hold her new baby brother for more than a minute.

Julie came round with Edward, an enormous bunch of flowers that they could barely get in through the door AND lunch – a delicious home-made salmon en croute with vegetables AND

PUDDING. Why doesn't Mum ever cook things like that? She was wearing this really cool dress, must have been designer because it fit her perfectly. Dad opened a large bottle of champagne and let me have a glass and Mum got completely pissed. Her cheeks went really red. Soooooooo embarrassing. I wanted to talk to Julie about Life and fashiony sort of things, but Mum sat next to her the whole time discussing labour and the wonders of epidurals (Sooooo disgusting – I'm never having a baby) and the only thing she asked me was whether or not I was pleased to have a brother. Well how would I know? He's only been here about ten minutes. Duh . . . Why do grown-ups ask such dipshit questions?

Edward looks taller than he did in the summer, which means I might move him up my list of top ten boys and put him in second place after Simon. He's quite sweet really, he has these funny little sideburns that he's obviously really proud of, although they look as if he's got a bit of bum fluff for facial hair, and he kept stroking them, but otherwise he was really kind to Lola, and he managed to make me laugh by talking about the bummest Christmas presents he'd ever been given. He has an aunt that used to give him a Spirograph every year when he was younger. Now she's taken to giving him deodorant and aftershave.

Dad went a bit over the top at lunch though, about having a son. I mean what the fuck difference does it make whether it's a boy or a girl, when he's spent the last few months saying he doesn't want it anyway and that it isn't his? HE HATES FOOTBALL AND CRICKET, so what is he going to be able to do with a boy that he can't do with me and Lola? Bond I suppose. And how do you think that makes me and Lola feel? He's here, pretending he's never been away, now that there's another boy in the house, but he didn't love either of us enough to stay before. Thanks Dad. I took Edward up to my room and played 'The Idiots' CD really loud. He had some cigarettes, so we sat on the windowledge of my room, wearing fingerless gloves and blowing smoke out of the open window. His mum doesn't know that he smokes either.

From: Sue James
Sent: Saturday 22 December 10.12
To: Angela James
Subject: IT'S A BOY!!!!

On the small side (5lb 10oz) but perfect! The most beautiful baby and I'm completely smitten. Don't ever want to put him down. Funny how things change – with Frankie I was desperate for space and solitude because that first baby changes everything, but with this one I'm blissful, for the moment that is. It really is different with boys. Frank and Lola can grow up, leave home and rule the world, but this small boy is my boy. I just want to wallow with him, feel his little body curled in my arms, watch him feed and sleep when he does. On day 3 when the milk came, the hormones dropped and I looked down at his perfect little face and began sobbing at the thought that I could never ever possibly love my future daughter-in-law. Pathetic isn't it?

I don't feel tired, just high and triumphant. Birth easyish too, just one small tear now that my pelvic floor has been stretched wider than the English Channel by two other babies.

This one practically fell out. And the really weird thing is he looks just like a small version of Matthew. The same high eyebrows, the same wide lips. We got out pictures of Matthew as a little boy last night and the resemblance was uncanny. It's either Tom or Max. I think we're moving towards Tom. What do you think?

Matthew is now behaving as though the past six months never happened, which is just astonishing. Does he think I'm a total moron? He wasn't much use at the birth either. He stormed in, furious, with his briefcase, said he had an important meeting with a client at 11, and when exactly was I going to have this baby? So I told him to go, and come back later with the juiciest, most gossip-filled magazine he could find to take my mind off things between contractions. I didn't want him anywhere near me. He held the baby first though. Tom clamped eyes with him before me, and in hindsight, although that happened quite by chance (the midwife simply dumped the bundle in his arms), it was one of the best things that could have happened because he's smitten with the baby. Tom slept with me last night and M slept on the sofa, but otherwise he's behaving just like he always did when he was living here – slumped on the sofa in front of the news, slumped over the newspaper in the morning, and completely deaf to anything the children say to him while he is involved in either activity. 'Is this a father for life or just for Christmas?' I asked him yesterday, as he held Tom in his arms and peered down lovingly at him, talking to him quietly about some of the future wonders of the male world no doubt.

'How can a father be for anything other than life?' he replied crossly.

'If you are the father that is.' Joke didn't go down well. He stormed out of the bedroom with the baby, and I was the one who had to go and apologize to HIM . . . I haven't yet got the energy to face him with 'us' and 'our future together or apart'. I suppose I'm sort of waiting for him to say something, since he's the one who left. I'm not expecting him to fall down to his knees and declare his undying love for me after nearly two decades of marriage (although that would be nice – if men only realized how far a little romance can take them . . .), but I am owed something – an explanation, an apology, just asking if I minded if he stayed would be nice. He clearly loves the baby, but does he still love ME? He gave me a massive hug after the birth, but has ignored me physically ever since, although he has been trying to be kind and considerate, so I'm not sure what to think any more. Is he back, or could he be off again tomorrow on that Harley Davidson? Maybe he's just doing the right thing, rather than being here because he really wants to be?

Anyway, I've decided that all I can do is just lie low and rest with the baby, and hopefully we'll have a really celebratory Christmas with Frank and Lola. I'll try and ping you before Christmas . . . Matthew is off to get Mum tomorrow morning. Frankie is kicking up rough about moving out of her room, but Lola's bed is much too small and un-comfortable for Mum . . . but if we don't ping each other before then, we'll talk on Christmas morning. Much love Sxxxxx

xxxxxxxx

Dear Diary,

Sunday 23rd . . . Only 2 days to go. Lola's already looked at tomorrow's date on the advent calendar, I can tell because it's sort of creased up. She's tried to press it back in, but it doesn't look new any more. I used to do that too. Too old for it now, unless of course they've got chocolate in them. I've searched the house for presents but can't find anything. Do you think Mum actually got it together in her state before she had the baby? She had better have got me something good. Wouldn't mind money if she hasn't though.

Granny arrived at lunchtime, which has meant clearing up and clearing out of my room. I can't see why she'd mind a few clothes lying around, but Mum insisted that I hung everything up and cleared space in and on top of the chest of drawers so that Granny could put her things there. I have to sleep on a mattress on Lola's floor. I still can't see why I'm the one who has to move, when Lola's room is prettier AND nearer the bathroom and the ground floor, so fewer stairs to climb. I'm sure if Mum actually ASKED Granny she'd say she'd prefer that. Absolutely all of my friends are away or grounded until after Christmas, but I'm texting

Ruby and Fran about the party, and we're making plans on MSN messenger. The plan for New Year's Eve goes as follows

10 a.m. To Ruby's house to wax legs, curl eyelashes, massage each other's faces, exfoliate and make ourselves look as sexy as possible.

4 p.m. All to Fran's to decorate house, put out food and continue to make ourselves as sexy as possible. Also sort CDs. Mustn't forget to take *Saturday Night Fever*.

AIM OF PARTY To drink, dance all night and flirt with as many boys as possible. I'm going to ring Edward and see if he wants to come. So far we've got about 25 girls coming and only 4 boys worth having.

From: Sue James
Sent: Monday 24th December 16.19
To: Angela James
Subject: Happy Christmas!

Well I think Mum's happy. She's already complained about the fact that we don't appear to have the tea bags she likes best, and supper was a little too late for her liking, wiped her finger disapprovingly over every surface, said the garden was in need of a good weed (whereas I think of them as plants), pronounced Tom (for it is 'Tom') to be a little small, and Frankie's room to be much too far away from the bathroom, when Lola's room would have been just fine, so I'd say she was on top form wouldn't you?? There's stacks of food in the house, a lovely fire burning in the grate, a giant tree in the hall, *White Christmas* has just been on the telly and she's never without a dry sherry in her hand. So what's to complain about? The tea bags!!! 2 or 3 times an hour!! And then she couldn't resist having a go at North Butting at lunch today, because I was the one who had to make the decision to send her there. She says the food is disgusting and the company boring, and that all those old biddies make her feel old. 'You're no spring chicken yourself Mum,' I muttered as I cleared the table, which sent her into one of those angry silences that make me want to strangle her. Honestly, she's lucky if that's all that's wrong with the place. I saw places where people looked like they'd been dead for days without anybody noticing. Why is it that there is nobody in this world who is capable of making my blood boil like our dear mother?

It's lovely to have her here, of course it is, but why is it that she always has to make me feel as if I owe her something for having been born and brought up by her? Why is there always this feeling of unrequited debt, as if I have somehow disappointed her expectations? I'm a fully qualified GP for fuck's sake! Hundreds of people queue up to see me in the misguided belief that I can help them feel better (who knows maybe they even do as they walk out the door). I've even saved the odd life or two, but that's nothing apparently compared to the value of having 'Mother at home when the children are small'. She wanted to know if I was going back to work, to which the only answer was 'Yes of course', but that seems to offend her as it did after

Frank and Lola were born. 'Angela knows where her priorities lie. She'd never leave the twins with a stranger,' she said, and then twisted the knife even further by saying that she thought Frankie was looking terrible, and was at the age when she needed her mother to help her learn how to make the most of herself, but of course I couldn't do that because I never was much interested in how I looked when I was her age – always had my head in a book, while you of course looked immaculate and had manicures and pedicures, and that if I wasn't careful Frankie was bound to become a drug addict . . . AAAARGH!

Frankie hasn't made things any easier by stumbling into her bedroom last night looking for something after Mum had gone to sleep. Mum woke up, complained about Frankie's manners, the state of her clothing and her attitude for most of this morning and swore blind that neither of us were that had as teenagers. If only she knew!! What amnesia! Completely forgotten how you and she used to fight, and how I used to have to sort things out between you, but when I reminded her of that she said, 'Angela and I *never* fought!' and then looked hurt for the best part of an hour, as if I'd said something really shocking, like you were on the game to fuel a drug habit because she was such a bad mother. Honestly, is it just old age that makes people cantankerous or is she particularly difficult – don't answer that, I know, I know. Can we come and live with you in Australia???

When Mum isn't complaining about Frankie, Frankie's complaining about how unreasonable Granny is, how is she supposed to be able to think ahead and anticipate her every possible need for the next 3 days and remove it from her room, for which I have some sympathy. She has a point but . . . AAARGH!!!!!

Family Life! Christmas – a time of peace and harmony, a time to cease hostilities, soothe hatreds and remember the love of one's fellow man . . . What would we do without it? Talk to you in the morning. S xx

✉

From: Sue James
Sent: Tuesday 25 December 22:21
To: Angela James
Subject: phew . . . it's over . . .

Darling Ange,

Brilliant of you to get the twins to babble at her over the phone this morning. She'll be able to talk about that for months to come. She was sitting on the sofa right next to the phone when you rang. Instead of answering it, she just shouted 'PHONE!', as if we hadn't noticed. Matthew was on the floor searching for a crucial piece of Lego under the Christmas tree and I was feeding the baby. When I said, 'You couldn't answer it could you, Mum?' she came out with a classic – 'Well it isn't going to be for me, is it?' – 'It's probably Angela,' I replied, 'you know, your daughter,' as Frankie picked up the phone. It was so funny I couldn't be angry.

The day got off to a cracking start at 5.45. Mum complained about the tea once again, and insisted that each child showed her everything that Santa had brought before they opened the next one, when actually what the kids really wanted to do was rip everything open with squeals of excitement, so the whole Santa thing took nearly two hours . . . Then there was breakfast and Church (Frankie at least had the decency to leave her mobile at home), and then back here for presents, which of course produced the usual round of disappointments as well as the odd delight. Matthew has given me the most exquisite antique embroidered throw . . . it's really lovely. Quite moved me. Is this love or guilt? It's certainly beautiful.

Matthew's parents arrived bang on one o'clock when Matthew and I were rowing about the lunch in the kitchen. There was no way that lunch was going to be ready a minute before 4, (fine by me but not by Mum) simply because of Church and Matthew insisting that the turkey had to have stuffing underneath the skin as well as up its bum. So I made rounds of smoked salmon sandwiches and we all got completely pissed on champagne. Peter was sweet, insisted on holding Tom for hours, and Granny Wilcox had tears in her eyes because he is the spitting image of Matthew. 'It's uncanny,' she kept saying, 'sooo like Mattie.' There was only one difficult moment, when they produced some very expensive bath oil for

Mum. It was exactly the same bath oil as they had given her last year, but instead of saying 'Thank you' and 'How lovely, my favourite', she pointed out their repetition and described at length how she had almost broken her arm falling over in the bath with the last lot and had had to throw the rest away. I could have killed her. Granny Wilcox looked deeply embarrassed.

They did bend over backwards to be nice to me though. Heaps of smellies and stuff for Tom, and even offered to come and look after the kids for a weekend when Tom's a bit older so that we could have a weekend away, which is an unprecedented offer in 17 years of marriage . . . Matthew must have filled them in on the past few months, although I doubt he's told them that it's all his fault . . . He says the late night movie's started so I'd better go. Mum's in bed, so we thought we'd snatch a little peace with a box of chocolates. I'll ping you tomorrow.

Masses of love S xxxxx

Dear Diary,

Boxing Day morning, which has to be one of the most boring days of the year, and it isn't even lunchtime yet. Why is it called 'Boxing Day' anyway? Probably because families fight like boxers, because it's completely unnatural to force people who don't actually like each other into such a confined space for 24 hours the day before, when all of the shops are shut and there's nothing but the Queen and *The Sound of Music* on TV. There's nothing to do now but look at your presents, which seem less exciting than they did yesterday when they were all wrapped up. I can't even hide from Mum and Dad bickering because I haven't got a bedroom until Granny leaves. Talk about feeling homeless in your own home.

Christmas Day was the same as it always is. First of all Mum always gets more excited about Father Christmas than Lola, who stopped believing in him ages ago but keeps the whole thing going because Mum loves him so much. So there's all that stuff about 'clever Santa' and 'doesn't he know you both well', when he quite clearly doesn't deliver to every single child in the world because he forgot Tom, as Lola pointed out when she reached the satsuma at the bottom of her stocking. Then when she saw Mum's face she reassured her with 'Maybe the elves forgot to tell him about Tom, he's only just been born and he was supposed to come after Christmas.'

Then there's the usual hysterics about the lunch. Dad cooks because, unlike Mum, he knows how to, but she can't stop herself from interfering, gets in the way and drives him psycho. They argue about things like whether the carrots should be cut in rounds or long sticks. Can you believe it? Every year they have this same boring conversation. When she's not trying to ruin the cooking she's fussing over Granny and resenting every single minute of it. She's not that bad as old ladies go. I've seen smellier ones on the bus home from school. I think her blue rinse is really cool, a bit punkish in fact. It sort of shimmers under the fairy lights of the Christmas tree. I think I might have a pink one when I'm her age. She just always wants to move on quickly to the next thing – 'Isn't it time we opened the presents under the tree/had lunch/turned on for the Queen/for the children to go to bed?' She says 'Isn't it' almost all day long. Funny how when you're old like that, and you've lived so long, you seem to want to wish away the little time you have left. Instead of just ignoring her like I do, Mum can't resist reacting. She hisses 'Yes, Mum, in a minute' at her with such anger that she really could explode. Honestly you'd think at their age they'd have worked it out. She ought to just let her sit and chill in front of the TV, like old people are supposed to do. They've lived long enough, they're entitled to a little peace I would have thought.

I sit there watching whatever's on, while they rake over some incident or other in the past and pick away at it. Was it 1986 or 1987 that Auntie Angela had that trouble with her back? Who cares? And then there's always the story of how our car broke down one Christmas Day when we were on our way to Granny Wilcox for lunch and we sat in the car, starving for four hours waiting for the AA. Mum's been so traumatized by that event that she refuses to go anywhere now on Christmas Day and they have to come to us. A bit extreme, since that sort of disaster never strikes twice, but that's grownups for you – over-anxious and neurotic. And why is Christmas exactly the same every year? The presents are kind of great and it's still kind of exciting, but it's not THAT exciting any more, which is kind of scary because the day is exactly the same as it always was so it must be me that's changed.

I got:

• A Top Shop voucher from Mum and Dad for £150!!!!

- £20 from Granny.

- A CD Walkman from Grandpa and Granny Wilcox which is cool cos my one's broken. Mum must have told them.

- A really horrible sweatshirt from Clare and her Mum next door which I'll never ever wear.

- Lots of bath stuff and make-up from Santa, which is what I really wanted, AND an eyelash curler, which is maybe why Mum wouldn't buy me one when we went shopping.

From: Sue James
Sent: Wednesday 26 December 19.27
To: Angela James
Subject: Boxing Day

I'm hiding behind the computer so that I don't have to do anything for anybody or talk to anyone. The tension is so thick you could almost cut it with a knife. Mum didn't sleep. Says Frankie's bed is much too uncomfortable and that she had chronic indigestion from yesterday's lunch, which was of course much too late for her. She spent most of this morning reclining on a sofa looking tubercular white and sighing pitifully, as if this was her last few hours of life from a curious wasting disease. She's a brilliant manipulator. She manages to produce two extreme and completely contra-dictory emotions in me – extreme anger, even hate, at her childish selfishness, and extreme guilt that I'm not doing enough to make her life happy or even comfortable. She picked up at lunch though, ate through two portions of fish pie, even though she said she wasn't hungry, and stirred things up nicely when she asked Frankie if she was anorexic just because she had left half her food on her plate. Frankie did not take this well and started scowling and breathing heavily. Matthew then cleverly rubbed salt into the wound by saying that with such a magnificent bottom Frankie could never be anorexic. I married a moron. Frankie called him a pervert and shouted obscenities at him and then stormed out of the house with such force that she knocked a bottle of red wine all over the carpet as she got up from the table and dislodged a picture in the hall as she slammed the front door behind her, smashing glass all over the floor. Mum then began a lecture on what a difficult girl she was, and that perhaps she needed to see a psychiatrist or go to one of those American boot camps to be put right, and how rude young people were today, which made me just want to hit her. If Stan and Ollie were teenagers she would, I swear, have said something along the lines of 'I bet they never behave so badly because of course Angela is at home to offer some sort of moral guidance.'

Matthew cleared up the wine, I cleared up the glass, Lola cleared off to her room for a bit of peace and Mum finished up all the pudding on the table. If she doesn't have indigestion again tonight it'll be a miracle. Frankie stayed out for nearly two hours, refused to talk to anyone, and ran herself a bath so that she could lock the door behind her. Matthew idiotically tried to confront her in the hall and get her to apologize, and I think if Mum hadn't have been here he and I would have had a full-scale row about it. If anyone needed to apologize it was him, although her behaviour was of course inexcusable. He also tried to insist that she came with us next door (HND invited us all for tea, groan), but Frankie shouted through the bathroom door that she wanted to do some coursework while the house was quiet, to which of course there was no reply.

Mum behaved herself next door, although she did manage to call her Freesia instead of Fuchsia, and has of course been going into overdrive ever since we've been back about how charming she is, how wonderfully clean and tidy her house is etc . . . and such a shame we haven't got a conservatory like that out the back . . . Do you think the government will ever be persuaded of the benefits of euthanasia?????

How was your Christmas??!!

S xx

Dear Diary,

27the December. Had such an exciting day at Top Shop. I spent all of the money that Mum and Granny gave me. I've never bought so many things in one day in my whole life! It was such fun and gave me such a warm full feeling inside, staggering home with so many bags and such lovely things. Now I can't decide whether to wear the dress Dad got me before Christmas or this amazing silk skirt and pointy boots that I got today to Fran's party.

Being out is like such a sharp contrast to being in. It's sooooo boring here. None of my friends are around, and I watched four videos back to back yesterday when I should have been using this dead time to do some coursework, only I couldn't be bothered. Ruby's back from her grandparents' tomorrow, so hopefully I'll see her then. This is supposed to be a happy time, but all Mum and Dad seem to do is bicker. They waste their time squabbling over tidying up, who does what, and how to do things, when what really matters are the big things in life, like living and going out.

Dear Diary,

Friday. Dad's been trying to be nice to me which means that Mum's had a go at him. I'll never forgive him though for what he said about my bum. He can't ever know how uncomfortable it is to feel so out of proportion, so big round my hips with nothing up top. What does he know about how I feel?

He did take us all ice skating today and that was fun – he's quite good at it really, for someone so old, showed me how to go backwards, and pulled Lola along really fast till she screamed at him to stop. Mum didn't skate. She sat holding the baby next to Granny, who kept complaining about the loud music and the fact that she was cold. She's always holding the baby, and then when he's asleep she's asleep and we all have to tiptoe round them. All Dad seems to say is SSSHH DON'T WAKE THE BABY. Turn down the music or you'll wake the baby. When I'm going hyper with my friends on the phone it's SSSHH DON'T WAKE THE BABY. Sometimes just walking round the house makes him say it. Well, forgive me for breathing, Dad. Maybe I should just move on out and give Tom my room now.

Dear Diary,

New Year's Eve and I can't wait to get out of here!!! I've been stuck in this mental hospital for over a week now without seeing a single friend, and I'm so bored I could kill myself. Mum's not interested in anything or anyone but the baby. He's kind of sweet, but nothing special really. Lola spends the whole time either holding the baby, singing to the the baby or wanting to help Mum look after it. All she ever says is 'He's so Sweet' in a squeaky, babyish, sick sort of voice. Dad spends the whole time shouting at me about not tidying up or helping enough, and when he's not telling me off, he or Mum are asking me to do something, like find a nappy, go out and buy nappies, or, worse still, stick one of his stinky nappies in the bin (at least she hasn't asked me to change him yet, but that'll come soon enough). Then I have to help Lola, make her a sandwich (isn't she old enough to make one herself?), help her with her shoelaces, help her when she's stuck with some crappy toy that someone gave her for Christmas. Both Mum and Dad have decided that it's my job now to take out the rubbish, which is just not fair since Dad's back (it seems) and he always did that every morning on his way to work. Am I the only one now who ever does any work around here? It's child exploitation, they don't even pay me. When they're not ganging up against me they're rowing about something stupid, particularly now that Granny's gone back to the old-age dump and they can let their true feelings really rip. Yesterday Mum actually had a go at him for bringing in some mud from the garden, when he was out there doing some digging because she'd asked him to, and then when he asked her if she'd made any coffee, she told him to make it himself, that she was fed up with looking after everybody else, and took Tom out for a walk in his snuggle sack. Honestly, Mum should really have grown up a little more by now.

Ruby's coming over this afternoon to help me get ready. I still don't know what to wear, whether I wanna come over as grungy and couldn't care less cool, or really dress up and make a sort of statement that this is New Year's Eve and from now on I look sexy because I'm gonna have sex, want sex, be sexy all this year. It says so in my horoscope for the year. Geminis are going to have a really cool year, particularly if they get it together with Leos. Whatever I wear, the padded bra plus half a roll of bog paper is a cert.

From: Sue James
Sent: Monday 31 December 21:02
To: Angela James
Subject: HAPPY NEW YEAR

Frank walzed out of the house just over two hours ago in a haze of deodorant ('smells like farts' said Lola) in this AMAZING dress. She looked fantastic! So elegant, womanly, stylish, with her hair caught up in a sort of comb things, and her neck's become so long and elegant. Stunning. Made me quite tearful. She looked so sexy, such a change from just a few months ago when she would have gone to a party with trousers halfway down her bum and a crop top. And seeing her like that made me feel so UNSEXY. I've been slobbing around in one of Matthew's shirts since Boxing Day, with Tom attached permanently to one or other boob, every bit of me wobbles vigorously when I walk, I'm in a muck sweat half the time, I've still got chloasma over my cheeks, stretch marks all over my stomach and I'm so tired I can barely open my eyes. She's off to a party oozing sexuality and all I want to do is go to bed, whenever possible, and sleep. We're so middle-aged now I can't bear it!

The Christmas tree is beginning to look even more tired than I am. There are more needles on the floor than on the branches and I'm sick of all the cards cluttering up the mantelpiece. I'm longing to sweep the whole lot away into the dustbin, but of course can't because of the kids until just before they go back to school. Lola is gradually and methodically working her way through her presents, and must be growing up because we haven't had any tears. Usually there's always something upsetting, either because whatever it is she's been making from one of a host of horrid craft kits doesn't match the image on the box (because they're made by experts and she's just a child), or because something she really loves gets broken or stolen by Frankie, but it's been calmer this year, maybe because we're all more preoccupied with Tom.

Matt took Mum back to North Butting on Saturday. She's been a nightmare, of course she has, and it is blissfully peaceful and more relaxing without her, but she looked so sad as she got into the car, so frail and old suddenly. It's as if just the thought of going back to all those 'old sods and biddies' as she calls them makes her older and weaker. She needs to be there, we can't look after her 24/7, and she knows that, but I just felt so guilty saying goodbye. I can't ever win with her, nothing I ever do is good enough it seems, and I know it is too late for her to change. It just makes me sad that's all, our relationship ought to have been so much closer, much more loving, like we are with our kids, but it is hard for her, even now. Still, she had a good time I think. She loved her canvas and oils. She plans to paint us a family portrait from a photograph, which is sweet.

Baby's crying so gotta go, but hope New Year was good. Did you go out??? Love S xxx

Dear Diary,

IT'S A BRAND NEW YEAR AND FROM
NOW ON IT'S A BRAND NEW ME!

I danced so much last night that my legs ache,
and that new deodorant's complete crap because
I stink as well!!!! Dad picked me and Ruby up
at about 1 in the morning and she's still asleep
next to me. It was a good party, but we still
could have done with a few more boys. The
ones we know well from school seem so shallow
and boring and so YOUNG! They still think its
funny to fizz up coke and shower it all over a
girl's hair. Serena was covered and had to wash
it during the party it was so sticky. So pathetic.
  Saskia's dad gave her a camcorder for
Christmas – how lucky is that, she's soooooo
spoilt – so we spent a lot of time dancing for
the camera and pretending to be movie stars.
And then at midnight Fran's mum let off fireworks in the garden and opened some
Champagne. Now it's a whole new year and my
star signs are good. 'Close relationships will get
a makeover and new ones will intensify' (which
means good news within the gang); 'your
professional life isn't going to sleep' (does this
mean GCSEs?) and 'love is likely to blossom

after Saturn's ball and chain has been shed in February'. Gd.gd. And when it comes to predictions for people born on my actual birthday it's even better. 'The intensity of your emotions will surprise you this year, and lead to many positive changes in your relationships. The more you strive to understand other people, the easier it will be to live with them, and the easier it will be to live with yourself.' As for resolutions that's a hard one. Can't give up smoking because I've only just started.

1) Mustn't bitch
2) Try and get on with Saskia, be more mature than she is
3) Save money (need jeans)
4) Keep up to date with homework
5) Make an effort to understand maths
6) Get serious about GCSEs
7) Find a boyfriend
8) *Give my undying love and affection as well as all my best clothes to Ruby* (This is Ruby's handwriting. Dream on Ruby and piss off, this is my diary and it's PRIVATE!)

✉

From: Sue James
Sent: Saturday 5 January 18.13
To: Angela James
Subject: Re: HAPPY NEW YEAR

Ange darling,

You're so brave!! Having to leave one child
screaming at a nursery on their first morning
alone is bad enough but to have to leave two
screaming 'Mummy' and clinging to your legs
like limpets must have been sheer hell. Did
they have enough nursery workers to free you
so that you could leave??? You're SO SO
brave and I'm not surprised you felt bereft,
even if it was for just an hour. The idea of ever
having to leave Tom, to go back to work, fills
me with such gloom that I can't bear to think
about it. (Mum'd be thrilled if she knew this,
so I'm not going to tell her!)

He's getting really chuchy cheeks and
feeding so much that he's practically growing
in front of my eyes. He's long, with very long
elegant fingers and toes. Completely edible. I
think he might be tall like Grandpa Wilcox.

I'm just loving every moment of being with him. I didn't expect it to be this exhilarating. I'm incredibly lucky. I could hold him all day long, and resent having to put him down to do something as mundane as load the washing machine. Amazing. Never felt this way with either of the two girls when they were this small. It must be my age and the circumstances. While everything else seems to be in a state of stagnation (Matthew/career) or decay (girls growing up and more argumentative, body in inexorable decline), Tom is the only one who just loves me unconditionally and doesn't answer back.

Matthew has gone back to work and I've hardly seen him. Leaves early, comes in late, long after I've snuggled down with Tom, so we still haven't 'talked'. I just lose myself in this baby. It's liberating to have absolutely no routine. We just slob about the house and eat at odd times of the day, and even though I'm still a bit sore from the labour, the hormones are flying high and I feel content and almost young again, even though I clearly look an absolute sight. As for my size, well I must be well into the outsize department by now. What's different about this baby is that I don't feel any pressure to get back to work to prove anything.

I've been given a whole new lease of life as a mother, and it isn't exhausting or over-demanding (yet). I'm just blissfully happy.

Frank and Lola go back to school on Tuesday so I'm searching the house for gym kit and buying pencil cases – Santa completely forgot to visit the stationery department. Frank's at Ruby's, Lola and Matthew are at the cinema, and I'm supposed to be cooking supper for their return, so I'd better crack on. Loads of love and keep strong . . . Sue xxxxx

Dear Diary, Tuesday

I wish, I wish I WISH I hadn't spent every
single penny of my Christmas money so quickly.
Why didn't anybody tell me to save some,
because I need new tights (and all the ones in
Mum's drawer are manky), and a padded bra
AGAIN, because I've lost my one somewhere at
Ruby's, and I could really do with some new
jeans because my thighs and bum seem to be
spreading and my old ones feel tight. I look in
the mirror and feel like Alice in Wonderland
must have done when she drank that potion
and grew massive. I don't recognize myself in
the mirror sometimes, and there isn't a drug
that will make me smaller, except ampheta-
mines and they turn you psycho.
    What's to say? It's January and dark and
raining. Yuk. I'm back at school. YUK. They're
piling on the pressure now about coursework.
YUK YUK. Saskia's being a complete bitch
again, surprise surprise, but I'm trying to rise
above it and be nice. Mum and Dad seem to
barely notice my existence. They're so obsessed
with this baby that anybody would think they'd
never had one before. Bet they weren't that
fixated on me. Whenever they talk to each
others it's about Tom. Dad comes home from

work and the first thing he does is ask Mum how he's been today, but he doesn't ask me anything, which just makes me feel like I could grow an extra head and nobody's notice.

BUT there's this new boy at school and he's SOOOOO fit and he's in my form NOT Saskia's!!!!!! Perhaps that's why she's being so mean. She keeps on giving me these evil stares. He's tall and dark with shiny, clean black hair, large brown eyes and this really sweet smile. He is so beautiful. His name's Chattie. Great name since he hasn't said a word yet to anyone all day.

Dear Diary,

Wednesday, January 9th

I think I'm in love!!! I can't get him out of my
head. I can't take my eyes off him when he's in
the same lesson as me, and if he's sitting behind
me I have to really stop myself from turning
round. When he smiles at me my cheeks burn,
and I'm so embarrassed I just want to run
away, which is so pathetic. Why can't I just
smile back and talk to him like I do with everybody else? Ruby reckons he must like me, but
how can I really know?? It's so scary.

Dear Diary,

Thursday January 10th. The trouble with Dad is that he's stupid. He thinks he's really clever because he's a lawyer, but actually he doesn't see how totally imbecilic it is to come home from work and expect all of us to be interested in what he's been doing, when he's never interested in whether or not any of us narrowly escaped being run down by a lorry on the way home, or the fact that GCSEs are next year, or that I wasn't picked for the spring musical. They've offered me lighting, but I'm not going to do it. He's so selfish and distant. He never hugs me any more. The trouble with Mum is that she lets him get away with it. She never ever says anything to him about the really important things in life, like being interested in one's children. She just lets him have his way, and when I told her that, she just said she was too tired to argue with anyone at the moment, but I think she's scared he'll leave again. I mean what exactly does she DO all day when we're at school to make her so tired? She's stopped telling him what she really thinks. She's not being honest with herself. And when she does take issue with him over something, its so totally trivial, like the fact that he's forgotten to do something he'd said he'd do, or he said he'd put Lola to bed but he's left her in the bath so long that it's gone cold and she's fallen asleep in the water. They bicker about this totally pointless stuff, needle each other and squabble over stupid stuff, because they don't wanna talk about the big things, like whether or not they still love each other or whether or not he's going to leave. When they're not bickering about domestic crap, they're focused on the baby. He's never out of Dad's arms, when she lets him hold him, and you don't have to be Freud to work out that they're channelling all of this love and attention into this baby so that they don't have to really look at or talk to each other.

BUT I had this amazingly powerful dream last night that has stayed with me for most of the day. I was floating, flying really, and then I got cornered by this really strong fire and just flew away from it. I've never seen such vivid colours in a dream before. I told Ruby and she said it absolutely had to be about Chattie, because when you have sex with someone you love it feels as if you're on fire, she'd read it in a magazine. He was wearing this really nice baggy top today and jeans. Saskia thinks he used to live abroad and has just moved back to this country because his clothes don't look familiar. Put it this way, they didn't come from either Top Shop, Gap, or down the market. He has his own style. I like that. Saskia thinks we should follow him home and see where he lives. Fran goes why waste the time, he's not THAT fit – just ask him.

Dear Diary,

Saturday SATURDAY!!! And I managed to sleep until 11.30 which makes me feel a lot happier, but for some reason seems to drive Mum mad. She said half the day was gone, wasted in bed, when it's my day, one of only two free days a week, and if I chose to spend the morning asleep what business is it of hers? Anyway, I didn't know I'd slept that long until I woke up, how could I? She goes to bed with the baby whenever she likes. She doesn't even bother to get up at all now in the week if the baby's asleep. She used to get up to see us off to school before the baby was born. Now she says we're old enough to do it by ourselves, and anyway Dad's back and he can do it, but he's so busy rushing round the house, looking for a clean shirt and shaving and complaining about the fact that he's bound to be late for some meeting if he takes Lola to school, that I end up having to do everything for Lola and me. I sometimes think Lola'd go to school without breakfast if I wasn't there. Mum bends over backwards to do things for Dad and Lola (when she can be bothered to get up), but I can't remember the last time she did anything for me, like help me tidy my room, or talk to me about something important instead of just giving out orders.

I NEED to talk to someone, any one of my friends, to find out what's happening, but can't get through to anybody – Ruby, Fran, Saskia are engaged and Serena's gone to her Granny's for the weekend. She's sent me four text messages she's so bored.

Dear Diary,

Sunday and I've had a really crap weekend. Nobody's answering the phone so they're probably all out with each other and without me, or they see my number and just don't answer. Why do I always have this feeling that they're talking about me behind my back? There's nothing to do. Ruby spent the night with Fran; Hayley and Nat went to the cinema with their boyfriends and I really didn't want to tag along, and nobody else would pick up, so I spent Saturday night at home alone. How sad is that? Saturday night! I mean that's all there is, the best night of the week and I stayed in to watch the lottery, knowing that all of the others were out somewhere, having a really good time without me. I know they don't mean to leave me out, but it felt that way. And being alone, without anybody, just made me feel well bad about myself.

Dad was out somewhere and Mum went over to Julie's for dinner and took the baby with her. It was her first time out since giving birth and I could see that she was really excited about it. She didn't even ask if I wanted to come along too, just said there was some pasta in the fridge and went. I know it would have been a bit sad, spending Saturday night with a bunch of middle-aged saddos, but it would have been a great deal better than staying home alone. Even Lola wasn't here to keep me company or argue with. She went next door to Clare's for a sleep-over. So I sat smoking in front of some crap weepie movie. At least it meant I could smoke indoors which is something, I didn't have to go out to that freezing bench. It felt really odd, sitting smoking on the sofa with an ashtray on the arm. Mum's always home, now that she's had the baby, so I kept jumping whenever I heard a noise and had to remind myself that Mum wasn't about to come in and freak.

I raided the fridge for beer, ate an entire can of Pringles, felt sick, and then wished I hadn't eaten them. I thought about sticking my finger down my throat and throwing them up but couldn't be bothered. I started sorting out my room, which should make Mum pleased (when she finds the time to forget about the baby for one minute and actually come into my room and notice). I want to redecorate my room. The walls are going to be deep purple and the window frame black, and I'm going to get some bright pink silky fabric to make cushions for the bed, so that I can sort of sit up at the end and read or what-ever. I put all my CDs into alphabetical order, which means it's much easier to find them. I also found three history homework assignment sheets and my maths books underneath the chest of drawers, which explains why that sad Mouldy cow is on my back again, because I thought I'd done them and handed them in. She threatened me with a detention just for arguing with her. How mean is that?? I'm never going to find the time to do them. I put my maths book in my bag and the history sheets in the bin.

Neither Mum nor Dad got back before midnight and I couldn't get to sleep until I knew that there was someone else here. I think it was Mum who got back first. The silence was kind of creepy, so I lay in bed imagining ways to ask Chattie out, and then kept drifting off, imagining how he really liked me and not Saskia and that he was actually staring at my bedroom window at that very moment, or that he was planning to take me away for the weekend to this really amazing party at a large country house with a heated swimming pool and NOT Saskia, and then I remembered that I hadn't got rid of the smell of cigarettes in the sitting room and raced downstairs to open the window, but that's no good when it's freezing in January, we'd only get burgled, so I sprayed the room with cat flea spray to make it smell different. It was the closest thing I could find to air freshener, which of course Mum never buys because she says it's carcinogenic and very bad for your lungs if your breathe too much in. Saskia's Mum doesn't think so because she has cans of it under her sink. And why have we got cat flea spray when we've never owned a cat? I just managed to chuck the can into the bin before they came back.

Dear Diary, my one and only Diary,

Tuesday. If I don't make myself scarce in my room there's no peace. Mum and Dad had this massive row tonight over the state of the kitchen. Dad reckons that if Mum's home all day she ought to be able to do a little clearing up. She reckons that if he could achieve the simple tasks she set him, like remember to get Lola to school on time with the right PE kit, when she can barely walk, then maybe he'd have a right to criticize. What a pathetic thing to row about. Why don't they just say sorry and make up? The rest of the house doesn't feel like home any more. It's covered with baby things, baby smells, baby noise and Mum clearly resents me getting in the way. As soon as I got in the door yesterday she asked me if I could hold the baby and try and stop him crying, so that she could wash her hair. I mean, excuse me, I'd hardly got in the door. Then she asked me if I could peel some potatoes for tea. How, when you're holding the baby? And when exactly am I supposed to do my homework or talk to my friends, who incidentally don't seem to want to talk to me. Nobody wanted to come back to my house on the way home today, nobody. They all went to Saskia's, even though I couldn't go because I'd promised Mum I'd come straight home. They said to come back for a bit, but that felt wrong, so I went home when I could have been with my friends, and all Mum's done is go on at me to help Lola with her homework, when she's only 10 and homework doesn't mean anything when you're that age. I've got GCSE coursework to do. Who's going to help me with that?

Dear Diary,

Wednesday.

What is going on with my friends? I tried to talk
to them at break and lunch about what was
going on at home, but they didn't seem to
understand. I said how everything was messy
and covered with baby stuff and it stank of baby
lotion, and Fran goes, 'Well at least she can't
have a go at you about your mess then.' When I
said that she never seemed to want to put the
baby down and hug me, Serena goes, 'Well what
do you expect, babies need to be held all the
time, otherwise they feel insecure and grow up
even more fucked up than they're bound to be
by how shit life is.' And Ruby goes, 'Hug your
Dad, at least he's back home, I haven't a clue
where mine is.' It's like I know that I'm lucky in
so many ways, but I don't FEEL lucky. I feel
lonely. I can't remember the last time Mum was
pleased to see me or told me that she loved me,
she's so wrapped up with the baby. And if my
friends don't understand that, and aren't being
supportive, I feel even more lonely, like I
shouldn't be complaining, like there's something
wrong with me for feeling this way. They just
wanna have a laugh at the moment, they don't

wanna be dragged down by my problems. And Saskia is getting on really, really well with Chattie, they seem so at ease with each other when all he ever does with me is smile (oh so sweetly). He says he wants to come to the cinema with us on Saturday night, and Saskia can't stop talking about what she's going to wear and whether or not she's going to pull him. It's like she's assumed they're about to go out before it's even happened, and all the others just go along with it. It's like she's decided he's hers before it's even happened yet. He is so fit. I can't actually take my eyes off him when he's around. I can't concentrate in lessons. He's different to all of the other boys in school, more mature and sooooooo buff! If he actually liked me, if there was any chance that he actually liked me and wanted to be my friend, at least then everything would feel much better, much less bad. I could cope with Mum, the baby, the coursework and everything, I know I could. I think his birthday is in September which means he's a Libra which is a good fit with Gemini. The trouble is that Saskia's a Gemini too.

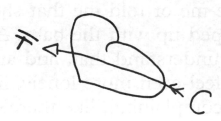

From: Sue James
Sent: Wednesday 16 January 12.02
To: Angela James
Subject: trying to get back to normal, whatever that means!

Darling Ange,

I think I'm becoming addicted to daytime TV! It's amazing, why does it feel as if you have these people sitting in your own front room? The sofas? The cosy chats? I don't know, but whatever it is it's addictive and I feel as if I've joined a club I never knew existed before. I sit there with Tom, either feeding or asleep, with cups of tea and packets of biscuits, completely happy. Sometimes I think I really ought to load the washing machine or put away the children's clothes, and just occasionally I remember the practice waiting room full of patients, and what I would've been doing if I hadn't had Tom, and relish the thought that I don't have to go back until June. Before you know it I'll have HND in here as well for coffee mornings! I bet she has the TV on permanently. (Only joking, I'd have to spend about six hours tidying up the place first, and there's this ghastly lingering smell in the sitting room. I wondered whether maybe there was a dead mouse under the floorboards, but Matthew reckons it's more like insecticide.)

Matthew comes back at 10 or 11 most nights. Says he's got a big case on. Stayed up last night and tried to talk to him about things, but he just said he was too tired as he kicked off his shoes, which threw me into a blind rage. How dare HE talk to ME about being tired when I never get more than two or three hours sleep and HE sleeps through the night on the sofa! How dare he just waltz back in here as if nothing has happened during the last six months, without so much as an explanation or an apology. He just sat there with his head in his hands and said nothing, until I asked him if he'd have come back at all, if there hadn't have been Tom, and he just said quietly, 'I don't know, Sue, I just don't know', at which point I burst into tears, and even that didn't prompt him to comfort me. I just feel all over the place, Ange, so sensitive. I feel like I look worse than Hagrid at the moment, and I really need him to just be loving and supportive, to at least pretend to care even if he doesn't, and if he can't do that then maybe we would be better off apart permanently?

The girls are thrilled to have him home and it's only because of them that I haven't kicked him back out already, and I suppose he is being helpful when he's here, although I spend so much time nagging him about stuff that sometimes I just think it would be easier to do it myself. Iris is being wonderful, but he seems to think that just because she's here and I'm not at work, he doesn't need to do anything at all without being asked. Also, I know I shouldn't say this but, when he is around, he is just SOOOO irritating I wish he wasn't here at all. He's like this huge presence, throwing his weight around, making constant criticisms, goading the kids into even greater rebellion and wanting sympathy for problems which I cannot even begin to comprehend. Clients are difficult, because they are stressed by their own difficulties with the law, they pay him a ton of money to sort out those difficulties, so for him to moan on about this seems to me to be about as pointless as a plumber moaning on about the number of blocked drains he's had to clear in a day.

All I actually want to do is hug my baby boy. I don't wanna talk to him and listen to him moaning. I don't want to sympathize, or even have to deal with his presence if he can't blend in with the walls and be easy to live with. Does that sound too harsh? Tom is so delicious, all I need in the way of male company. He fixes his eyes on me when he's awake and it's just love, pure love. It's uncanny how much like Matthew he looks, but he has Frank and Lola's mouth with those deeply sexy downturned corners – I think that comes from Dad. God how I miss him sometimes. I miss his sense of humour. He could keep us all up and running with that quirky way he had of summing up the absurdities of life, and all that sharpness Mum has would simply melt away. Do your boys have those lips too? I have no idea what they look like really. The photos are always so flat. Not long now though, two months and you'll all be here. Can't wait, and of course you can stay here, you can have Frankie's room and we'll put the twins in with Lola. I won't hear of you staying elsewhere, because how else are these cousins to get to know each other? If you're in the UK I want every available minute with you!

I've been picking up Lola every day this week from school and loving it. I just slob on down there with the other mums and nannies, with Tom in a Snugli, and chat at the school gate about school politics, how they're doing, and the inevitable – what school are you hoping to get her into next? Now that I'm a fulltime mum (for the time being anyway), I feel like I'm just one of them, available for consultations on temperatures and scratches, and happy to hug my girl as she comes running out of her classroom and then hold her hand as she skips back home. Even HND seems happy to chat to me as we wait for them to come out. Her latest fixation is that Clare might have a peanut allergy (not judging by the quantities of Snickers bars and Nutella she consumes in our house), and she has written to the head about the school lunches, wants her on a special diet. Head says she can bring packed lunches, which for some reason offends her. Can't think why.

MASSES of love S xxxxxxxx

Dear Diary

Friday. The entire gang seemed to need to go home to do their homework (What? Why bother when you can just not do it and get a detention instead?). Saskia said that she had to go straight home in order to be allowed out on Saturday night to the cinema and then on to Fran's for a sleepover (I think she's hoping that Chattie'll come to Fran's too), so the others all decided to do the same. I couldn't face going home. Dad's back home late tonight, says he has a meeting, Iris doesn't come and cook on Friday's so the place'll be in a mess, it'll be pasta for tea again and Mum'll be on my back to help. So I decided to go to Top Shop and cheer myself up, except that it's kind of depressing that you know it so well that you can find your way round it with your eyes shut. I tried on loads of things, but none of them seemed to look any good, except this T-shirt which was sort of tight but shaped, so it made my tits look bigger, and then I don't know what came over me but I just got this urge to stuff the T-shirt into my bag. I didn't even want it particularly. It was like I was challenging something to happen to me, and in that moment, when I walked out of the shop, with

my adrenaline pumping, wondering whether I
had been spotted and was about to be arrested,
it was all that mattered. In that moment I felt
powerful and I forgot about everything else –
Mum not really caring, the baby, Dad not
really being there or really carin g, the fact that
everyone else has or has had a boyfriend when
I haven't, the fact that everyone else is happier
with nicer things. I could forget about being
the boring old Frankie for a while. I didn't get
caught, the T-shirt looks great (surprisingly),
and now I'm going to practise with some
make-up, to see if I can get myself looking
really, really good for Chattie tomorrow night.

Dear Diary,

Sunday January 20th 10.30 at night. Mum and
Dad think I'm asleep, but I can't. I can't stop
thinking about Chattie. Saskia made sure she
sat next to him in the cinema, but I managed to
sit on the other side and just the smell of him
made me feel faint. I have no idea what the
film was about. Toby, Will, Sean and Simon
were there too, but sitting down the front
chucking popcorn at the screen, laughing and
back-chatting the film, which made Saskia tut
with disapproval about their immaturity, when
only ten minutes ago she couldn't stop talking
about how fit Simon was and how much she
fancied him. She's so two-faced. Fran sat on the
other side of me with a huge tub of popcorn,
which we shared. It meant I could turn into her
and away from Chattie because every time my
leg or arm brushed against him there was like
this zing of electricity and I thought I was going
to die. Fran was also dying of embarrassment
over Sean. 'I can't believe I actually kissed that
guy, several times,' she kept saying. I don't think
she saw much of the film either.

 After the film was over, Saskia hung around,
hoping that he might suggest something else, but
he didn't. She invited him over to Fran's for a

sleepover, but he said he couldn't because he had to get up early for his riding lesson. RIDING! Do you think Dad'd give me lessons if I asked him at a good moment? And THEN he said that he really liked my T-shirt, the one I nicked from Top Shop. He said that he thought it was cool and suited the colour of my hair! How amazing is that . . . that he even noticed???

Dear Diary,

Tuesday. I can't believe I got another detention today. I'm stacking them up so quickly that I'm beginning to spend more time at school than I do at home. Still, it does mean I can use the computer in the IT room and catch up on some coursework, and of course it does mean that I don't have to be at home to help with the baby. Mum and Dad were so horrible to me last night that it would actually have been preferable to spend the night at school. First Dad had a go at me about my appearance. Since he's been back, he seems to think he has a right to comment on what I wear or choose to put on my face. Last night he said I was wearing much too much make-up, which was rubbish, and that he found all piercings abhorrent, and that if I ever even thought of getting a nose ring I could pack my bags right now. Well that's charming that is. Didn't even ask me what I thought about piercings (when I think I hate them because Chattie does). And then Mum, who hadn't heard all this because she was next door collecting Lola, chooses suppertime (a disgusting meat loaf with spinach, yuk, because Mum says she's anaemic after the baby – so why do we have to eat it too?) to lay into me about the phone bill, which she says is at least £90 higher than it was last time, and that I really was going to have to spend less time talking to my friends, when we don't talk about anything important anyway and I see them all day long. Well, what does she know, she who hasn't got any friends anyway? What does she know about friendship and how important it is to talk? Sometimes I really hate living here. Sometimes I wish I could live somewhere else. Maybe Fran or Ruby's mum would like to take me in as a lodger, or adopt me.

From: Sue James
Sent: Tuesday 22 January 19.42
To: Angela James
Subject: Re: trying to get back to normal, whatever that means!

That's fantastic that the boys now ask to go to nursery – congratulations! A real break-through . . .

  We're going through what must be termed one of the lows of family life – teenagers! Frankie is more grumpy, stroppy, rude and unhelpful than I've ever known her, when this is exactly the time when we really need her to be easy to live with. Can't ever get her up in the morning without shouting in her ear ten times, dragging off the duvet and putting on the radio at full volume. When I ask her to help clear up something, she says the mess wasn't hers, which is what 5-year-olds say, and she was unbelievably insulting at supper last night. Said it was like eating pig's shit when I had actually made an effort to cook something proper for the first time since Tom was born, so that was kind of hurtful and hard to stomach (ha ha!), and then she has a go at me about not having any friends, which is also kind of hurtful when I would have a lot more if I didn't spend all my time either at work or at home looking after my children, and then she stormed off, screaming and shouting that we didn't understand her, that she hated us, that she wished she lived somewhere else, which is also deeply hurtful (although not a bad idea, now I understand why they farmed children out as apprentices before we had compulsory schooling). I had planned a different meal. Matthew was home early for once, I feel stronger, able to cook and be motherly, and it is ages since we have just been together as a family at supper. Everyone is usually off doing their own thing. But it was not to be. Shame. It's teenagers I suppose, the 'age' as they say. Hormones. Still no sign of a period though, perhaps it'll get better once she has one.

Tonight, everyone is calmer, both girls are watching *EastEnders*, Frankie is sullen but polite, and I daren't bring up the subject of the exorbitant phone bill again in case we have another row. Matthew said we were lucky it wasn't £150 more than the usual amount, rather than just £90, and to let it go, we can afford it, but I kind of feel that there's a principle at stake here. Otherwise, life with Tom is blissful, there are crocuses coming up in the garden and I'm planning to take up walking for at least an hour a day to get my strength up and shift a little weight.

Much love Sue xxxx

Dear Diary,

Friday. January 25th. Midnight. I think Mum and Dad are asleep. Tom certainly isn't, he's been crying for hours and neither of them have got up for him. I'm not going, he's not my responsibility. Saskia's been a complete bitch all week. Ruby must have told her that I fancy Chattie because Saskia makes a point of talking about him whenever I'm around. She goes on and on about how he's asked her if she'd like to go riding with him, because of course Saskia knows how to ride, and how brilliant he is at football, because she stayed behind after school on Wednesday to watch them play. Then, whenever he's anywhere near us, she throws her arms around his shoulders in this really embarrassing way, like she owns him or something. So I've kept away from them both. If he does fancy her, and it's hard to see why anyone would fancy her (she's not THAT pretty), then he's welcome to her. I just don't like the way that makes me feel about me. I may not be as pretty, but I am MUCH nicer than Saskia, not smug and spoilt like she is, and if he can't see that, if he can't see me for who I really am, then maybe nobody can, and that's kind of depressing. If he could only see me for who I was, then maybe everything else would be better. Ruby swears she never said anything to Saskia, but I don't believe her. And that's also kind of depressing, being betrayed by your best friend.

Went to Top Shop again this afternoon. Friday afternoon is a good time to nick something because it's kind of like your reward at the end of another boring, depressing week. I nicked a lacy top and a jumper. It's SOOOO easy . . . and I really wanted this wide Sixties belt, right by the entrance, but there was this security guard hovering there and I got scared. Might go back for it next week.

Tom is STILL CRYING and nobody's picked him up. Do you think I should?

I've brought him back to bed with me to try and shut him up by bouncing him around on my shoulder like Mum does, but he won't. I think he needs feeding. He's lying on my bed now with a bright red face. I wish he'd shut up. You can see why people shake babies. It would be so easy just to kill him right now. He's so fragile and defenceless. Imagine that, he has no idea that he could be just seconds away from death because he's just a tiny baby, yet just 14 years on I know. I know the only thing between life and permanent darkness is my desire to keep him alive (and not end up in prison for the rest of my life. Do you think teenage sisters can get off on compassionate grounds on the basis that their lives have been completely fucked up by the arrival of this unwanted sibling?). Better wake up Mum before this line of thought goes any further.

Mum just grabbed him from my hands and shut him up with one of her tits and didn't even say thank you. Charming.

Dear Diary,

Saturday. I've spent all afternoon trying to write him a letter and it keeps going wrong. I mean how DO you tell someone that you really like them? My bin is full of rejects. I've tried 'Would you like to come out with me next weekend?'; 'I can't get you out of my head, I think I love you'; and I've even copied out a Shakespeare sonnet and thought about sending it anonymously, but what good would that do if he doesn't know who it's from? He might even think it was from Saskia. I can't stop thinking about him, and I feel slightly sick when I do think of him. I've lost my appetite, even for chocolate and biscuits. Maybe I shouldn't even try and let him know. Maybe it's pointless. What would someone like him want to do with someone like me anyway?????

Dear Diary,

Saturday night. I've just had a massive row with Ruby over the phone. Instead of being supportive and understanding, she's SOOOO defensive. She goes that I am the one who is not being a good friend by not believing her. Says that a true friend would not accuse her of lying, when I know that a true friend does not talk about you behind your back and she DID. I've been crying and crying, can't stop crying. I rang Fran and she said she thought I was being oversensitive, and what did it matter anyway if she had told Saskia, because she probably knew anyway, and that it was better with boys to stand back a bit and let Saskia make a fool of herself. At least that way he actually gets to know who I am. Thanks Fran. Now I feel like they've all been talking about me behind my back, about how stupid I am, and I don't want to see any of them. I just want to stay here in this room. It's safe here. Nobody can see me. Nobody can see me crying. I wish I could stop crying. My face has gone all blotchy and my nose is red. Maybe I am oversensitive? Why am I such a cry baby? Why do I feel so alone?

Dear Diary,

Saturday. 2 a.m. I've read a whole book about dating and my star sign for the week, and it's clear that I should do absolutely nothing at all about Chattie, just sit it out, but it is hard to concentrate on anything else. I tried to do some history homework this evening, but I couldn't really concentrate on anything but him. I feel so wiped out, and then trying to do some work just made me feel worse because I didn't achieve anything, couldn't even find my notes. I'm just a loser. It doesn't help that Mum's so obsessed with the baby either. 'Not going out?' she asked after supper. There's no need to sound quite so surprised, Mum. In fact it's surprising that she's even noticed. I think that's the first thing she's said to me all day. I told her I had some homework to do and ran back up to my room. Now it's 2 a.m. and I can't sleep and the baby is crying AGAIN. Why do they never wake up any more. Why do I have to deal with this????

Dear Diary,

Sunday. Woke up to find blood all over my pyjama bottoms but not on the sheets. Period number 2. Mum's been up since 2 a.m. with the baby and she's walking round the house like a zombie with her eyes barely open, so I didn't bother telling her, although I did wonder about my pyjamas. How do you get bloodstains out? If I put them in the washing machine they could make everything else bloody (how disgusting), so I took them straight out to the dustbin and threw them away. The first period is exciting. The second's just manky and I wish I didn't have to have them. It feels like I'm walking around the house with a mattress swinging between my legs.

I can't believe I wasted the whole of yesterday thinking about Chattie. I rang Ruby to apologize, but she was out and her mobile was on voice-mail, so I rang Fran and she said I should just forget it, she'd get over it. I don't know though. Ruby and I have never argued like that before.

Dear Diary,

Sunday evening. Mum's asleep, Dad's shouting
at Lola for no apparent reason other than that
she's ten and irritating and spoilt (which is all
his fault anyway), there's fuck all on the TV
other than pop videos on MTV, and Dad won't
let me watch them, so I'm trying again to do
my history homework. I've got to write an essay
on Victorian attitudes to morality, which means
sex, and I can't find anything that even refers to
it in the coursebook. All I know is that they
wore horrible clothes to cover up their bodies,
which must have made teenage angst about
body image a great deal easier to deal with
when you just can't see it at all. I think I'll go
and run a bath. Periods make you feel so dirty.
The blood smells horrible.

From: Sue James
Sent: Wednesday 30th January 13.12
To: Angela James
Subject: sometimes I feel like dancing (if only I could trust my pelvic floor)

Ange darling,

Life during the day with just Tom and me couldn't be simpler or more blissful. If the sun's out and it's not too cold we go for a walk. I'm beginning to feel the muscles of my legs working again. If it's not nice we stay in. I can sort of cope with just the two of us and our minimal needs, and I've now got the energy to cook and clean up when he's asleep, but the evenings and weekends, when everyone else is around, send me into a blind panic. Suddenly life gets more complicated. Lola's rowing with friends at school and snappy at home (sibling rivalry?), and I don't know how to sort it out for her; Frankie's monosyllabic and sulking (sibling rivalry? How can I even begin to fathom what's up with her if she won't even speak to me?); and Matthew is patriarchal and demanding. He hasn't asked me to cut his toenails yet, but it's only a matter of time . . . (sibling rivalry?)

Matthew has now reassumed his place in the marital bed. When I asked what this signified he simply said, 'Well I'm back now, and that sofa's bloody uncomfortable.' Typical pragmatic male mind. When I said that it would have been nice if he had asked if I wanted him there, since he was the one who had left it, he just looked hurt and I'm the one left feeling guilty, FOR WHAT???? Every time I try and talk to him about what's going on, he either avoids me or accuses me of being overanalytical. Patronizing bastard . . . I'm desperate for a really big row to clear the air and move things on, but every time I try he just walks away from it. He WON'T talk about it which is just MADDENING.

It's really odd having him there at night. I've got used to sleeping alone and rather like it. The bed suddenly feels minuscule, and I lie there long after Tom has gone back to sleep and look at this stranger in my bed, this man I thought I knew so well. I'm tempted to buy a king-size, now that I am king-size (separate beds feels like too radical and irrevocable a statement).

We've moved Tom into a cot on the landing,

just outside our bedroom, because Matthew's worried about squashing him and thinks that if we don't move him out of our bed now, he'll never move out. I felt like saying, 'That's fine with me, why don't YOU move out into the cot on the landing,' but bit my lip. I missed him, but I did sleep. If it had been my first baby I would have been up all night, hovering behind the door. Since it was my third, I fell straight into a deep sleep and poor Frankie had to get up for him. She wasn't pleased, but she was awake anyway, and since she does absolutely nothing around here to help otherwise, I think she's got a bit of a nerve to complain about that. (She mentions it every night now before she goes to bed.) Since then Tom's settled into sleeping alone a little better, I've got up at the slightest sound from him, Frankie's slept, and Matthew feels he's won a small victory.

Mind you, I have been very tired. There's been panic at the surgery – there's a major flu epidemic in London at the moment, three doctors are off sick, and they simply can't cope with a waiting room splitting at the seams and enough patients demanding home visits to choke up the switchboard. So I've been back in a bit, for a few hours between feeds, to try and ease the flow, but the most upsetting part was visiting a woman today who wasn't much older than me I suppose, with two children a bit younger than Frank and Lola. She died from the flu about half an hour before I got there. It happens occasionally, she probably had a weak heart. Her husband was distraught, her two children in shock, and there was nothing I could do. If someone from the surgery had got to her the day before with a massive dose of antibiotics and taken her into hospital, she might have survived, but I didn't say that, obviously. I sat with them awhile, tried to help with tea and sympathy, but just felt helpless, hopeless and very shaken. She was so young, pretty, important to her family. It could have been me. That could have been Frank, Lola and Matthew crying at my bedside . . . puts everything into perspective somehow . . . We may be having a turbulent time, but death would end all of it . . . cliché but true.

Having this baby has definitely aged me by at least a decade in less than a year – stretch marks steadfastly refusing to go, and I've begun to get those fine wrinkles on my upper lip (you might not recognize me at the airport). Every time I look in the mirror I seem to look older. HND says collagen cream is the answer. Botox is attractive but must be devastating for the liver.

Lola and I are off down to see Mum on Sunday, so I'll give her your love. Frank refuses to come. Says she has too much home-work. Any idea yet when you'll be here?? Good Friday is on March 29th this year (Is it different there? I've never understood why the date moves around so . . .), so presumably the week before????
Masses of love Sue xxxxx

Dear Diary,

Thursday 31st January. I can't believe a whole month has gone since Christmas, which means there's only 2 weeks to go until Valentine's day (I've bought six different cards and can't decide which one to send to Chattie), five months to go to my 15th birthday and 11 months to go until next Christmas!

Ruby and I have just about made up. We've hugged and all that, but there's still this residual resentment, like she can't quite forgive me for believing she could tell Saskia, so maybe she didn't. Maybe Saskia just knew. It's hardly difficult when I blush and go completely silent every time he's near me. Ruby's coming over on Saturday, and we thought we'd check out this café he says he loves to eat in because the fries are fresh and there's this really cool art all over the walls. So maybe I'll really feel as if we've made up then.

Dear Diary,

Friday. The others were all going to Saskia's to watch a video, but I didn't want to go. I don't really wanna be around her when all she can talk about is how Chattie said this to her and Chattie did that. I pretended I had to get home to look after Lola, but went to Top Shop instead. I sort of feel pulled there, it's like my secret. And it is Friday. I haven't even told Ruby. I hope she doesn't feel that's a betrayal. You're not supposed to keep anything from your best friend. But it's funny how it doesn't feel THAT exciting any more because it's so easy. If anything it feels kind of grubby and pathetic that I'm doing this on my own, rather than with a gang of friends for a laugh. I tried on some things and didn't like any of them. There wasn't even anything I really wanted. I got away with the wide Sixties belt without anyone noticing, although I did feel scared as I left the shop. Maybe I should stop this. Maybe I should make a definite plan with someone for next Friday so that I don't end up in Top Shop *again*.

Dear Diary,

Sunday 3rd February. Chattie's favourite café really is cool. No wonder he likes it so much. We share the same style, another indication that we are meant for one another. The seats are furry, fake leopardskin and the walls are painted matt, dark grey so that the black and white photographs displayed on them seem highlighted and stronger. They're really powerful images of animals with people, where the animals look strong and big and the people look weak and small. Very deep. He must be an animal lover. I mean, how many teenage boys go riding? Maybe he keeps all sorts of weird pets like ferrets and salamanders. I'd better read up on them. Saskia says he wants to be a vet. Perhaps I should think of doing that too?

It was weired being there though. I kept looking at the door, thinking that he might walk in at any moment, and what would we do then? Ruby said we should pretend that we'd always loved this place and had been here lots of times before, and that we should study the menu and the prices, so that I'd have something to talk about with him if the café came up in conversation. We shared a plate of fries and had a milkshake each.

310

From: Sue James
Sent: Monday 4 February 11.12
To: Angela James
Subject: Re: It's March 22

FANTASTIC! Can't wait to see you! Good timing too, with a few days to get over jet lag before Easter. Haven't told Mum yet. What do you think we should do? Get her here as well for Easter weekend? (God knows where she'll sleep, although come to think of it she could have our bedroom and Matthew and I could sleep in the sitting room.) She seemed frail yesterday, said her hip hurt and was rather vacant, a little depressed perhaps. She was pleased to see me and the baby, but then she just sat there, staring out of the window into the middle distance, and complained repeatedly about the weather (which is grey, wet and typically February). I quizzed the nurses, who said that she hadn't had a fall, but that she had been a little quiet lately. They weren't concerned, but she worried me slightly. She seemed smaller, she's aged a lot just in the past month and doesn't seem to have that energy or sparkle that is Mum, with

311

an interest or an opinion on everything. She didn't even have the energy to have a go at me, which (as you know) is unprecedented.

Matthew reckons it must have been quite a blow for her, going back to North Butting after Christmas. Last year she had Harry and Jack to go back to, now there are fewer and fewer of her friends left. I also think that she's taken one of those great leaps down that old people do from time to time – they age suddenly and then stabilize for a while. Old age is no fun a lot of the time. If only I could move her somewhere nearer – perhaps now is the time to investigate alternatives in London again, before I go back to work – but she did make it clear that she wanted to be in the country, near where she used to live with Dad, and I couldn't persuade her otherwise. The trouble is that there really isn't any alternative to her being in a home. We'd have to sell here and find somewhere else with another bedroom if she was to live with us (and even though I think she'd probably quite like being with us, we're urban London and the Common hardly ranks with Gloucestershire), and I'm not sure that it's fair on the kids, or on me . . . except that at least there would be less guilt. Let's see how she fares over the next couple of months. I said

I'd go down and see her the weekend after next. She has started her painting of the five of us . . . absolutely hideous . . . for some reason she's decided to put us all on a bench on the street and Matthew looks like he's about 8-foot tall with a giant egg head, but it's a really good likeness of Lola. So far I'm just sketched, so no doubt she'll turn me into some fat, ugly gargoyle!!! It's impressive though, her dedication and her skill. I expect she'll do you four next, better bring some of your best photos with you to maximize your chances of a flattering likeness.

Tom's crying so I'd better go, and it's STILL RAINING damn it! I wanted to take him out for a long walk. Haven't managed to shift any weight at all and beginning to feel DESPERATE! All my really nice clothes are still much too small and I'm sick of wearing baggy jumpers.

Talk soon. Loads of love S xxxxx

Dear Diary,

Tuesday. 8.30. Saskia went riding with Chattie on Saturday and she can't stop talking about it. I hate her. I really, REALLY, REALLY hate her. Now all she can talk about is how much she loves horses, when she's never, ever even thought about them before, let alone LIKED them. Honestly, she's so two-faced. I don't wanna be anywhere near her and hear her boasting like that, but the trouble is that everyone else seems to be attracted like a magnet to her, and I don't want to be completely on my own. They hang on to every word she says and she's just lapping up the attention. Ruby asked her today if he had kissed her yet and all she could say was 'Not exactly'!

'So what does that mean, Saskia? Exactly?' Ruby replied, which made her storm off. Thanks Rubes.

It just makes me feel like I'm not worth anything, that's all. I'm not worth anything because he wants her rather than me, and I'm now labelled as a loser by my best friends because they all know how I feel about Chattie and that I've lost out to Saskia. I HATE HER I HATE HER I HATE HER!

Dear Diary,

Wednesday. 9.30. What a disgusting supper.
How does Mum manage to ruin even a roast
chicken. Doesn't she know that the skin is the
fattiest bit, and that it is guaranteed to give you
a heart attack in about ten minutes if you even
just look at it? She dumped masses of the skin
on to my plate because she says I love it, and
then looked all hurt and offended when I said I
didn't want it. I used to like the skin, Mum,
before I knew better. Anyway, we shouldn't be
eating chicken at all, because they're raised in
barbaric prison conditions, and fattened up
with hormones and antibiotics, rather than with
any real food, and then we get to eat them.
Great. Anyway, Mum gets the hump all
through supper, just because I didn't eat a bit
of skin. It's pathetic. As if I haven't got enough
to worry about with my GCSEs coming up.
What am I going to do with my life? What
happens if I fail all my GCSEs and end up
unemployed, homeless and miserable on the
streets? Do you think she'd notice then? How
can I concentrate on my GCSEs when I don't
even know what I want to do with my life, and
whether or not these are worth my while
studying for? I mean geography, it's all right,

it's quite interesting sometimes, I'd like to go to some of these places, get away from here, but is it really relevant to my future? Does it really matter?

Dear Diary,

Thursday. 2.30. The café on the Common. I couldn't stand it in that place a minute longer, so I've snuck out early for a cigarette and a bit of peace. I didn't even tell Ruby I was going. Sometimes I just want to be left alone. I don't want anybody to see me, think about me, I don't wanna have to talk to anybody, worry about making a mark on the world, making an effort, keeping my end up. I just wanna be somewhere where I can be me. Whoever that is. It's really cold. This coat is much too thin for this icy wind, and it's not raining yet but the sky looks dark. I could go inside, but they won't let me smoke in there and it's more peaceful here. No one around to look at me. The hot chocolate's warm enough. Can't think why I haven't come here before. It's peaceful. Pretty even. There's geese and ducks on the pond. They stick together, they don't judge each other, not like people do. I'm alone here, but then again we're actually always alone in life. Funny that. As a child you don't ever think about being alone in the world, unless you get lost and scared and then someone finds you, but when you get to this age you feel lost all the time, because the world suddenly seems so big out there and there's no one really rooting for you all of the time like when you were younger. You're alone with your weaknesses and your mistakes, they're all yours, no one else's. You're expected to do things for yourself when maybe you don't want to, maybe you can't, maybe you don't know how.

From: Sue James
Sent: Friday 8 February 23.12
To: Angela James
Subject: shoplifting

Got a call at about 5.30 from Westminster
Police to say that Frankie had been caught
shoplifting and could I come down to the
station. I dumped Lola with HND and of
course couldn't say why, just that there was a
slight emergency (luckily she was in), took
Tom with me in the car, and sat in this horrendous traffic jam for about an hour because it's
Friday night. When I finally got there Frankie
looked completely distraught. She'd been
crying, her face was smudged and her hair
dishevelled. She hadn't been put in a cell,
thankfully (are they allowed to anyway with
minors??), and the policewoman was actually
quite nice to her, gave her a cup of tea and
some biscuits. However the humiliation and the
anxiety of having to face me with this shameful
behaviour, and then having to wait for over an
hour to see me because I was stuck in traffic,
was evidently too much for her. She burst into
this awful anguished, heaving sobbing when

319

she saw me, and I didn't know what to do. Instinctively I wanted to just wrap her in my arms and tell her that everything was going to be all right, but actually the stupid girl had just been caught stealing, which is a serous criminal offence, and I felt that I had to show some sort of parental disapproval, particularly in front of a policewoman. So, I sort of hovered uncertainly, and it was the policewoman who sat down next to Frankie and put her arms around her shoulders and said, 'There, There, Love,' which made me feel completely inadequate because it should have been me. I'm her Mum.

They let her off with a caution because of her age, but said that if she ever got caught again she would be prosecuted. She's bloody lucky, the stupid girl was trying to steal a coat the size of a house, with several security tags on, so it would have been a miracle if she hadn't got caught. Why a coat for fuck's sake??? She's got two perfectly good ones. I carried her bag for her back to the car and we sat in the dark for a while, in silence, and then I just lost it, Ange, I don't know why or where it came from. I was expecting her to say something like 'I'm sorry' or even 'Thank you for coming to get me', but she didn't, she just sat there hiding behind her hair. I asked her why she needed to steal, we're not short of money, and she said that she didn't know why, that it just felt right at that moment. Perhaps it was just the casual indifference of her response that made me incandescent with rage, or maybe it was just that at that moment everything about living with a selfish, morose, monosyllabic teenager, a new-born baby and an emotionally detached quasi-autistic man, came to a head. I just blew up, shouted at her, called her stupid and selfish and burst into tears. The baby bellowed from sheer shock, and Frankie screamed back at me before storming off into the night. I shouldn't have, I know. She needed me to keep it all together at that moment, but stealing, when we're not short of money, when she doesn't actually want for anything, when so many other people have so much less than she does and don't steal, and not to even know why, and because it felt 'right'?? What does that say about me as a mother? How can she not know in her bones that it's wrong, always wrong?

So I stormed off into the night after her, with the baby crying, and found her sobbing at the entrance of a mansion block, and I ended up having to say that I was sorry to her in order to get her back to the car. By the time we'd crawled back home through the rush-hour traffic we were on speaking terms again. I asked her if the coats she had were warm enough, and said that if she felt she needed a new coat she should have asked. She said she didn't need one. I asked her again why she'd done it, and again she said that she didn't know why, that maybe if she knew why she could stop (which means she's done it before) and that it was good for a laugh, and that at that moment she could forget everything (forget what?). It just feels like such a kick in the stomach, Ange, just when I'm vulnerable. I'm still so angry with her that I can barely look her in the eye. It's like I don't even know my own child any more. How could she be so stupid? How could she?

Maybe they're all at it? Maybe that's how teenagers get their kicks these days? I suppose it's better for their health than smoking or drugs, but it is illegal, and what's more it's wrong. I thought I might ring Ruby's mum and see if she's been aware of any shoplifting, but that means fessing up and I'm not sure if that's wise. Do you think I should? I feel I ought to, as a responsible parent, but it might make Frankie feel as if I've betrayed her confidence. She asked me not to tell Matthew. They've not been getting on that well since he left, and she just doesn't want another row – facing up to me is enough I can see that – but I'm not really even sure about that either. He ought to know, he's her dad, and then what happens if he discovers somehow and realizes he wasn't consulted? Teenagers, Ange, why is it all that much more complicated when they get to this age. You've got it easy when they're young, enjoy it.

Love Sue xxxx

Dear Diary,

Sunday February the tenth and I've been
grounded all weekend. Dad won't even let me
go over to Ruby's. He's just a weird, saddo
psychopath and TOTALLY STUPID, because
grounding me doesn't teach me anything at
all. It doesn't teach me not to steal, it doesn't
make me see the error of my ways and repent.
It just means I can't see my friends and I feel
even more lonely and bored. It just means I
have to spend the whole weekend in my
bedroom, to avoid seeing my own father. It
just means I sit here and smoke more. I know
I shouldn't have done it, I've said I'm sorry,
I've promised I'll never do it again. What
more does he want??? Does he think that I
need to be PUNISHED for this, that being
caught by a security guard, frogmarched
through to the back of Top Shop, driven
through London in the back of a police car
and then having to wait for two hours at the
police station for Mum to be bothered to
come and get me isn't enough??? I never ever
want to go through that again. Did he never
do anything just a tiny bit wrong when he was
young? Come to think of it, probably not. And
why is my getting caught stealing stuff any

324

worse than him puffing away on illegal drugs on a Saturday night after Lola's gone to bed? Then he started having a go at Ruby, blaming her for the fact that I've been nicking things, which is so mad it's funny, because she doesn't even KNOW. I told him that, but he didn't believe me, doesn't believe anything I say, and at lunchtime today said he wanted me to stop seeing Ruby, that she was a bad influence, which is even madder because she is the only person in this world that keeps me sane because she's my best friend. He can't stop me seeing my best friend.

Mum promised me that she wouldn't tell Dad. I knew he'd over-react like this, but she just couldn't keep it to herself, so that's the last time I trust her with anything. I could hear them rowing about it late into Friday night from my bed. He was furious, really angry, frighteningly so, and he blamed Mum, said that it was her job to make sure I stayed out of trouble, which is hardly fair since she didn't ask me to steal something and she isn't with me every minute of the day. Mum went mad at that, and said that since he was the one who had disrupted family life by leaving us, then maybe he ought to think about meeting his responsibilities before he accused her of failing hers. I could hear her crying, like she used to when they rowed before he left. I hate hearing her cry. Parents are supposed to be the strength that you rely on, and it's my problem, not theirs, so they shouldn't be this upset. I wanted to go down and tell them to shut up, that it was rude to talk about me like that behind my back, that this concerned me, that it was all my fault, and they should talk to me rather than argue, but then I heard Mum tell Dad that she found me unbearably selfish and unreasonable at the moment – 'She's an absolute nightmare most of the time and does nothing but add to our difficulties with a new baby. The last thing I needed on a Friday night was to have to drive up to town to collect her from a police station' – but I was a teenager now and that he had to expect some trouble. Teenagers get up to things, experiment.

Well thank you Mum. It was really upsetting to hear that. Like I'm not as important as the other two, like my needs don't matter any more now that I'm fourteen, like I've let them down. I can't help being the way I am, I don't even really know who I am. Like everything is all my fault, that I'm the one who makes everything bad around here, when she was the one who went and got pregnant by mistake and ruined everything. What you need when you're a teenager is really supportive parents, not rowing ones, parents who say they love you, no matter what, because there's so much other shit to deal with at school where you're bored stupid and rowing with your friends. I haven't told them that I heard them. I just sat there on Saturday morning and let Dad rant at me, took the lecture like a punch on the cheek and left it at that. What point is there in arguing with him when he never listens? I said I was sorry, that I'd never do it again, but he just went on and on, banging on about WHY? And HOW COULD I BE SO STUPID? When I don't know why I did it, and I'm not that stupid. Why do grown-ups always have to insist that there are reasons for things, when sometimes there aren't any? Maybe if I knew why I'd done it I wouldn't have needed to do it at all in the first place, but you can't say these things to Dad because he never listens, so I went to my room and kicked the wall. At least I had a full packet of cigarettes to keep me company. I've got three left. It's too cold to smoke out of the window, and I really don't care any more whether or not they find out. What could they do to me now?

From: Sue James
Sent: Monday 11 February 12.52
To: Angela James
Subject: Re: shoplifting

What do you mean 'don't take it so person-ally'? How can I not when she's my daughter and my responsibility? And I'm not being THAT hard on her, Ange. The idiot has just been caught shoplifting, which is a criminal offence. I'm amazed that you used to do it when you were only a year or two older than Frankie, and no I never knew. Did Mum ever find out? Did you ever get caught? What else did you get up to? The worst thing I ever did was drink so much vodka one Saturday night that I threw up all over a parked car before collapsing, and Jack had to drag me home, poor boy. I felt so ill it was months before I could drink again, and even now the smell of vodka makes me feel sick. I'm such an inno-cent STILL, and so trusting. What's amazing, when I think back, is how much I took the flak from Mum for you when I was the good one!

The truth is, that I don't actually know

what I'm supposed to do with Frankie, as her mother. I can't stop her from stealing, or doing anything else for that matter, because I'm not with her most of the time, and she doesn't confide in me any more. Matthew hasn't helped by being so heavy-handed with her this weekend that she retreated to her room and refused to come out to eat with us. I heard her sneak down to the kitchen at about 10 last night to raid the fridge. I know that teenagers just do this sort of thing from time to time, but actually what I can't shake from my mind is that in some ways it is all my fault, that maybe Matthew *is* right and I am to blame for not bringing her up well enough to KNOW that what she has done is wrong. Fear of getting caught isn't enough of a deterrent (although I suspect it will work in Frankie's case). I want my children to have a deep knowledge in their hearts and bones as to what is right and wrong, where the lines of good and bad behaviour lie, how to treat people well, and I'm not sure that Frankie does have that. Doesn't she realize that the mistakes you make at this age can stay with you for the rest of your life? Obviously everyone is an individual, and children are their own people, but there is no substitute for good parenting, and how people bring up their children makes an enormous difference. So how have I failed her if Frankie feels that it's perfectly OK to steal? Has she stolen things from us? Is she innately criminal, or is this just a phase she's going through? And who do I talk to, who do I ask for advice as to how to bring her back on track? I have no idea. No one tells you how to do this bit.

Maybe it isn't fair to blame her for rocking the boat right now, but things were just beginning to settle down with Matthew and now he's walking around like an active torpedo. You should have heard him leave this morning on his motorbike. He made so much noise it was like Concorde taking off. HND was round within minutes to complain about the noise. I wish I hadn't told him. Frankie was right about that. Their relationship is now at rock bottom, Matthew has found another stick to beat me with, and Frankie scowls at me silently whenever we pass on the stairs. It's going to take some effort to get us back on to an even keel. I really don't need all this right now, but at least I'm not at work as well, so there is a bit of time to try and sort things out. Thought I'd surf the net a bit this afternoon

and check out parenting groups for advice.
At least it's anonymous.

Lots of love Sue xxx

Dear Diary,

Valentine's Day.

Didn't get a single card in the post so one thing's for certain – Chattie didn't send me one. I on the other hand sent him six. Couldn't decide which was the nicest card, or the one that was most 'Me', so in the end I sent them all. Now I realize that was a really stupid thing to do, because all this attention is just going to make him big-headed. He'll think there are all these girls out there fancying him, which means he's even less likely to want me.

Saskia of course got one and brought it to school. Even Hayley got one and no one's EVER said they fancy her, let alone kissed her or sent her a card. She was so excited about it she said she was going to buy a frame for it. Everyone it seems got a Valentine card except for me. I think if this goes on for much longer I really will have to kill myself.

From: Sue James
Sent: Thursday 14 February 15.21
To: Angela James
Subject: Valentine's Day

Dearest Dear,

Well, I simply can't move in this house for
flowers, there are boxes of chocolates piled
high on the kitchen table, expensive perfume
and bath essence, cards and gifts flooding in
through the letterbox . . . how was
Valentine's day for you? Matthew completely
forgot. I think that was conscious, wilful
forgetting, because actually you can't forget
these days. Every shop window has red hearts
on it, the radio never stops talking about it,
and Lola's made about a dozen different cards
in the last three days. I, on the other hand,
found the time to buy him a pair of red satin
boxer shorts and a card.
   You're right, ignore him for the moment
and concentrate on Frankie. The trouble is
that she makes herself scarce as much as
possible. She's coming in late from school

(says there's a swimming gala coming up, but leaves her swimming costume at home) and spends every single moment either on the phone to her friends or locked away in her bedroom. I went in there last night and tried to talk to her, but she just screamed at me to go away. As I looked into her face, filled with hate for me, I saw myself at her age screaming at Mum. God how I hated her for making my life a misery, for dumping so much family stuff on me, treating me like some sort of housewife maidservant, just because I was the eldest, when I wanted to be out with my friends. And then she could never resist that swipe about my appearance, just because I was on the big side like Dad, rather than thin like you and her. Now, here is my own daughter, someone I have loved more than life itself, hating me, pushing me away, cutting me out of her life like I did with Mum. That hurts. Still, she is eating with us again, which is a bit of a breakthrough, and I suggested she had some friends over sometime soon, for a back-to-back video sleepover with as much popcorn as they could eat, which produced an 'OK' and even a 'Thank you', so hopefully that's some basis of communication to build on.

Better go and get Lola from school. I was so late yesterday that she was the last one left. I intend to be first today, S xxx

✉

From: Sue James
Sent: Friday 15 February 02.31
To: Angela James
Subject: you were right

Not only did Matthew fail to remember Valentine's Day, he didn't come home until 11.30, shouted at me when I told him that I thought that was a fucking shitty thing to do on this of all nights, and then he laid the whole ugly scenario in front of my eyes and wiped my nose in it. You were right, Ange. He's been having an affair with a 28-year-old legal secretary at work for the past six months, and he was with her tonight. He says it's over, but it clearly isn't for him because he was with her instead of me. He says she has put an end to it because she wants to find someone her own age with whom she can have children. 'I don't expect you to have any sympathy, Sue,' he said sheepishly, 'but I'm gutted.' HE'S gutted!

I was quite surprised by my own reaction really. I didn't cry or feel particularly upset at first – just a sense of overwhelming relief, peace even, that the truth was now out and

336

that I wasn't being paranoid or neurotic, because I finally had an explanation. Then I just sort of exploded – that I had to be the one to be reasonable when HE was the one who had got us into this mess, just because he couldn't keep his fucking pants on, seemed so unfair – that HE had the nerve to tell ME that he was gutted by her leaving, when actually HE was the one who left ME when I was pregnant with his child. It wasn't jealousy so much as the betrayal of it, the fact that he could be so selfish when I was this vulnerable. Then, after I exploded, I started crying and couldn't stop. I sat there sobbing, feeling so alone, so old and unattractive, so stupid for having been such a fool. He tried to put his arm around me, but I didn't want him anywhere near me, and then he started crying and saying that he was sorry, that he had been such a fool and that he loved me. Honestly, Ange, I don't know what to think any more. I'm so confused and tired through lack of sleep, Frankie's exploits, Tom, that I don't know what to do about it. Nothing probably . . . he's back on the sofa – not asleep, I can hear him listening to the World Service – and I said we'd talk some more in the morning, after the kids have gone to school.

You get first prize for intuition Sis, quite
something when you're on the other side of
the world. S xxxxx

Dear Diary,

Saturday 16th February.

Dad's letting me out this weekend and expects
me to be nice to him as a result. How can you
attach that as a condition? Being nice to your
parents should come naturally. You should want
to be nice to them because they are tolerant,
understanding, considerate and nice to you, not
because you're bribed to do so with the promise
of escape. He has no right to lock me up here
anyway, like Rapunzel or something. The other
conditions are that I go nowhere near Top Shop
– is he mad or what? Why would I want to go
near that place at the moment? – and that I
stop seeing Ruby, which is so absolutely unfair
I'm not even gonna consider it. She's my friend,
not his, and I love her. I need her.
   All week there have been his jokes and jibes,
like 'Had a good day? Steal anything worthwhile?' It's like I'm not ever allowed to forget
my 'crime' and move on. I forget about it and
start trying to do some homework, and then he
reminds me of it and makes me feel bad about
myself. What is the point in even trying to do
some work if he's labelled me as the bad seed
of the family?

Ruby and I are going to the cinema and then back to her house to sleepover. I wanted to go back to Chattie's café, just in case he was there, and then on to that nightclub place that lets you in for free before 11, because I could do with some excitement to take my mind off all this, but Ruby didn't want to. Fran and Serena might come too. There really isn't that much to do when you're 14, other than go to the cinema or sit in McDonald's, looking out for fit boys. Everything else costs too much, or it's for older teenagers. Haven't told any of my friends yet about what happened. Said I was ill last weekend, which was why I couldn't come out. Not sure how to tell them or what they'll think. Saskia of course is going riding again today with Chattie. Bitch.

Dear Diary,

Tuesday 19th February. Café on the Common. Left school early because I haven't done the maths homework and can't face the prospect of yet another detention, so I reckon it's better not to be at the lesson at all so that she doesn't notice. It's a bright, sunny, cold day and I've got four cigarettes, a tiny piece of dope that Toby gave me in exchange for a kiss and a bit of a feel in the darkroom yesterday (just as disappointing as the first time, I really don't fancy him), and 56p, which isn't enough to buy a hot chocolate. The trouble with being at school is that all it does is remind me of how much work I'm not doing, rather than making me do the work. I know my grades are dropping because I'm not working hard enough and I'm just no good. The trouble is that time is running out, and if I don't find a way to catch up soon, I'm never going to. I go up to my room, intending to study, sit down at my desk, find it hard to find the right books, find it hard to concentrate, so I don't do it, and then I really hate myself and think of all the ways in which I'm just a loser. If I knew what I wanted to do I could focus on the future and work to achieve something, but I don't know what I want to do, I don't even know who I really am. It's like I'm different people with different people. I put on this act that I'm fine and cheerful, but I'm not really, deep down. It's like I'm walking around in this fog, struggling to find a way out – some door, some path that will lead me on. If I had just one thing to cope with at a time then maybe I could deal with it. If I only had school and GCSEs and not all the other stuff – Saskia, Chattie, Mum and Dad's rubbish and a baby in the house – if I had breasts and proper hips to swing, then maybe it'd be easier to deal with GCSEs.

Something weird has just happened. I'm sitting here, writing in my diary, and this old saddo sits down next to me. Said I shouldn't be smoking, and then asked me if I could spare her a cigarette! I said that I've only got 3 left, and she goes that's all the more reason to give her one because she has nothing at all. Then she goes why aren't I in school anyway? Like it's any of her business. So I shoved the packet in her direction and she took one, but instead of going away like I wanted her to, she stayed and offered me what looked like water from a bottle, but actually it was vodka. It tasted disgusting, but it did help take the cold away. Then she starts lecturing me about how I'm too young to be sitting here on my own, that she could tell from my clothes that I came from a good home, and I should go back there where it's warm. 'How bad can it really be there, that you'd rather be here?' she asked. 'Bad enough' was what I wanted to say, but I didn't answer her. It was none of her business. I just wanted her to go away. Then she goes on about how she wasted time when she was young, thought she had years ahead of her, but the thing is that if you don't make the most of what's on offer while you're young, you can't catch up when you're older, and that if I didn't wanna end up like her I should go back to school. How weird is that?? Like some sort of omen or something?? I told her I didn't need lectures from her, and that I wanted to be left alone. The creepy thing is that I really don't wanna end up like her, but I wasn't about to tell her that, and going back to school isn't the answer. I don't know what is. I rolled a small joint after she'd gone and that calms you down, makes you think less.

From: Sue James
Sent: Wednesday 20 February 13.47
To: Angela James
Subject: Re: you were right

No I haven't been avoiding you because your advice is categoric. I'm just drained, confused, busy, that's all. You may be right again. Perhaps I should just kick him out, but I have three children now to consider as well as me, and what say do they have in all this??? Plus he is trying: he is coming home from work before Lola goes to bed, he has apologized, repeatedly, and seems to want to make amends. I feel terrible, of course I do, hurt, rejected. The most depressing aspect is the whole middle-age thing of feeling like one's body is less sexy than a sack of potatoes, rejected for a body nearly 20 years younger, when as an intelligent, mature woman (and a doctor) I ought to know that doesn't matter at all, and life begins at 40 etc. Well, does it???? He's still sleeping on the sofa because I don't want him anywhere near me, but I can't just kick him out. S xxxx

Dear Diary,

Thursday 21st February. Saskia has started slagging off Chattie in a really weird way, like she doesn't like him any more, like something's happened, only she won't say what. Ruby reckons that it's probably that something *hasn't* happened, like he hasn't kissed her, that's really bugging her, but I think that's too much to hope for. I still can't bear to be anywhere near him at school or in the playground, because I don't trust myself not to blush or say something stupid. I really hate myself that I can't. I mean, why can't I just pretend he's a normal boy and talk to him like I do to all the others?

Got called in by Miss Lesbian Moulder this afternoon. She says I owe her three letters from Mum, explaining my absences, and if I'm off school any more she'll have to ring home. She also said I'd been seen smoking leaving school, when what I do outside school is none of her business. Then she starts going on about how my health matters, and how silly it is to start smoking at this age because it's much harder to stop as you get older, and she knows because it took her the best part of two years to give up, and now she feels much better. Well, good for her, but what does that have to do with me?

Then she starts lecturing me about how I might think that I've got my whole life ahead of me, but that the habits you start at this age easily become entrenched, and that I was intelligent enough to look after myself, so why didn't I? Patronizing cow. How dare she talk to me like that? Who does she think she is, my mother? Fran, sensible Fran, says she was only trying to be kind, and that I've always been her favourite, and that she cares about me, but why do grownups think they know it all? They may look back with regrets, but that's their fault. This is my life, to live how I like, not hers.

From: Sue James
Sent: Saturday 23 February 20.56
To: Angela James
Subject: aubergines – never bake them without pricking them first

Ange,

I'm not being weak and denying my own feelings. I FEEL THIS, ANGE, EVERY MINUTE OF THE FUCKING DAY. The affair is over, I know that. He was a fool, and he knows that – although if she walked back into his life and he had to choose, I'm not sure which way he would fall. I'm just being pragmatic. Kicking him out wouldn't solve anything, just make everybody even more miserable, and perhaps if marriages are to last the course, we have to accept that there are times when we are weak, that we all do the wrong thing, and that we need to forgive mistakes for the greater good. Plus, if I ever get my shape back and feel good enough about my body to have an affair with someone younger and sexier, I might just do it now!!!! All I can do is take things a day, a week, at a time, and for the moment he's here, still trying hard and still on the sofa.

Otherwise . . . Mum is thrilled that it's only a month to wait until you come, although she did find it hard to understand why you were coming on your own with the boys. I had to explain three times that it was hard to get on to flights, and that Spike was happy to stay at home. She never travelled anywhere without Dad, so the idea that you could is baffling, or maybe she's going just a little bit deaf. She was generally much happier last Sunday – the news that you're coming has helped. Also the sun has been shining and the daffs are popping up outside her window. I've been trying out a few recipes, thought it would be good to use the time to try and expand my repertoire and give Frankie something to thank me for, but I'm not sure she's noticed.

Last night all three children were crying at the same time. Lola caught Frankie wearing one of her favourite tops and tried to take it off her, and then, as far as I can gather, rather than giving it back to her, Frankie kicked her. Lola came running to me screaming. I told Frankie off for kicking her, Frankie burst into tears because apparently I always take Lola's side and I don't understand what it's like having a pesky little sister that much younger than her

(oh believe me I do, don't I, Ange!), and why
can't I stop picking on her just because she is
the oldest? At which point I put down the baby
to try and give her a hug and he started
screaming as well. Two arms between three
children simply won't go. I left the baby and
Lola, and followed Frankie up the stairs, but
she slammed the door in my face before I got
there, and shouted at me to leave her alone so
angrily when I opened the door that I did.
When she's in that sort of a mood she makes it
impossible for anyone to get close to her. So I
went back downstairs, fobbed off Lola with a
packet of crisps, Tom with a bit of boob, and
completely forgot that I had put an aubergine
into the oven to bake. Apparently, if you bake
them first, you can then chop them up and put
them into creamy pasta sauces and it tastes delicious, according to HND. Lola's been nagging
me to make it, says she loves it when she has it
next door. When I finally remembered, it was
black but still perfectly formed. I stuck a knife
into its side to see if it was cooked, and there
was a huge bang as the bloody thing exploded
all over the kitchen. It was definitely cooked.
Aubergine splattered the walls and floor and
scalded my face. The noise was so loud that it
even coaxed Frankie out of her room and into a
sympathetic human being for about ten

minutes, when she saw that my cheek had been burned and that I was in real pain. She wrapped some ice into a tea towel and made me sit down and hold it against my cheek. Now I have this large, red, pustulating sore that looks like a cross between a large spot and a sarcoma, and I've had to retell the story all day long because everyone I meet stares at it in this rather anxious way. 'No it's not a spot or full-blown Aids. I was baking this aubergine . . . and actually what I didn't know is that you have to treat them just like sausages and prick them first . . .' Now it's not just my body I have to worry about disguising, it's also my face!!! The only person who managed to see the funny side was HND, who laughed so hard that tears ran down her cheeks, and then she said that maybe it was time I went back to work since I was obviously a better doctor than a cook. Since she's always given me such a hard time for working at all, I consider this to be a major breakthrough.

Relations between Frank and Matthew are still at on all time low. He comes in from work and demands to know where she's been and who with, like the Stasi, and then he can't resist winding her up with some jibe about stealing. If he can't find anything at all in the house for just one moment, he says,

'Frankie must have nicked it,' and it's beginning to really get me down, so Frankie must be livid. I've told him to lay off, that it isn't funny, and that he has to put this firmly in the past and forgive her. She is just a teenager and every teenager makes mistakes, how else do they learn about life? He's certainly made enough in his adult life – how would he feel if I continually reminded him of those?

I'm looking for an improvement all round in family life before you arrive . . . and if not, perhaps your arrival alone will prompt better behaviour. Let me know your flight times and I'll pick you up from the airport. Masses of love Sue xxxx

Dear Diary,

Sunday. I can't believe what happened last
night, and I know I can tell you because, unlike
all my friends, you can keep a secret. Toby had
a party at his house, and Saskia wasn't there
because she was away for the weekend with her
parents, but Chattie WAS! I had to have at least
three vodka and cokes to even be able to look
at him, let alone talk to him, but with Saskia
not there I just knew I had to do something.

I was sitting on the stairs with Ruby, and
Chattie passed us going up the stairs and like
smiled at me and I like smiled back without
blushing because my cheeks were red anyway
(according to Ruby) from the vodka. When he
came back down the stairs my legs were like
right across them, and he had to step over me
and didn't quite make it and kicked me, and was
so apologetic you'd think he'd just stabbed me in
the back or something, when he hadn't hurt me
at all. Ruby told me later that she thought he'd
done it deliberately. Anyway, he sat down next to
me and kept saying he was sorry, and like was I
all right, and then we just started talking about
stuff. I didn't know it was possible to talk to a
boy like that. He started telling me about how he
was a bit upset at the moment, because his horse

was lame and so old now that the vet was recommending they put her down, and he'd had her since he was like 8 and really loved her, and he didn't want to have to do it. It felt like such a grown-up thing to have to decide and he wanted his Mum and Dad to do it for him, that was what he was going to tell them tomorrow. I mean how awful is that??? Having to decide whether or not to murder a horse that you love so much it's like part of your family!!! I was like really sympathetic and said I was really really sorry (Ruby thought I went a bit over the top about it), and how I couldn't imagine what that must be like. Then I asked him what it was he liked about riding and he was really interesting about the symbiosis between man and horse and how you kind of control the horse when you're on its back through trust and relationship rather than through fear, spurring it on, or whipping it, and it sounded so cool because he really thought about things, meaningful things, rather than worrying about being macho and cool like all these other dipshit boys. It was really easy to talk to him. He asked me about my family, and I told him about the baby and how hard that was to live with because it changed everything, and he said he understood because his parents had adopted a baby girl three years ago and every-thing had changed for him then, only he couldn't really complain about it because the poor girl had nobody at all to love her, but that he'd got

353

used to it and now she was such a strong part of his life that he'd be devastated if anything happened to her. We talked for ages on the stairs until he had to go home, and he said it'd been really nice talking to me and he'd see me at school.

I couldn't believe it! Not only did he know me, he seemed to even like me, he liked talking to me! And I didn't feel the least bit shy or embarrassed because of the vodka. Alcohol really does make everything easier and more exciting. It even made me forget the fact that I had just started period number 3. Why do we have to have them every month?? You just forget about one and then bang, there goes another one, and of course I hadn't expected it so I didn't have any pads and had to borrow one and my pants were all bloodstained and disgusting. Euggh I really hate periods. They seem much more exciting and grown-up before you get them, but then as soon as you do, they're just a pain.

I stayed the night at Toby's with Ruby, because it seemed easier than trying to get back to her house. We slept on the sofa, only I hardly slept at all. I couldn't stop thinking about him. I couldn't stop talking about him with Ruby. I kept waking her up to ask her things or relive our conversation one more time, and she got really cross with me. We were both like really tired, stiff and grumpy this morning, but it was worth it. That vodka really helped, even if I did throw up in the middle of the night.

Dear Diary, Tuesday February 26th

Life at home is just crap – I feel like I'm
completely alone here. There's such a big age
gap between me and Lola that she isn't the kind
of sister I really need at the moment – someone
to confide in, like maybe a twin. Mum is trying
to be nicer to me, and her cooking has improved
a bit since she's been at home, but she's always
with the baby and she ALWAYS ALWAYS takes
Lola's side in things just because I'm the oldest.
She just refuses to see how the spoilt brat winds
me up sometimes. As for Dad, he's best avoided
altogether. I just let him say his bit, lie for an
easier life, and get away from him as quickly as I
can. His latest obsession is sleepovers with boys.
He thought I was at Fran's on Saturday night
(had to lie about planning to stay at Ruby's
obviously, since he thinks she's SUCH a bad
influence), when actually it was too much hassle
to get there from Toby's so we just crashed
there, and it was a mistake to let that slip
because he just went crazy again. Should have
lied about that too. So what is the big deal
about sleepovers when there are boys there? Why
are parents so against them? Like we might have
sex or something! Shows what's on his mind. He
might I suppose. Judging by the way he flirts

with some of my friends (he just adores Fran —
so sensible, *so* grown up) he might find it hard
to sleep in a room with a load of them, but
we've been like in the same classroom, playground, parties with these dipshits for years.
Why would we let them have sex with us when
we don't want sex with them???

Now that things with Chattie are a zillion
times better, all of this stuff at home doesn't
worry me so much, it's like I can deal with it
better, let it get to me less because I know HE
likes me. He was off scholl yesterday because he
was so cut up about losing his horse, but he sat
with me at lunchtime today and we talked some
more about it. It was harder to like talk freely
without the vodka, but it was just so nice being
with him. It's like when he's with me, that's all
that matters. There's just him and me and I
forget about everything else. Even my tits!!! Still
hunting for that perfect bra.

✉

From: Sue James
Sent: Friday 1 March 11.19
To: Angela James
Subject: Pinch punch first of the month and no return!

I don't know what it is about today's date, but it just seems to hold so much promise. January and February are done with for another year and there's nothing but spring and summer to look forward to. Maybe you have become sufficiently ozzified not to feel this way any more. It is after all hot enough out there for bush fires at this moment . . . are they anywhere near you? Now that it's March I'm beginning to make plans for your arrival. Matthew had a brainwave and suggested we rented a house large enough for all of us, somewhere in the country for a week, that Mum could come to, and that way we'd all have a bit of a break, by the sea perhaps . . . I'm looking into it. I've started cooking for the freezer (what do your boys like to eat??), Mum's already packed her suitcase, and Frankie's saying that she might as well leave home now if she's going to have to give up her bedroom every holiday. Talk about melodramatic! She wavers between being so ecstatically high, energetic and sexy that she makes me feel like a dried up old hag and very tired, and becoming so morose and distant that I immediately want to hit her and I jump to hysterical conclusions – Drink? Drugs? First period coming on? First love? Unrequited love?? Trying to understand a 14-year-old is a bit like trying to understand another species. I'm sure we weren't like that at her age.

Clare's got chickenpox and HND has of course been behaving as if it were meningitis . . . I've been round at least 6 times to check the spots. I did feel sorry for her though, because she has been trapped indoors for nearly a week with Clare in quarantine, so I looked after Clare here on Friday so that she could get out and do some shopping, get her hair done, go to the gym or whatever it is that she normally does with all that time when Clare is at school. She was so thrilled by my offer that she bought me this huge bunch of flowers and I think relations are at last beginning to improve. Tom obviously hasn't had chickenpox, but Clare's way past the infectious stage now anyway, so if he does succumb, might as well get it over. It also gave me a brilliant opportunity to really go through Clare's hair and get rid of all her nits. I sat with her in front of *The Sound of Music* and painstakingly removed every single egg I could find. Now Lola stands a chance of being completely nit free for a while.

Let me know if there's anything that you want to see/do while you're here. We could even pay Frankie/bribe Matthew somehow to stay in with all of the kids and you and me do something girly together . . . I haven't left Tom yet with anybody, but I think I could just about manage to tear myself away from him for some time alone with you. And yes, Matthew is still on the sofa, but he brought home a fantastically expensive bottle of red wine last night – smooth like velvet, without the faintest kick of cider vinegar or bicarb or whatever it is they put in wine these days – and we drank that together after Tom went to sleep, and talked, reminisced really, about life before babies. Milk might curdle for Tom tomorrow but what the heck. He's monstrously big, way off the scales at the baby clinic for 10 weeks.

Lots of love Sue xxxx

Dear Diary, Tuesday 5th March.

I've been at school for one whole week and 2 days . . . I've even been to every lesson, and it's all because of Chattie. I want to be there because he is. I can even like just about concentrate in the lessons because he does, and when I asked him yesterday whether he'd taken any notes for the history essay on the Victorians that I was supposed to hand in before half term, he said he'd lend them to me and help if I liked, which is really, really nice of him. He doesn't like wanna be with us as a gang at break or lunch, but he does talk to me when we're like on our own or walking in and out of lessons, and yesterday he even sat next to me in maths, which destroyed my concentration altogether. There was like this electricity flying between us, even though our bodies weren't even touching. Saskia is now pretending that she never liked him that much anyway to the others, which is pathetic because they're definitely not stupid. They can remember that she couldn't actually talk about anything else BUT Chattie just over a week ago. She avoids me completely, won't talk to me at all, which kind of says to me that she does still like him.

Wednesday.

Dear Diary,

CHATTIE RANG THIS EVENING!! I was so nervous talking to him that I could feel myself wanting to run away and just put the phone down, and I had to squeeze my nails into my palm to remind myself that this was real and that I mustn't blow it.

HE'S ASKED ME OUT THIS SATURDAY!!! DID I WANT TO GO TO SEE A MOVIE WITH HIM? DID I!!!!

But I didn't say that of course. I was like, 'If you like.' This is the first time I have ever been asked out on a date. I can't believe it! As soon as he put the phone down I rang Ruby, Fran and Serena to tell them, and then couldn't decide whether he'd meant just the two of us (which is kind of scary), or whether he wanted us all to go out like as a gang, like we would normally do. Ruby reckons we should all go, to make it easier for me, but I'm not sure, he might not like that. I've read through the whole of *Time Out* and can't decide which film we should go and see, and I've gone through my whole wardrobe and can't decide what I should wear. The only thing that's certain is Ruby's padded bra.

From: Sue James
Sent: Wednesday 6 March 21.27
To: Angela James
Subject: Dorset or Wales?

Dearest Dear,

Last-minute properties have come up with two
options with enough bed space for all of us.
One is about twenty miles from Lyme Regis,
expensive and quite ritzy by the sound of
things, but rolling green countryside. The other
is on the coast of North Wales near Harlech.
Much cheaper, by the sea, which is always
lovely, but it'll take hours to drive there –
Matthew reckons six to eight because once you
get into Wales the roads are slow, narrow and
windy. Matthew thinks we should consult
Mum, since this could easily be her last holiday
ever (cheery isn't he?), and that if we don't let
her have some say over it she'll just find even
more things to complain about, but I'm not sure
that that's necessarily true, and since we're the
ones who'll have to do all the work etc . . .
Also, I'm not sure I've got time or the energy to

go through all this over the phone with her before both properties get snapped up. Which do you like the sound of best? Ping me back soonest. Otherwise I'll just book one. S xx

Dear Diary,

Thursday. Saskia's been slagging me off
behind my back. She's even told Lesbian
Moulder that I've been smoking in the year
10 toilets, which is just pathetic because
everybody who smokes smokes in there, so
that can't be news to her. But you know what?
I just don't care. She can be immature and
spiteful if she likes, but I'm just not gonna
rise to it. Still can't decide what film or what
to wear, but at least I know he means just me
on my own because he said he wanted to
meet me at his favourite café first, which is
really great because A) I know where it is and
B) I can pretend that I love it too and that'll
give me something to talk about. I'm
SOOOOOOO nervous and SOOOOOO
excited. I've been lying in bed for nearly two
hours now, unable to sleep and unable to get
him out of my mind. I just wanna touch him,
kiss him, feel him, and it's like lightning bolts
of electricity through my body whenever I
think of how he might do that. I imagine him
kissing me and I just want him. I've never felt
this sexy, this in lust before. And we've never
even touched, other than knees on the stairs
at Toby's party. Maybe if I tried to think

about something else I could get to sleep.
Here goes. And there goes Tom, crying again.
I'll get him up and give him to Mum.

From: Sue James
Sent: Thursday 7 March 09.45
To: Angela James
Subject: Re: Dorset or Wales?

OK Dorset it is then. I'll book it now and ring Mum and talk it through with her. S xxxx

From: Sue James
Sent: Friday 8 March 13.25
To: Angela James
Subject: Re: Dorset or Wales?

Right, it's booked for us from Saturday the
30th until the following Saturday, the 6th
April, which means you've got about a week
with us in London to get over your jet lag,
and we'll drive up and see Mum together. She
won't be able to wait a week to see you,
knowing you're in the country, and both
Frank and Lola will be off school that week
so we can take them too.

   The house sleeps eight with one double four
poster bed (ours!) and three twins, which
begs the question as to where we put Mum.
Matthew reckons she'll want the four poster
to herself (Yes?? Or tough??). I think we put
Mum in a twin of her own, move beds around
or take a couple of lilos with us for the kids
to sleep on, so that they're all in another
room, and then you can have a room all to
yourself and sleep late every morning as the
children amuse themselves in front of the television (it's got satellite, therefore cartoon

369

network and MTV!), while Granny cooks them breakfast (joke). The alternative is you sharing a room with Mum which you may or may not want. Think about it.

There's a garden with a swing in it and a pond with frogs which is hopefully not deep enough for Stan and Ollie to drown in, but we'll stand guard just in case, and there's a microwave which is making Matthew almost orgasmic with excitement because he thinks that means we can fill the back of the car with instant M&S meals. I have steadfastly refused ever to have a microwave in my kitchen because it's yet more radiation and completely unnatural (I know, I know it makes many a working mother's life much easier – HND swears it's bliss for quick baked potatoes and reheating pasta – how disgusting REHEATING pasta?? Isn't it just as easy to make fresh?). Anyway, Matthew thinks that living with one for a week is going to make me change my mind. Ha ha. Over my dead, fat, stretchmarked, blob of a body.

Frank has gone into one of those blind panics over clothes that are at their most acute when you're 14. She has absolutely 'nothing to wear' (stomps around almost naked in her bra and knickers to prove the point) and everything I own is either 'hideous'

(Nicole Farhi hideous?) or 'outsize' (your standard average 14). She's been in a fury for the past 24 hours, and then exploded, practically kicking down a wall, when I told her that we were going to this house in Dorset for Easter. 'How dare I make plans without consulting her'; 'how would I like it if she just told me we were doing something'; and then 'Well, I'm not coming, I'm staying here on my own,' to which of course the only answer is 'Oh no you're not. You're only 14, it's against the law and they'll take you into care.' I tried to reason with her – it was only a week, her friends would be away too, there was a phone plus satellite television – but all she could say was 'I have plans.'

'What plans?'

'None of your business.'

'It is if you're telling me they're better than going on our first complete family holiday with Auntie Angela, the twins and Granny, ever.'

'ANYTHING WILL BE BETTER THAN THAT.'

Honestly, Ange, why does family life get so bloody complicated with teenagers? They maintain it's an abuse of their civil rights when you change the colour of the bog paper without consulting them. I could strangle her.

Anyway, she's coming. I'll just let the subject drop for a while until nearer the time.

Must go . . . booked into our first mother and baby swim class. I just hope it's not one of those where they expect you to chuck your baby into the water without armbands to see if they float. Not sure I could do that.

Lots of love Sue xxxxxx

Dear Diary,

Sunday. 11 a.m. Bed.

I can't believe how happy just being with Chattie made me yesterday. I was really really nervous at first. Had to walk round the block and smoke three cigarettes before I felt brave enough to walk into the café at all, and then I got really worried about the beige raincoat I was wearing that I'd nicked off Mum and wished I'd worn something else, something less smart, more casual, but he said how much he liked it as soon as I sat down at the table opposite him, and he smiled at me with those big, brown watery eyes and immediately I knew it was going to be all right. He's so fit, I feel better looking just being with him, and he's so easy to talk to. Is this LOVE?? I mean am I in love with him? I can't like think of anything else but him, I don't want to do anything other than be with him, and I keep wanting to write his name all over everything. Chattie . . . I THINK I LOVE YOU!!!!
I picked at a salad and then ate most of his chips, which made him laugh, and then we had this like really deep conversation about all the animal photographs on the walls. He said he

liked the photo of the rhino best, because it had to be one of the ugliest animals on the planet, and yet somehow in black and white, towering over this fat, ugly mug of a white man with a gun, the rhino looked much more beautiful. He thinks it's a really profound comment on the modern notion of beauty, how in fact ugliness is the new beauty. I'd never thought of rhinos that way before.

We went to see this really silly romantic comedy, and he paid for everything (which felt kind of nice, even though I know you're supposed to insist on splitting everything to like keep your distance, so that you don't owe him anything). And THEN . . . he held my hand as we walked home. I mean boys aren't normally like that – the dipshits at school aren't. They'd NEVER pay for a girl and not expect her to give them at least a wank afterwards, and they'd never walk you home, unless THEY were scared that they were going to get mugged without a girl there to protect them. He didn't kiss me, but I wanted to, I really wanted to kiss him, but then maybe holding hands is enough right now. I think he likes me, and because he likes me it's like the only thing that is really real in my life right now. He brings things to life. I must ring Ruby and tell her how it went.

From: Sue James
Sent: Monday 11 March 11.56
To: Angela James
Subject: Re: Dorset or Wales?

OK, if you want to share with Mum, that's
what we'll do. I've talked to her about six
times in the past 24 hours about the plan for
the Easter Holiday. She's thrilled, but determined to adopt that irritating hurt and
rejected tone simply because you're going to
be here for a week first without her. I've told
her that we're coming up to see her for the
day as soon as you're over your jet lag and
can tell the difference between night and
day. I've told her that there simply isn't room
in our house to have her there beforehand.
I've told her that she's going to have a whole
week with you and the boys in Dorset. All
perfectly reasonable replies I would have
thought, but not for Mum, Oh No! I've had
a lot of those tense, silent conversations
where her sense of hurt rejection oozes down
the phone, trying to cripple me with guilt
when all it does is make me want to kill her.
Typically, she insists on seeing it selfishly

rather than appreciating the fact that I have organized a major treat and that we both have a great deal to do simply as mothers of small children. 'I'm sure that's not what Angela would want if she were here or could talk to me,' she said, all clipped.

'Well it is, Mum, and you can talk to her, just pick up the phone and ask her for yourself.' But she refuses to believe that's possible. Somehow, phoning Australia is as difficult and expensive as flying a rocket to the moon. Funny how it still makes me jealous, this feeling that she prefers you, admires you, would rather spend time with you, when actually her attitude is just so childish, it's laughable. The one thing mothers ought to be selfless enough to do is to encourage their children to like each other, and want to be with each other outside of parental influence (although it is a little hard with mine since the age gap is so big and Frank and Lola fight so over clothes, but I hope they like each other when they're older). You grow up through life with siblings and have to deal together with parents when they're old, and that's hard enough in itself without all those old childhood resentments resurfacing. It's amazing really that you and I get on as well as we do, given how she's continually tried to set us off against one another. One advantage of you being in Australia for the past 4 years is that that hasn't really been possible. And she hasn't seen you for so long so I suppose it is understandable that she's working herself up into a state about it. I just hope that doesn't mean REALLY bad bahaviour on her part to make up for lost time!!!

Spring's here – daffs out, forsythia, blossom, sunshine, not quite warm enough to go out without a coat, but definitely not winter any more, so you won't get too much of a shock weatherwise. Much love Sue xx

Dear Diary,

Tuesday. If we're going out, when do I start counting the days from? Saturday when we went to the cinema? In which case we've been going out for 4 whole days today, which is the longest I've ever gone out with anybody (because Toby only lasted about 6 excruciating minutes when he kissed me at Saskia's party). The longest any of us has been out with anyone is Fran (with Sean). She says it was nearly two months. Chattie rang last night and tonight and we talked and talked, until Dad shouted at me to get off the phone for supper, but he like sort of avoids me at school, smiles and says hello but doesn't like wanna sit with us at lunchtime or anything. Ruby goes that's because he doesn't wanna lose face with the boys. Saskia goes that's because he doesn't think he's even going out with me at all, and then flounced off. She's just jealous, and now that I know that Chattie likes me, now that I can actually talk to him about things, I really couldn't care less and I feel much stronger about everything. Anyway, it's time she grew up a little and realized that she just can't have everything she wants. Spoilt brat.

Dear Diary,

Thursday 14th March. 6 days today! He's said he's going to invite me to come and stay in his cottage in the country. I'm so excited, but he hasn't said when, and I know that I'm going to have to lie to Mum and Dad about it. Ruby says I can pretend to be staying with her, but that's no good, only I can't tell her why, which makes me feel bad, and I like need to know soon so that I can set it up. Ruby goes I should just ask him when, but that feels really pushy. He doesn't realize that my parents would just go apeshit, like I was being invited to an orgy or something rather than a weekend away with his parents. And I'm really, really worried that he's gonna ask me to go during the holidays. Mum's planned this family love-in with Granny and Auntie Angela in the middle of nowhere, and if going means I have to miss out on Chattie then I'll just have to run away to do it.

From: Sue James
Sent: Thursday 14 March 23.19
To: Angela James
Subject: Re: Dorset or Wales?

What do you mean you never thought you were her favourite? Of course you were, you were prettier, more astute at smoothing her over, telling her what she wanted to hear. You always seemed much closer to her, more affectionate with each other, you did all those girly things together like mothers and daughters are supposed to do, like shopping and dyeing your hair together, while I swotted to get into/through medical school. During that awful time when I had to move her out of home and into North Butting she was so furious with me at one point that she even said that she wished it had been me that had emigrated instead of you. I don't think she really meant it. If it had been you here, packing her off like that, you'd have got just as much flak as I did, but it was an interesting Freudian slip nevertheless.

We ought to talk more and chew the

family cud when you're here, just you and I. You do miss out on a great deal of all the detail about Mum's life, and I guess it must be easy to just forget about it all when you're such a long way away. I really don't resent it, Ange, believe me, because there's no point, but it does make me laugh sometimes and I often wonder whether I am passing on similar discrepancies to Frank and Lola. I love them both to bits, and equally. It's just that Lola is with me and seems to need me so much more at the moment, just because she's younger, and Tom needs me even more. I just hope that Frankie doesn't misinterpret that.

A boy called Chattie has been ringing her every night this week, and she's wandering round the house in this sort of dreamy state and rushes to do 1471 whenever she's been out, to see if he's called. Matthew asked me last night if I'd had a 'talk' with her about contraception. I told him I was sure she knew it all from school anyway, but that I would raise it if the right moment came up. How do you talk to your own child about safe sex and contraception? It's easy at work, because that's other people's children and actually you don't really care what they're up to, but when it's your own child . . . Anyway, she's much too young . . .

Talking of bed, it's time I went there . . . Masses of love S xxxx

From: Sue James
Sent: Friday 15 March 22.51
To: Angela James
Subject: Re: What's 1471?

If you dial 1471 an automatic voice (are they real people???) gives you the time and telephone number of your last call. Only if it's anyone really interesting she says, 'The caller withheld their number', and then you waste ten minutes thinking through everybody you know, wondering who it could possibly be.

I'm glad Mum writes lovely things about us to you. Bring the letters with you if you remember. I'd love to see what she's said. I think that generation really believed that if you praised your children to their face they'd grow up spoilt or boastful. Now we know different. S xxxxxx

Dear Diary,

Sunday. We went for a walk on the Common, holding hands, but he still hasn't kissed me, although I felt he wanted to. We were deep in a conversation about school, like trying to imagine how the teachers spent their weekends and what they would be if they were animals (Lesbian Moulder was definitely a chameleon – style all over the place and pretends to be one of the kids), when I realized that we were walking in step and at the same pace. It felt so comfortable, our hips like practically touching. If he'd only kiss me, then I'd know that we were really going out, that he really liked me. If he wasn't quite so tall, maybe I'd be able to kiss him first, only that's really really scary. I think I'd need to have a drink or two first.

For some reason Mum keeps making these cryptic comments like, you know that sexual intercourse under the age of 16 is illegal don't you? And I found all these leaflets from the Pregnancy Advisory Service lying around on the kitchen table. I mean what is she like? Does she think I'm a complete retard? She's the one who got pregnant accidentally. I'm nowhere near having sex with someone. It's what he's gonna think when he feels for my

384

tits and there aren't any that worries me. He still hasn't mentioned exactly when he's inviting me away for the weekend, and I didn't like to ask.

Dear Diary,

Monday. Saskia has started on this line that
I'm so obsessed with Chattie that I haven't got
any time for my friends any more, which is
ridiculous because I love the guy, I'm not
obsessed with him, I can think about other
things (just!), and I still love and need my
friends too. Why does it have to be one or the
other? Because she wants to exclude me from
the gang, that's why. Mean bitch. Ruby goes
not to worry about it, it's just Saskia being her
usual manipulative self, but how can I not
worry about it. Particularly since I need my
friends more than ever, simply because this is
such a massive new experience and I need to
talk about it with them.

Mum is going into neurotic, middle-aged
cleanliness overdrive, just because Auntie
Angela is coming with her twins. I mean don't
they have dirt in Australia?? She wants me to
dust my bookshelves when the woman's hardly
going to have the time to read. She wants me
to clear out my chest of drawers and clear a
space in my wardrobe when she's not coming
until the weekend, and where am I supposed
to put things in the meantime?? And why do I
have to move out of my room again? It's her

386

sister, why can't she and Dad move out, or move Lola in with them. Why does it always have to be me?

✉

From: Sue James
Sent: Wednesday 20 March 2.15
To: Angela James
Subject: Your imminent arrival

Mum is now happy I think. I've told her that you and I plus kids will be there on Monday or Tuesday, depending on how you're feeling, and that you will ring her as soon as you get back here on Saturday morning. I've also got some tickets for a concert in Cheltenham, in the week after we come back from Dorset, so that taking her back to North Butting won't be quite such a wrench, or, I hope, so difficult, because she'll know it's only a matter of days before she sees you again. God knows what I'll do with Tom that night. He's not weaned, so I can't leave him for that long in London, so I might just have to bring him and Matthew with us, so that one of us can sit outside, or let you do that one on your own, while I look after the boys at home. Let's see how things go. Mum's thrilled anyhow, so that's what matters, because it's her favourite Mozart piano concerto and she says that the only music she gets to hear now is Frank

Sinatra and Val Doonican. Perhaps we should do something about that – get her one of those portable CD players and some CDs and take it up with us when we go to see her next week? I never realized it was an issue, she hasn't mentioned it before.

I've shifted about eight bin bags of rubbish and clutter out of this house, so there should be room for you and yours. And Lola's done a great job in her bedroom, making a boys' corner so Stan and Ollie should have fun in there. Frankie is still acting as if I've asked her to change schools and never see any of her friends again rather than go to a nice house in Dorset for a week. Had another massive row about it last night. She won't tell me why she doesn't want to come, just that she has plans that she won't tell me about. I've even suggested that she brings a friend with her, but she just refuses to even countenance coming. She's vehement and very aggressive about it and I can't understand why. I haven't mentioned this to Matthew, and I'm relieved he wasn't here last night because he would have just poured oil on to the flames. She was also threatening to leave home if she has to move out of her room, and since she did have to move out at Christmas for Mum, and she has had to put up with a lot from Matthew continually winding her up about shoplifting and the state of her dress, I took you up on your offer and said that she could stay in her room and that you would sleep on the sofa bed. That compromise calmed her down a bit, but I'm not sure for how long. Out of all of us, she is the one who most needs her privacy, somewhere to go and do all that teenage contemplation, and it means that we don't have to listen to Eminem, which is an absolute blessing, so I hope that you don't mind.

Matt says he's never seen this house looking so tidy and that perhaps we are now ready to embrace Fuchsia and Robert for 'Drinks'. Maybe you're gagging to meet them after everything I've told you (but promise to behave). I've cooked up tons of cauliflower cheese for the freezer, since the boys love it, and I've doubled the internet shopping order. As this is likely to be my last e-mail, ping me back immediately if there is anything else I need to know/do before Saturday. Otherwise I'll be there at 07.30 on the other side of customs. I'm so excited, really, really looking forward to seeing you all. It's been so long.

Masses of love and not long now Sue xxxx

Dear Diary,

Friday 2 a.m. I can't sleep. I can't stop thinking about Chattie. I can still feel the shape of his hand in mine. But what worries me is that he still avoids me at school. It's like he's polite and all that and talks to me, but he won't touch me or be with us at lunchtime, and it's getting to the point where Saskia and Hayley don't believe that we're going out at all. And he still hasn't said anything about going away to his house in the country for the weekend, and Mum's got this awful family holiday planned next weekend, and if he's like gonna ask me then I have to know now, and have some time to construct a plan to get out of going with Mum and Dad. Ruby says that he's probably going somewhere anyway because it's Easter, but that if he does ask I can just like say that I'm going away with my family and sound a bit more distant, but I don't wanna miss anything. He might not ask me again, or worse still he might ask Saskia instead. Today was the last day of term so I might not see him again until the beginning of next term, and he hasn't suggested doing something together this weekend. I said did he like wanna meet up when he rang last night, but he said that he didn't know yet because his Dad was away and his Mum wasn't very well, so he might need to stay home and help look after her and his little sister, which sounds a bit unlikely. I mean, what teenage boy would want to do that? And then he didn't ring tonight. Maybe he doesn't wanna go out with me any more and doesn't know how to tell me? I'm getting quite good at rolling joints, but Toby's dope has almost gone. Must ask him for some more. I think I'm stoned enough now to be able to sleep. See yer.

Dear Diary,

Saturday. Dad woke me up at like 10 o'clock because Auntie Angela has arrived. How mean is that? Doesn't he know that teenagers need to sleep? So I staggered up, said hello, and then went straight back to sleep for three hours, when Mum woke me up for lunch. They're quite nice really. Angela looks much prettier and younger than Mum and the twins are sweet, definitely not identical. Ollie is bigger with a wider face and Angela doesn't dress them the same, so it's easy to tell them apart. They like fighting and hitting each other the whole time, which is kind of funny. Mum kept hugging Angela, which was really sweet. They were really pleased to see each other. I wonder if I'll ever feel like that about Lola when we're their age? Angela gave me this really nice chain necklace, a top and some cool flip-flops. Mum would never have managed to buy anything so nice on her own, so maybe Angela understands teenagers. She is younger than Mum after all. She said she wanted to take me out for lunch one day next week, or maybe in Dorset, so that we can just talk us two. I'd like that.

Ruby thinks I should text him and just ask him straight – Do U wanna D8 tnite – but that feels a bit forward. If he says no then there's absolutely no hope for the rest of the holidays, and then I'd never be able to go back to school, and actually it'd be better just to play it cool and wait for him to ring. Although I'm not sure for how long I'm going to be able to bear that.

Dear Diary,

Monday. The first day of the Easter Holidays
and already I'm so bored and desperate for
Chattie to ring that I can't seem to think
about or do anything else. Mum wants me to
go with them to see Granny tomorrow, but if
I go he'll ring, and anyway I'm gonna have
to spend an entire week with her in some
backward village full of the over 50s, so it's
like really appealing to go and see her
AGAIN. I mean, do I have to spend the
whole of my holiday just with Granny? I said
I wanted to stay home and do some coursework, but Mum just grunted disbelievingly
and said I'm not happy leaving you here all
day long on your own. So I said well you
were happy enough to leave me here with
Lola last summer, when you went to work
and we didn't have Iris, and that shut her up
quickly, particularly in front of Auntie
Angela. She's agreed to let me stay here if
Ruby's here too, so that we can work
together (!), and said she'd give us money for
pizza. So that's tomorrow sorted. Auntie
Angela's really nice. Much more understanding than Mum is. She took my side,
told Mum that it wasn't fair to make me

spend the whole holiday with Granny, and slipped me an extra tenner for some ice cream and a video as well.

Dear Diary,

Tuesday. Ruby MADE me ring Chattie as soon as Mum and everybody had left the house. I was so nervous I put the phone down 3 times before I'd finished dialling his number, and then when I finally got through, waiting for him to get to the phone after his Mum answered was simply agony. He sounded really pleased to hear from me, and asked what I was doing, and then said he'd come round and go to the video shop with us, but I broke into such a sweat while I was talking to him that I had to have a shower and change, shave my legs and smother myself in perfume. Ruby and I tried to do some work while we were waiting, but there was just so much to talk about, and then Fran rang and then we watched some TV. Everything seemed all right as soon as I knew that I was going to see him, and then when I saw him, well my legs just turned to jelly and I got all nervous again. The three of us snuggled up on the sofa in front of *Billy Elliot* with a giant packet of Haribo sweets, and then we got so hyper from the sugar that we had to leap around the room like ballet dancers. Chattie put a cushion over his head so that he looked like a face-less robot as he danced and then Ruby leapt up on to the sofa so hard she knocked it backwards and knocked over a table and a vase as well, which made us collapse with laughter. Chattie helped me to clear it all up when we'd calmed down, and then he hugged me in the hallway before he left. God it was AMAZING!!! Feeling his body against mine like that. I thought he was going to kiss me, he looked like he wanted to but he didn't. Ruby screamed as soon as he left. She was so loud that he must have heard her from the street. I hope he didn't think it was me.

Dear Diary,

Thursday. Chattie didn't ring yesterday or today and I CAN'T ring him again. I just can't. It makes me feel like I'm the one who's doing all the work, like I'm the one who wants him more than he wants me, and I don't wanna have to feel like that. It's like mega depressing to think that I only feel happy or as if life's worth living if I'm with him or if I know he wants to be with me. On Tuesday night I could cope with anything because I'd seen him and he still seemed to like me. I could cope with Mum having a go because I'd left the kitchen in a mess, Lola having a go because she found her favourite hair stuff in my room, and Stan and Ollie fighting like a pair of sumo wrestlers and kicking me in the shin as they trashed half my room. I could even cope with Dad stomping round the house like a policeman because he couldn't find a bottle of his best wine. Both Mum and I told him he must have drunk it, but he kept insisting that he hadn't and that I'd probably drunk it with some of my friends. On Tuesday night I just laughed, it seemed like such a silly idea, when he'd obviously drunk it and forgotten, but today it feels like a real insult, like how dare he accuse me and my friends of stealing his wine, like how could he think so little of me and am I never ever going to be any more than a thief in his eyes . . . All because Chattie hasn't rung . . . and that just makes me hate myself even more, for being so weak.

Dear Diary,

Friday. I can't decide whether or not I should sleep with Chattie. I don't actually want to. I'm not ready for that yet. Maybe I will be when I'm sixteen. It just feels like such a large jump to go from hugging to full sex when we haven't even kissed yet, but when I think about how wonderful it feels to be close to him, how like my whole body just wants to melt into his, I can't help but want to. Maybe he would like me more if I did? Ruby thinks I'm mad. She says you only have to read *Cosmo Girl* to know that as soon as you sleep with a boy they call you a tart, because boys just can't help bragging about it to their friends. Sometimes they even pretend they've slept with someone to make them feel bigger, and then the poor girl cops it in the playground when actually she's completely in-nocent. Wendy Mulford still finds it hard to shake off that image, even though she's now in Year 11, because it got round the whole school that she'd gone and done it with Jake Hastings when she hadn't. But Chattie's not like those other boys. He doesn't need to brag. But what if I don't sleep with him and Saskia does?

401

Dear Diary,

Saturday 30th March. Dorset, and it's raining so hard that you can't even get to the car without getting soaked, so we're all cooped up indoors after spending about then hours squashed in the back of the car. Mum said it was only three but it felt like ten. The windows were so steamed up from the rain that I couldn't see where we were or where we were going, and Dad and Mum kept arguing in the front about routes, and him going too fast in such 'treacherous' conditions, and 'was Angela still with us' in the car behind, and did we have enough petrol, or should we stop here or there for a break. Honestly, grown-ups talk about such boring things, and why do Mum and Dad always argue whenever we get in the car and go anywhere, when all you have to do is get in the car and drive. Dad suggested she went with Auntie Angela, but there wasn't room for the baby as well in her tiny hire car AND Granny, so Lola and I had to have both of them arguing AND Tom crying half the way, when actually life would have been much easier if we'd just had Granny instead, but they didn't listen to that suggestion.

The house is really big, almost grand, with this

huge wide hall, large squishy sofas in the sitting room and SATELLITE TV!!! (which Mum keeps trying to turn off, but what else ARE we supposed to do when it's raining?). All the furniture and curtains and stuff like matches, unlike in our house where everything clashes and looks messy and disgusting, and although it's not exactly my style, it's very old-fashioned with flowery patterns everywhere (I much prefer the modern look), it is at least tidy. I'm not sure how I'm gonna smoke here though. The cigarette'd get soaked through before I even managed to light it in this weather, and there are more people around to notice or smell smoke on my clothing, so I'd better be careful. Get some chewing gum perhaps. I'm sharing a room with Lola, which I thought would be awful but she's being quite sweet really. She's shown me all the things in her rucksack and wants to know which of her clothes I like best and which nail varnish she should put on, and then she wanted to talk about Stan and Ollie. Which one did I like the best? I expect I'll be bored stiff of her though by the end of the week. Do you think Lola could be trusted to keep a secret if I had a smoke out of the window? I'm beginning to really really want a smoke. I just wish I'd talked to Chattie before we left. I've texted him, told him I'm away until Saturday, but that's not quite the same thing. And he hasn't texted back yet.

Dear Diary,

Easter Sunday. Do you think he could like track me down by my text message? Wouldn't it be simply amazing if he like just turned up here because he couldn't actually bear to be without me for a whole week? Our star signs in the news-paper today talk about nothing but love . . .

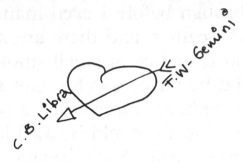

It's only Sunday and already I'm so bored I could kick in a window. We've been out for a short walk and to the pub for lunch, and I've only managed to sneak in one smoke since we got here.

It's been raining so hard that I feel as if I've been living in a goldfish bowl, only the water's on the outside and it's spot the lunatic on the inside. It's only when you're with your family all the time that you see how nuts they actually are. In fact it's amazing that Lola and I are quite so sane, coming as we do from that lot. Mum and Dad are trying hard to suppress their natural urge

to bicker because they don't want Granny or
Auntie Angela to see that their marriage is in dire
straits, when of course it's so obvious that they
practically have DIVORCING written across their
T-shirts. So they're not talking to each other at
all, and you can practically see their resentment
steaming out through their ears. Granny is
enjoying winding Mum up because that's how she
gets her kicks. Last night Mum produced this
disgusting supper, and Granny sat there talking
about how Mum never could cook, always had
her head in a book, never worried enough about
how she was turned out, unlike Auntie Angela.
Dad then weighed in with more unnecessary
hurtful honesty by saying that it was often like
that with sisters – Frankie's the one with the bum
and Lola's going to be the one with the legs. I
wanted to hit him. Surprised he didn't chuck in
something about my being a thief as well, only
that'd reflect badly on him wouldn't it? So we sat
there in silence, trying to digest this stodge, while
Granny went on and on about Auntie Angela's
perfect childhood until Auntie Angela told her to
shut up and said that at least Mum knew the
nutritional benefits of what we were eating, which
was more than she did. Mum looked really
crushed by Granny until Angela stuck up for her.
I felt really sorry for her, even if the food was
inedible. I made a point of eating everything on
my plate, asking for more, and saying how much
I liked it, even if it was a lie. At least Mum

tries, unlike Granny who's just decided that it's everybody else's job to serve and entertain her, and complains when nobody's brought her a cup of tea in bed in the morning by 8 o'clock. Why is it that families feel it's OK to be honest about things like this, which are in fact just rude and best kept to oneself, and dishonest about the things that really matter??????? I can't actually talk to either of my parents about the things that are really important in my life right now.

The sun came out this morning though, which made the grown-ups go on and on about how spring was finally here to celebrate the rising of the Lord, and Granny was ecstatic because it meant she could sit in the garden and watch the little ones do an Easter egg hunt. I helped Stan and Ollie and even found a few for myself. Lola did one of those pathetic pretend cries when she realized that the twins had more eggs than she did because I'd been helping them, and instead of just telling her to piss off and grow up, Dad produced a whole extra bag of eggs and dished them out. Talk about favouritism. The whole point is that you have to look for the eggs. If she can't cope with that tiny bit of competition how is she ever going to cope with secondary school? Granny gave me and Lola £10 each and some Lego to the twins, Auntie Angela gave us both vouchers for Virgin Megastores and Mum and Dad gave us each £20, so that harvest was well good.

406

Dear Diary,

April Fool's day and Dad has pulled such a mean trick I'm never going to speak to him again. I even think I hate him, which is not how you're supposed to feel about your father when you're 14. When I came down for breakfast he took one look at me and screamed, 'What's happened to your face?' Like a fool I fell for it and ran to the mirror. I was so worried I burst into tears. Dad and Mum thought it was really funny. Ha Ha. They couldn't see how upset I was, but Auntie Angela did. She followed me into the bathroom, hugged me while I cried, and told me they were mean bastards and I had a much better looking face than either of them had and did I want to have a look through her clothes and make-up and try things on. Chattie still hasn't replied to my text.

Dear Diary, Wednesday.

The trouble with Mum is that she can never resist the opportunity to dump some chore on me when I'm around, and then she wonders why I try to be away from home as much as possible. Home is supposed to be like where you rest, not work. Here I'm just completely trapped. Yesterday she made me make both our beds when I don't see why Lola can't make her own bed, tidy our room when it was perfectly tidy, help her and Auntie Angela peel about a hundred thousand potatoes, and then look after Tom for an hour while SHE had a rest! Today she's asked me to take him out for a walk in the buggy to get him to sleep, so that she can have another rest. I don't see why I should spend the whole of my holiday looking after her baby so that she can just lie around and do nothing. It did mean though that I could get to smoke in peace, even if half the village did look at me suspiciously like I was some saddo teenage mother. I'm glad now that I decided not to bring the rest of my dope, even if I could do with getting stoned to cope with the boredom. I'm never ever going to live in the country. There's nothing to do.

Supper was delicious because Auntie Angela

cooked, but tense as usual. Granny complained that they weren't getting out much, other than for walks, that we were watching too much television and that she'd like to go and see something culturally stimulating locally, like a gallery or a castle or something, that the children needed their intellectual horizons raised. I don't think she realizes how much stimulation we get at school these days. Mum went into one of those tense silences, which means she's going to say something horrid to Granny, because she hates it whenever Granny says something critical about her children, but Angela got in before her and said, 'What a good idea, let's have a look at some of the local guidebooks and see what there is.' Well I'm not going anywhere. I'd rather stay here and smoke.

Chattie still hasn't replied to my text message. Do you think I got the right number? Or maybe he just doesn't wanna talk to me. I KNEW it was a bad idea to come away this week. If I was at home I could ring him and meet up with him. Here, I'm just trapped, bored, lonely and miserable. If I was 15 do you think Mum would have let me stay at home? At 16 she definitely has no right to make me go anywhere. At least Ruby's replying to my text messages. She says she's gonna go and take a look at his house and check if they're there.

Dear Diary,

Thursday. Only two more days in this dull, depressing place and then we can go home. I wish I'd never come. I stayed in bed and slept in till lunchtime, so at least that meant half of the day was gone in this dump. Granny's OK really, a bit selfish like old people are. We have to turn the telly down when it's something she doesn't want to watch, or up when it's something she does want to watch. At least we don't have to turn it off, although she tried that one until Auntie Angela stepped in and said, 'I think that's being unreasonable Mummy.' Mum sits there and takes it, whenever she's being rude about her, but couldn't stop herself from lashing out at her this evening when Granny went on and on about how funny and attractive and clever the twins were, and how they were gonna kill the girls when they got older, 'unlike your Tom'. This sent Mum into such a rage that she accidentally on purpose smashed a plate against the wall in the kitchen and stormed off into the night. It was mean of Granny, but he is a really ugly baby. She's right there. And when he bawls I just wanna stuff an orange into his mouth to make him shut up. What I can't understand is why Mum lets Granny wind her up so much, and if she knows what it feels like to be the oldest and least well loved, why does she then go and dump all those same pressures down on me? She ought to know better.

Went down to the bench in the village this afternoon for a smoke. Auntie Angela spotted me and sat down beside me, which sent my blood pressure sky high until she said she'd promise not to tell Mum that I was smoking if I gave her a fag. We talked for ages, about how stifling family life can be, and how our family when they got together were enough to make the keenest teetotaller sneak down to the pub for a drink. 'Why do you think I married an Australian?' she said. She said that Granny loved Mum very much, and that she just felt threatened by her that's all, because she was clever and did something useful in the world, and that Granny's biggest problem was that she never did anything with her life other than have children. 'You won't have that problem with your Mum,' she added, 'and it's a big one.' I can see how that might make Granny meaner, particularly now she's old and knows that she's never going to be able to do anything useful before she dies. We walked slowly back up the lane and she asked me whether I knew what I wanted to do when I left school. When I said that I hadn't a clue and that it really worried me, she was so kind and understanding, said that sometimes people discovered things about themselves when they began working in the real world. It was nice having someone understanding to talk to, even if she didn't have any answers. I suppose, in a funny, weird sort of way, it's helpful to know that even grown-ups don't always have the answers. Maybe there just aren't any.

Dear Diary,

Saturday and home!!!!! Mum took Granny back to her old people's dump, so that meant I could go straight to London with Auntie Angela and the twins. We had a really good talk about life and love, and I told her about how I felt about Chattie and made her promise not to tell Mum. She said she had first fallen in love with someone when she was about my age and that she could still remember what that felt like. He had broken her heart because he hadn't wanted her. She said that although she felt terrible at the time – there really isn't anything worse than being rejected by someone you love – there was a certain pleasure in actually feeling anything real at all, even if it was bad, and that it was better to 'have loved and lost, than never to have loved at all'. How true. She said there was probably a really silly reason why he hadn't replied to my text message – maybe he'd lost his mobile or had it stolen, maybe he was away too for Easter with his parents, and hadn't taken his mobile with him – maybe she's right. But there isn't a message from him on the answerphone or on Messenger, and I think she was just trying to be nice to me, make me feel better. He could get in touch if he wanted to. There's payphones for fuck's sake. Ruby isn't picking up her phone and it's Saturday night and I don't really know what to think. Do you think I should phone him now?

Dear Diary,

Sunday. I finally plucked up the courage to phone and there was no answer. Ruby says she walked past his house and it looked like they were away. But he didn't mention that they were going anywhere. Why didn't he say? I smoked so much dope last night that I fell asleep sitting up in bed and it's all gone now. Toby said that if I met him on the Common he'd give me some more, but then when it came to it, he wouldn't just give me it, he wanted a blow job in return. How sick is that? I was gonna just run away, but then I thought, well, if I'm not gonna like get anywhere with Chattie, at least this way I'll have done something with a boy AND got something else out of it, and then if I do get anywhere with Chattie at least I'll be experienced. It was one of the most disgusting and embarrassing things I've ever done. I really wish I hadn't done it. I managed to pull away from him though, before he came. Imagine having all that in your mouth, must taste disgusting. It's made me feel well bad about myself, like I could do that. I thought about ringing Ruby, but if I told her and she disapproved, I might lose her and I can't risk that. So that's another secret I'm keeping from my best friend, but at least I've got lots of dope to smoke now to make me forget about things. I love the way a joint feels in my fingers when you roll the papers together to shape the tobacco, even before you lick it. It's sort of comforting that.

Dear Diary,

Monday 8th April and still no call. I go back to
school on Wednesday, and if I haven't heard
from him by then I've told Ruby that I'm going
to assume it's all over between us. All this
hoping and not knowing is too much to bear.
Auntie Angela may be right in that it is better
to have loved and lost than not to have loved at
all, but this is agony and I think it's better like
to have loved someone and won them. If they
don't really wanna be with you, what does that
say about you? That you're not worth being
with, that's what.

Auntie Angela took me out this afternoon,
which was really nice. We went shopping and
she bought me these really cool high heel shoes
and an off-the-shoulder top, and then we went
to see an 18 film. I've never been into an 18
before, I even hesitated but she like dragged me
in and said it was bound to be just a harmless
bit of sex since this was just a romantic comedy.
Mum would NEVER do that. In fact she'd
probably be furious if she knew I'd gone at all.
There was quite a lot of sex, which Auntie
Angela said spiced her up a bit after having
twins. 'Wouldn't it be great if sex really was like
it is in the movies,' she said as she slipped her

arm through mine as we left the cinema. 'There's always hope I suppose,' she laughed. I felt really like honoured that she should talk to me like this, it made me feel so grown-up.

'How would I know, I haven't done it yet!' I told her as we walked arm in arm to the tube station.

She said, 'Well don't expect it to be like that when you do. Firstly, they never look like George Clooney, secondly, they're even more scared than you are, and thirdly, they rarely know how to give a girl pleasure until she shows them how. Fourthly, never ever do it until you're really ready for it, really want it. They can wait, they have no regrets, but you might have tons, even with Chattie.'

I was so embarrassed I blushed. I wanted to tell her about Toby and how I kind of regretted that, but couldn't. But it was like really nice to talk about things with someone I could trust, someone who didn't judge me but trusted me to make the right decision and like cared for my welfare enough to make sure I was looking after myself. I really like Auntie Angela. Why does she have to live in Australia? It's a real pissoff that there's only one person in my family who like understands me – and she's leaving on Saturday.

Dear Diary,

Wednesday. Chattie said 'Hi' like he barely knew me in the playground today, and Saskia came right up to my face and goes how she had spent all week with him, skiing in France, and that I should lay off him. He didn't wanna go out with me, he liked her better. She said it so loud, like the whole world could hear her, and I knew right then that I was either going to punch her in the face or cry, so I ran off to the toilets on the third floor, locked myself into a cubicle and cried my eyes out. Fran banged on the door and told me to forget about her, that she was a lying bitch and I shouldn't believe her. When I wouldn't let her in she climbed over the top of the cubicle and sat there with me as I sobbed in her arms. Nothing she could say could make it any better. Saskia was right. He didn't wanna go out with me any more. He liked her better, the spoilt oh so pretty bitch who gets everything she wants. When the bell went Fran said she was going to English, but I wasn't shifting. My face was all red, I didn't wanna face anyone, I just wanted to stay there and cry by myself. I sat there smoking and crying until the end of the day. It meant I missed registration and that's another black mark on my attendance record. It meant I missed double English and yet another maths lesson, but I didn't care. In fact I'm not sure that I care about anything any more.

Dear Diary,

Thursday. Café on the Common.

Couldn't face the thought of going to school, so
I'm sitting here again in my favourite spot,
looking out over the common with all the
blossom out and people walking their dogs in
the spring sunshine, and I'm thinking about life
and what a bumshit deal it is having to live it.
It was hard going home last night and having to
pretend to Mum and Auntie Angela that everything was all right, and sit there over supper
while they laughed about old times over a bottle
of wine, when all I wanted to do was go to bed
and cry some more. Today's a bit better. I just
feel really really like DOWN, and even though I
knew this was going to happen – I had like a
premonition that Chattie actually wanting me
was too good to be true – it still really really
hurts and I can't face the thought of even
seeing him and Saskia at school. I know I look
terrible. I just wish I didn't feel so alone in the
world. Ruby texted me this morning at first
break, which was nice, and I told her I was fine,
but actually all I really want is someone to talk
to, someone who'll understand why I'm so
upset and say that it's OK to be upset because I

love him so much. Fran, Ruby, Hayley, Nat and Serena think I'm being oversensitive. Fran said yesterday that that was just what boys were like and I should just forget about him and concentrate on my work, find someone else, but I can't do it just like that.

Dear Diary,

Friday morning. It's raining and cold today.
Nicked a tenner out of Dad's pocket before he
went to work, for fags, cigarette papers and
lunch. He never knows how much money he
has in his pocket, and since he thinks I'm a
thief anyway, I might as well. I'm sitting in
Starbucks with a massive hot chocolate with
whipped cream and a lovely clean blank page in
my diary. I'm so glad I remembered to bring
you with me. It's cosy sitting here with you
while the rain lashes down outside. You're like a
constant friend in this existential world of
aloneness. I wonder what all these people
drinking coffee do with their lives? Do they feel
this alone all the time? If so, they must get used
to it, otherwise being a grown-up isn't all that
it's cracked up to be. It's kind of liberating,
knowing that nobody in the whole world who
knows me, knows that I'm here, liberating but
scary at the same time, like there's nobody
looking out for me. Ruby and Fran have just
sent me a text during break – 'M wants to no if
ure sick said not as sick as her.' Too right lezzie
saddo. So I texted back 'in starbucks join me.'
But they didn't.

1.30. Went to the amusement arcade for a bit and hung around there, which was kind of depressing because there were just a few sad old men in there, wasting away their lives hoping to win something when of course the machines are rigged so they won't, ever. I didn't dare smoke a joint. So I've smoked so many cigarettes my throat hurts. There was this really creepy man who kept looking at me and following me round, so I legged it back to Starbucks. It feels safe in here.

Dear Diary,

Saturday. Auntie Angela left today. Mum burst
into tears before they'd even got into the car,
Dad shouted at Lola completely unnecessarily
and made her cry as she was only trying to help
get the twins into their coats, Mum then
shouted at Dad, Dad stormed off down the
road without even saying goodbye to Mum's
one and only sister who lives in Australia, and I
was left to pick up the pieces – calm Lola
down, pack Mum, Tom, Angela and twins into
the car and wave them off. How come it's
always me that has to look after all the others
when nobody looks after me? Auntie Angela
gave me this huge hug before she left, and told
me not to think any more about Chattie (I told
her yesterday in the bathroom what had
happened and that I was gutted), and she goes
that I was a fantastic young woman and that it
was his loss, which was really sweet of her and
it did make me feel a bit better for a while. But
there's just this huge hole at the very heart of
me. He made it possible for me to feel good
enough about myself to go to school, face my
friends and do my work. Without him there I
can't see the point of even trying. So I waved
them off, and promised Auntie Angela that I'd

write and think about going to stay with them in the summer holidays on my own perhaps, or when I'm older I could go and be like their au pair, and then I took Lola inside and we dragged her duvet down and curled up underneath it in front of Saturday morning TV with a large packet of popcorn.

Dear Diary,

Sunday. Went to Ruby's last night. Couldn't stand to be here alone with them rowing again. Dad came back just before Mum did from the airport, so she wouldn't know that actually he'd been out all along. He'd obviously been to the pub because his breath stank, and when Lola let it slip that she and I had had a snack lunch together in front of telly on our own, and Mum realized that he hadn't been there at all, she went apeshit, like nobody else in the world has ever done anything so bad. I don't think I've ever seen her THAT cross with anybody. Must be a reaction to saying goodbye to her sister. He got all that pent-up emotion instead of us. Then she went on about how the place was an 'absolute tip' because there had been so many people in it, and that he could have been there to start clearing up, and he goes 'well she's YOUR sister', which sent her into outer space with anger, and then I knew that we were about to get it in the neck, and I've done enough work around here over the past few months, looking after Lola, holding the baby, clearing up her mess because she can't be bothered to do it, so I ran up to my bedroom, slapped the music up so high I couldn't hear her calling me and packed a bag to go to Ruby's.

Her mum had the decency to go out and leave money for pizza, so we had a much better time there than we would have done at my house. It was really nice to see her again. We got incredibly stoned and giggly, looking through old photographs and talking about old times – how we had gone for an illegal midnight walk once when we were away on a school field trip, and Ruby had tripped over a tree root and landed face down in a cow pat; how silly I'd looked in those stripy tights that I just thought were so so cool, and then Ruby gave me a makeover and curled my hair into ringlets. She said I had to come back to school on Monday, that it was only a question of time before I got into real trouble, and that she'd make sure Saskia didn't go anywhere near me. I'll see. I think I could manage it if I knew that he wasn't going to be there, but facing them together would be just too painful. I wish he'd never come to my school.

✉

From: Sue James
Sent: Sunday 14 April 22.46
To: Angela James
Subject: Hope the flight back wasn't too horrendous with twi . . .

Ange, darling, I miss you already and I'm sorry that Matthew chose the moment of your departure to behave so badly. He left the girls here alone the whole morning and propped up a bar somewhere through lunch, which has provoked another row, and I'm still not really talking to him because I'm so cross about the fact that a fully adult middle-aged man could have such bad manners. He could have held it together until after we had left for the airport for your sake.

The house feels empty and eerily silent now that you've gone. Frank disappeared to Ruby's last night, Matthew sulked in front of the television, and Lola and I played Scrabble on the sitting-room floor. You've also done brilliantly with Mum. I rang her this morning and she was thrilled by the whole thing – Dorset, you and the twins, the concert in Cheltenham – she even said 'Thank You' – a

429

first I think??!! So . . . in the unlikely event that she should drop dead tomorrow, we needn't feel (that) guilty. Talk soon. Masses of love S xxxx

Dear Diary,

Monday. The Café on the Common. There's like this huge black ball of emptiness inside. When I was with Ruby on Saturday we had such a laugh, such a good time, that this black emptiness disappeared. When good things happen it like wipes out the bad, but the moment I came here, instead of school like I ought to have done, I felt it come back again. The black hole inside. Maybe it's just loneliness. I miss my friends badly. I miss being part of a crowd. I miss the playground. I even miss sitting in those classrooms staring at the board, because at least you have to think about something. I even kind of miss Miss Moulder, because even though she is a meddling cow at least she cares about me. It's like without all that to take your mind off things, all you're left with is yourself, and the fact that you can't do stuff at school, and Chattie doesn't want me, and then this black ball just explodes inside me and the only thing that helps it go away is dope. Being stoned helps you think about it all that much more clearly. I can't go home because Mum's there all the time now with the baby. So this is my new home.

Dear Diary,

Tuesday. Café on the Common. The longer I'm away the harder it feels it's going to be to go back, walking through that gate and facing all those people. Chattie still hasn't called to see how I am, so I've been trying to write him a letter, trying to explain how I feel about him and asking him to just come and talk to me, here on the Common, so that I can really understand what's going on. The trouble is, I don't really know what I feel any more. I don't know whether or not this is love (is it?). I just feel so wiped out by this, and every time I try and write something, it comes out wrong so I scrunch it up and chuck it away. And why would he want a letter from me anyway? Why is it that we have to work out these really important things in life on our own?? How does anybody really know what is exactly the right or the wrong thing to do in life? WHY DOESN'T ANYBODY EVER TELL YOU HOW TO COPE WITH BEING DUMPED BY SOMEONE YOU LOVE BECAUSE IT REALLY REALLY REALLY HURTS.

I walked along the paths where we walked arm in arm like a couple this morning, and I could remember every single moment of it, how good it felt to be held by someone, how lovely it was, how nothing else seemed to matter. It was still so vivid it was like it had just happened.

From: Sue James
Sent: Tuesday 16 April 14.12
To: Angela James
Subject: Re: Hope the flight back wasn't too horrendous with twi . . .

OK, you're right again. I am angry with him for how he treats me, I'm livid, but that doesn't mean I can't get angry with him for behaving badly towards you. I'm not denying one to express the other – I can feel both at the same time but, unlike my own dear husband, know that it is good manners to consider others before yourself . . . And was it really that obvious, in Dorset? The marital disharmony? How excruciatingly embarrassing – do you think Mum noticed?

Sorry to hear about the vomit all over your best trousers when you were only ten minutes into take off. What a total, fucking awful bore, with only another 24 hours to go without being able to change your clothes. I suppose the only silver lining is that they weren't both struck down by travel sickness!

Dear Diary,

Ruby had a real go at me on the phone last night, said the only person I was really hurting by staying away was myself, that I needed to face up to things and not run away from them, and how they missed me. I wanted to cry when she said that. But when I asked her whether Saskia had talked about Chattie, she said she had, and that Saskia had been a right bitch and said I was obsessed and that I was deluding myself because he didn't like girls with big bums. Bitch. Why should I even want to be there when she talks about me like that? I shouted at Ruby when she told me that, and then she got cross with me and said, 'Don't blame me, I'm just trying to help you', and that they had all told her off for being so horrible, and how would she like it if one of us criticized her for having calves so wide she can't wear boots, when actually that's not nearly as bad as having fat on your bum that ought to be on your tits. I think she must have slept with him and that's why he wants to be with her, not me. I should have gone further with him that day, when he came over at the beginning of the Easter holidays. It's all my own fault.

Mum and Dad went to parents' evening at

Lola's school and just expected me to look after Tom and Lola for an hour while they were gone. I mean what if the house burnt down? What would I do then, I'm only fourteen. They just expected me to do it, they didn't even ask if I was free. Ruby rang and when they came back Tom had vomited all the way down the front of his Babygro and they were furious with me. Dad said he could have died if he'd breathed in his sick and I hadn't even noticed. Well how was I to know that? How was I supposed to do anything about it, when I was on the phone? When he heard I was talking to Ruby he of course blamed it all on her because she's such a 'bad influence', which is just so pathetic I can hardly believe he could be that stupid (well actually, come to think of it, I can). How can she be responsible when she wasn't even here???

They then had one of their ridiculous rows where Mum gets bossy and tells him what to do, and he tells her to shut up and that he doesn't need her to run his life for him, and then the baby starts crying because they're shouting at each other about absolutely fuck all that matters, and I just want to scream, bury my head under a pillow and smoke a joint.

Dear Diary,

Thursday. I'm never ever going back to that school. Toby's been bragging round the playground about how I 'give good head', and every single one of my friends rang last night to ask me if it was true. I lied of course, but I'm not sure that Ruby believed me and I'm certain that Saskia didn't. She called me a slag, said she wasn't surprised Chattie had dumped me if I thought Toby worth sucking off, so I slammed down the phone before she could say any more. I don't care what she thinks, but Ruby sounded really shocked and hurt that I didn't tell her. If I don't have Ruby as a friend then there really is no point in ever going back to school. It's so embarrassing I just want to die. I never ever want to have to show my face in that playground again.

From: Sue James
Sent: Thursday 18 April 23.16
To: Angela James
Subject: Re: Hope the flight back wasn't too horrendous with twi . . .

Matthew's calmed down a bit and actually apologized, so perhaps he's learning . . . so I've calmed down a bit too, but as soon as marital relations relax, parental/teenage tensions soar. We left Tom for just an hour last night with Frankie and came back to find him almost drowning in sick and looking green. She must have seriously overfed him. Matthew went ballistic. Accused her of being irresponsible, how could she ever go out and earn money babysitting when she couldn't even look after her own brother etc . . . I tried to restrain him, but I was upset about it too. She just forgot about him because she was on the phone to one of her friends – she's so wrapped up with herself at the moment, nothing else seems to matter. But then Frankie went ballistic back, screamed that she hated us, and that we didn't understand her or even know what she was going through,

438

and I thought she's right, I don't know because she never talks to me about anything any more. I never see her alone or spend time with her, and I just feel so awful about that, Ange, and I don't know how to reach her any more. It's like she's slipping away from me. I tried to talk to her after everybody had calmed down a bit, but she told me to go away and to stop prying, and that nothing about her life was any of my business any more, but that isn't true and I told her so. She just screamed at me, 'My happiness isn't your problem, it's mine and I'll deal with it, so FUCK OFF AND LEAVE ME ALONE.'

Looking at her hating me like that reminded me of myself when I was only a year or two older than she is, arguing with Mum, hating Mum, wishing I was a million miles away and able to live my own life. I can't bear to think we could have come full circle so quickly. I always thought it'd be different with my own daughters, that I'd understand them, stay close and loving, so that they wouldn't feel this way about me, but I've failed on that front, Ange, and that makes me feel so sad . . . She's still awake, I can hear her pacing about upstairs . . .

love S xxx

✉

From: Sue James
Sent: Friday 19 April 23.56
To: Angela James
Subject: Frankie

I think I'd better start at the beginning, otherwise this is likely to come out as an incomprehensible mess.

Had a phone call from the school this morning to say that Frank hadn't been there at all since the start of the term and was she ill/did I know?? At first I just didn't believe what the woman was telling me. Frankie had left every morning with her bag and come home at the normal time. Nothing seemed out of the ordinary. But she insisted that Frankie had not been marked down as present at a single registration this term, and that there were a number of unexplained absences last term. If she wasn't at school, where was she? What had she been doing?

I didn't know what to do or where to start looking. I had no idea where she could possibly be, and it was at least six hours before she was likely to come home. I tried to think back over the past few weeks, to see if I could pinpoint anything out of the ordinary, but there was nothing, just the usual sullenness, the rows. But last night she seemed so upset, and I remembered how she'd said that her happiness was not my problem, and I began to wonder whether there really was something wrong, so I went up into her room to have a look around.

I found a packet of cigarettes in her knicker drawer, which really upset me. She knows how much I hate it, and she always promised me she wouldn't. So I looked around some more and found her diary. I know I shouldn't have, Ange, I know it's private, I know it's not what you're supposed to do, but I just couldn't not, simply because of that phone call from the school. There's so much going on here that I'm not aware of, and as her mother I need to know so that I can even begin to start dealing with it. I sat on her bed and just cried as I read, Ange. She's been so unhappy, so lost. She's also been dealing with so much on her own – Matthew and me rowing, him leaving, the baby, bitchy girls at school, growing up. There's a boy that she really likes, but she doesn't think he likes her. She knows she's behind with her coursework and can't find her own way out of this hole. She's been smoking dope and she's even started her period, Ange, and I never knew, and that's what really breaks my heart. I should have known, Ange, as her mother. I should have been there to help her, buy her pads, make her hot water bottles, answer her questions, but she never even asked. She coped with it all by herself. I've let her down badly and I feel terrible about that. I ought to have known better. I spend my life at the practice trying to read signs in people, interpret symptoms, yet I couldn't even recognize them in my own daughter.

She mentions the Café on the Common quite a bit, so I put the diary back where I found it, strapped Tom into his buggy, and headed off to see if I could find her, but she wasn't there. I sat around drinking coffee for a while, hoping that she might turn up, but she didn't. When she finally came home at about 6, I told her gently that the school had rung and that she hadn't been there since the beginning of term. She told me they were lying, they'd got it wrong. I said schools got things wrong but not that wrong, and where had she been, why didn't she want to go? She said that she didn't want to talk about it now and headed for her room. Now that I really knew what was going on, I read the signs differently. She wasn't just being surly, she seemed almost depressed. Her face looked anxious and tense, and she didn't want me to get too close in case I could smell the cigarette smoke on her breath. So I said OK, we'd talk about it over supper with Dad, and that made her come back downstairs pretty damn quick. She didn't want to tell me why she didn't want to go back to school, and I can understand that. I'd love it if she could talk to me about Love, but given how things have been between us, even I know that's an unreasonable expectation on my part. However, she did promise me that she'd go back to school on Monday if I didn't tell Matthew about the phone call. I said that we could get her a tutor if she was finding the work difficult, and she said she'd like that. So maybe, just maybe, fingers crossed, things will be a little better from now on. But of course I can't sleep. (I can hear her talking with Ruby upstairs, funny to think that her best friend now knows more about what's really going on than I do.) I can't sleep because I feel I've really failed her, and I'm not quite sure how to make it up to her, or whether she'll even let me try. Much love S xxxx

From: Sue James
Sent: Saturday 20 April 19.23
To: Angela James
Subject: Re: Frankie

I know it is theoretically never too late to say
'I'm sorry' and 'I love you', and you're right,
I'll try that, but at the moment it feels as if
there is such a huge chasm of misunder-
standing between us that I can't even get to
that point. I will also suggest that she and I
go out and do something fun together –
you're right about that one as well, because
we haven't since her birthday last June (God
that feels like an age away and so much has
happened since then) – just as soon as we get
over this immediate crisis and she's talking to
me again.

Lola of course overheard our conversation
last night and over lunch today let slip to
Matthew that Frank hadn't been at school,
which set off World War 3. I could have
killed her. Just as things were beginning to
loosen up Little Miss Big Ears sticks a knife
in her sister's back. Matthew reacted as you
would expect and Frankie stormed off to her

room, refusing to talk to him if he was going to shout at her. Matthew then shouted at me for not telling him. So I followed Frank up to her room and hugged her. She sobbed in my arms and I just held her until she calmed down. She said she was really frightened of going back to school, that the teachers would make snide comments, and she'd be so behind with her work, and then there were her friends . . . 'And Chattie?' I said, and she nodded and then said, 'How do you know about Chattie?' and pulled away from me. 'Have you been reading my diary?' I lied at this critical point – who wouldn't have? – but she didn't believe me. 'How did you know about Chattie? I haven't mentioned him,' she continued. 'You must have been reading my diary, how else could you know?' At which point she began packing a bag with her diary and some spare clothes, and said she was going to stay at Ruby's. How could I have been so stupid, Ange, as to let that slip? She was just beginning to relax with me and then I had to mention fucking Chattie.

Anyway, she's not at Ruby's, because I've rung, and she's not at Fran's, Serena's or any of her friends' houses because I've rung them all, and she's letting her mobile go on to voicemail whenever I ring. She can see it's our number when I call. I even went down to the local phone box to ring, so that she wouldn't recognize the number of the incoming call, but she still wouldn't answer. She's been gone for four hours and I haven't got a fucking clue where she is. I've called the police, but they say that she isn't a missing person yet and that she'll probably come back later this evening when she gets cold and hungry. But what if she doesn't, Ange? Anything can happen to a 14-year-old girl between now and then! She could already have been abducted by paedophiles. I'm beginning to get desperate. Where is she? God how I've fucked things up, they couldn't actually BE much worse . . . Talk to you later, as soon as I know anything more. S x

Dear Diary

Chattie's café. I feel so completely, utterly and totally alone in this world. My whole family seen to have turned against me. I've let them down by not doing my work, being the brilliant person they want me to be, or going to school, which is the only thing I'm supposed to do each day. If I can't do that, how am I ever going to be able to work and support myself? Sometimes I think Mum actually cares more about her patients than she does about me. I'm sitting here, sort of hoping that Chattie will come in and we can talk, pick up where we left off and sort things out, maybe even find a way of being friends again. I'd like that, I miss talking to him. But I've had two cokes and so far he hasn't showed up. If he just was here, I could talk to him about everything, and he would tell me to go home and face them, sort things out, but without him here to give me the courage I'm not sure that I can do that on my own.

From: Sue James
Sent: Sunday 21 April 22.16
To: Angela James
Subject: Frank

What a night . . . I never ever want to have
to live through such anxiety again. I've practically gone grey. She finally came home at
2 a.m., so drunk that she was vomiting all
over the front hall and staggering. In fact I'm
not sure how she made it back at all.
Matthew and I had had such a row, fuelled
of course by our anxiety, that he did at least
listen to me when I told him to shut up, not
say a word, and let me handle this, as I
bundled her into the bathroom and locked
the door behind us. The one thing he knows
he can't hold an opinion on is the state of our
children's health. I let her puke some more,
washed her face and neck with ice-cold water
and then, when she'd stopped puking, gave
her a massive dose of Andrew's liver salts to
try and wake her up a bit. I wasn't going to
let her sleep until she had sobered up some
more and stopped puking.

We spent most of the night in the bathroom.

I sat hugging her from behind on the floor, leaning against the bath, in case she should be sick again, and rocked her as I sang lullabies to her like I did when she was tiny. I told her stories from her childhood, how we'd spent a week in bed together when we both had flu, and watched Disney videos back to back, and how we'd fallen about laughing at the end of the week when we finally felt better and saw how messy the bedroom was. How we'd built sandcastles in Cornwall, and massive mermaids in the sand with shells for scales and seaweed for hair. How she had loved her ballet classes so much when she was six that she spent each and every day in her tutu, ballet shoes and tights, and how I used to have to wash and dry them at night when she was asleep. The memories came back so fast and were so vivid it was as if they had just happened. She dozed and groaned against my arms. She kept saying that she felt ill, and that she was sorry, and then sobbed occasionally in the way that very drunk people do. She said she was so sorry about everything, for keeping me up like this, for having failed me and let me down. She said she was sorry that she had left Tom, and that he had been ill, and that she felt frightened and thought he might die because of her. 'I can't even look after my own little brother,' she wailed into my shoulder. I said she could, he was never going to die, and that Dad had over-reacted. I cried a little and told her that I loved her passionately, that I was so sorry that she had had to cope with all of this on her own, and that I wouldn't let that happen again. I told her that she hadn't failed me, that I was proud of her for growing up into such a strong, independent-minded woman, that I adored her, and that if anybody was to blame it was me, but that it had been a busy and difficult year. 'I know, Mum, all I ever wanted to do was help you, and I haven't even managed to do that, I've just made things worse.' At which point we both sobbed so hard we ended up laughing and I knew she was sobering up.

I took off her clothes, washed her face with a warm soapy flannel and put her to bed in those lovely silk pyjamas you gave me, Ange. I lay down beside her and stroked her head as she slept, and dozed off myself. Matthew was so shaken by all of this that he gave Tom a bottle at 6 a.m. and didn't wake me for his early morning feed, which is a bit of a breakthrough. I think it may be time to just let him have tit last thing at night, which means I'll dry up completely soon, and then my tits and a little bit more of my life will be my own again.

We talked a little more today, but she had quite a headache when she finally woke up, so I just tried to look after her. Matthew managed to hug her and say that he loved her, and that he'd been so worried that he'd toured the streets until 1 a.m. on his motorbike looking for her, so that's good. I think he may have finally realized that getting cross with her doesn't help. It just pushes her away. Frankie has promised that she will go to school, and likes the idea of a tutor to help get her back on top of her work, so that's my main priority tomorrow, but I feel that we've only begun to scrape the surface of her turmoil. She is so much more needy than I ever realized. When you see poverty and neglect like I do almost every day on my rounds, you just thank God that your own kids are so much better off, and I suppose that I just assumed as a result that Frankie and Lola would be all right. But when it comes to teenagers, I guess the real truth is that you never really know what's going on in their heads, and that it is perhaps a mistake to ever assume anything . . .

Must try and sleep, now that the immediate

crisis is over . . . I'll ping you later in the week and let you know how things are. Masses of love S xxxxx

Dear Diary,

Monday. Went back to school today, and it wasn't nearly as bad as I expected it would be. Everyone was really pleased to see me (except Saskia of course), and nobody mentioned Toby, other than Ruby who called him a lying little dickhead fantasist. Mum wrote a really long letter to Miss Moulder, explaining that things had been really difficult for me at home, and that we were now trying to work things out together, and consequently, typically, Miss Moulder was all over me like a rash. Mum let me read the letter and approve it. I'm glad she didn't mention anything about Saskia or Chattie, because that really feels so much more private, given that everybody at school knows who they are, and I really don't want her to know anything about it.

Chattie came up to me at first break and asked me if I was feeling better. Ruby had told him that I was really ill with gastric flu (thanks, Rubes), so I thanked him for asking and said I was much better. So that was well good to see him again. Saskia just sort of snarled at me from a distance, but the rest of the gang kind of shielded me from her and made me feel like they really wanted me back. The only bad thing about today has been the lessons. I feel so behind, it was like they were talking another language. I had to really concentrate to understand what was going on, and hope that the teachers wouldn't ask me any questions. There was only one snide comment from the Geography teacher, and I can just about live with that.

Dear Diary,

Wednesday. Mum and Dad are being really nice to me. Mum bought lots of my favourite things to eat, including those lovely fan wafers to go with ice cream and strawberries. She's even suggested that we go shopping at the weekend – but the thing is, I don't really feel as if I deserve all this attention. I feel so bad about all the trouble I've caused. I can see how worried they are about me, and that makes me feel well bad, that I could be so selfish when they're good parents. They're having to pay for a tutor just because I've been missing lessons, just because I didn't go to school, not because I'm stupid or dyslexic or something and need remedial help. So I'm determined now to go to every single lesson, and make sure my homework gets done and in on time, so that they don't have to worry about me any more. Chattie is talking to me, but he's still kind of like distant – and I'm not sure why. I still love him, I think I'll always love him, but maybe it just wasn't meant to be.

From: Sue James
Sent: Wednesday 24 April 21.15
To: Angela James
Subject: I think we're making progress

The house is amazingly calm and Matthew is really making an effort with Frankie. He went to WH Smith at lunchtime today and bought her some GCSE revision notes and the latest Justin Timberlake album. I feel a bit as if I'm treading on eggshells with her though. I don't want to say or do anything that might upset her or make her feel like running away again. I just couldn't bear it. I'm watching her every move for signs. I think she's happier, and I've talked to the school. She has been there since Monday, so that is progress.

  I still feel really embarrassed and ashamed about the fact that we have let it get to this stage with one of my own children. And you know what's really pathetic is that I REALLY don't want HND to find out about this. We're getting on so much better, and I don't want her to gossip disapprovingly about me again at the school gate when I've gone back to work and left Tom with someone else. (I think I'm going to look at a nanny share this time, so that there's someone who can also be here for Frank and Lola.) They say that you find the worst plumbing in the houses of plumbers, and maybe I have been more negligent with my own kid's health than I would have been with others at the surgery. I should have noticed. I should have been less wrapped up with myself and Tom, but then I suppose you just think these are phases. That's what Matthew says anyway, still, that this is just a phase, that all teenagers have to do something to crash through the barriers, and that we're lucky it's not drugs. (I haven't told him that she's been smoking a lot of dope.)

Frank had her period last night, said it was really hurting and what should she do. I was cool about it, managed not to say, 'I wish you'd told me when you first started,' and gave her some paracetamol. I made her a hot-water bottle, snuggled her up in front of the telly with her duvet, and said, 'Welcome to the world of menstrual cramps and PMT.' She laughed and said that she hadn't wanted to bother me with it before. I asked her if she wanted me to tell Dad and she nodded. When I casually dropped the bombshell after supper, that his daughter could now actually get pregnant, he just said,

'Well that explains everything! All women go a bit bonkers before their periods.' Typical male reaction, blame it all on the hormones.

So there you have it, the latest update from family life with a teenager. I just hope that there isn't worse in store for us around the corner.

Much love Sue xxxx

Dear Diary,

Friday and I've had the most AMAZING evening!!!!! We all went ice skating after school and Chattie came too. Saskia, Hayley, Serena, Nat and Fran clung to the outside edge screaming for most of the time with their legs wobbling around out of control, which really, REALLY annoyed me because they didn't even try and skate and get good at it. They just huddled together, and screamed the moment someone lost their balance. They looked like such idiots. All they did was moan and Saskia was the worst. All she said the entire evening was stuff like 'My feet really hurt', 'I'm dying', 'I hate this, let's go and have a smoke'. I love skating. I love the swish of the blade against the ice and the way you get so hot when you get moving and the ice is so cold. Ruby wanted to learn, so I held her hand as we went round and taught her how to push against the ice. She fell over a couple of times, but she got it really quickly.

The others were deliberately being pathetic just because a whole load of boys from school were there too – Toby, Will, Sean, Simon, as well as that gang of midget boys from Year 9 who still think it's cool to wear football shirts.

Honestly, they are so immature. Toby kept trying to pull girls away from the side, so that they had nothing to hold on to but him, which made them scream even more. Then he thought it would be really hilarious to spin Saskia round which made her lose her balance and slip so badly that she banged the back of her head against the ice. Her dad'll be so cross he'll probably sue. Chattie helped her up and helped her off the ice to a seat, which of course she LOVED, but she was OK, and then he came back on to the ice. He's a really good skater, so elegant and graceful. What I love about him is that he's just normal. He doesn't need to brag like the other boys, or loon around like some imbecilic leprechaun to impress people. He's happy to stand back and be himself, which is SOOOO mature. He's doesn't need to slap hair gel on to his hair to make it stand up and make him look like he's seen a ghost or something. He has his own style, he doesn't need to wear what others think is cool. He has these beautiful, slendery fingers, gorgeous eyes and when he smiles I just wanna die!!!!! He is just SOOOO FIT! All the others went off the ice with Saskia. They were like relieved to be able to sit down without losing face, but as soon as I could see that she was all right, I pulled Ruby back on to the ice and we skated round. Chattie zoomed up behind us, turned in front of me, took hold of both my hands and skated backwards in large swirling loops pulling me along from side to side. It was SOOO sexy and he can skate BACKWARDS. It was like in that moment all that mattered was him and me. I turned to look at Ruby, but she was heading off the ice. 'I need a wee,' she screamed and then it was just him and me, alone in a crowd, skating together. I felt like we were in a movie or something. It was just so sexy. We crossed our arms and held hands like real skaters do as we went round the rink in perfect harmony, just like we had done when we were walking on the Common together and it just felt so right. I could feel all the others were looking at me, Saskia was probably bitching about me but I didn't care. This was heaven and I can still feel my feet skating. I can still feel the warmth of his body beside me and his hands in mine.

Dear Diary,

Saturday. Chattie rang today and asked me if I wanted to go to the cinema with him tomorrow afternoon, and I'm so excited I can't sleep. He rang this afternoon, when I was least expecting it and sitting in the bathroom plucking my eyebrows. Now I'm having hysterics about what to wear. I've got everything out of my wardrobe and spread it out across the floor. I wish I'd taken Mum up on that offer to go shopping, but my stomach has been so bloated with this period that I didn't feel like it, or think that I could get anything on that was worth buying. I think maybe I'll wear something that he's admired before. That way I can feel a bit more relaxed. After yesterday's electric skating this feels like a real date.

Dear Diary,

Sunday April the 28th and we are officially
going out again from today!!!!!!! I met him
outside the cinema and we were a bit nervous
of one another at first, but the film was so bad
that we ended up laughing so much that all our
nerves like disappeared, and then we went to
Starbucks for a hot chocolate and talked. He
said he'd thought I hadn't wanted to see HIM!
That he had been nervous about calling me,
and couldn't believe it when I said I had
thought the same thing about him. He never
got my text message from Dorset, and Saskia
had been telling him lies about me while they
were on holiday together – that I thought he
was a minger and I still fancied Toby. Bitch.
They went to the same ski resort by accident
and he said he couldn't get rid of her. They
were even in the same ski lessons. It's amazing
how so much bad feeling can just disappear
when you know the truth, but I haven't let on
how miserable I've been these past few weeks.
He still thinks I've been really ill. He thinks we
should be cool about it in school though, so
that Saskia doesn't make life difficult, and I
think that's a good idea. She is supposed to be
my friend, but after everything he's been saying

about her I'm never going to confide in her or be nice to her ever again. It's going to be really hard not telling her that we're going out again AND that he kissed me at the bus stop!!!!!! It was SOOOO nice. I didn't know that kissing could be THAT good. Every time our tongues touched I just felt my whole body melt into his. I just wanted every inch of our souls to touch. I just wanted him. It wasn't horrid like it was with Toby.

Dear Diary,

Monday. Saskia blanks me the whole time but you know what??? I just don't care any more. I don't need her as a friend. I have Ruby and Fran and the others. It's her problem, she's just gotta find a way of living with the fact that Chattie seems to want me, not her.

Dear Diary,

Wednesday. I've had my maths tutor for an hour every day after school this week and I really like her. She's young and really pretty, with clothes I'd kill to have, and she says I'm really good at school stuff and not that behind at all. She's probably lying, but it's nice of her to say that. Mum really likes her too. She stayed for supper with us and Mum practically offered her a full-time job looking after all of us before she had even finished eating. I was SOOOO embarrassed. Chattie is cool about everything at school. I still find it hard to concentrate sometimes when he's in the same lesson as me. He sent me a really funny text message during the most boring maths lesson in the history of the world today, which almost got discovered by Miss Smart. I really don't need my phone confiscated right now. Saskia and I just ignore each other. I haven't told her that I'm going out with Chattie, but I almost let it slip today when she was talking about skiing and how good she is at it. (He says she's crap at it and got moved down a class.)

From: Sue James
Sent: Friday 3 May 09.51
To: Angela James
Subject: Hi

Are we a family that things just happen to or
is this normal family life? HND always seems
calm, organized and together. I know she only
has one rather spoilt, easy child, but why is it
that we ricochet from one crisis to another?
We've had unsuspected accidental pregnancy,
major marital rows, adultery and separation,
shoplifting, alcohol poisoning, truancy, a
plague of nits – all we need now is for
Matthew to declare that he wants a divorce,
for me to lose my job and Lola to get expelled
and we'll have had a truly exceptional/normal
(?) year! Only joking. I don't think the last
three are likely to happen. I just can't wait for
everything to feel normal again, whatever that
is. Just a sense of equilibrium, that everyone
is basically OK and trucking along happily.
Now that things with Frankie have settled
down a bit I've realized that I haven't
discussed this with anyone, other than you of
course, because I sort of haven't dared really.

It's not like when they're younger and you exchange confidences with other mothers at the school gate about nappy rash or problems at school. This feels much more private somehow. And then I wonder whether we are the only ones coping with a teenager almost off the rails and whether that says something about us as failing parents because of course everybody else does it better than us if they don't have these problems or whether this is just normal and everybody has these sort of problems with teenagers only they just don't talk about it . . . Mind games!

I am now focusing on the future and the prospect of going back to work properly in the last week of June. Not looking forward to giving up Tom, or daytime TV, BUT it'll be good to have that feeling that my life is my own for part of the day. I think things will feel normal again when I am back at work. There'll be more balance between Matthew and me because we're both out there struggling with other people's difficulties, and feeling grateful that at least we don't have 'that' to deal with. There's just the perennial problem of childcare. I've stuck an advert up in the local toy shop and café asking for a nanny share, and I'm working heavily on the new tutor (who is heavenly and adored by

468

Frank) to see if she'd consider it for a while. I've offered her double the normal rate for six months. She's saving to go round the world with her boyfriend, so she might just take it up. The other issue is clothes. I'm still two stone heavier than I was before Tom and can't seem to shift it, so nothing work-like really fits me any more. But it's a lovely sunny, spring day so I think I'll go now for a long walk across the Common . . . if I can avoid eating until suppertime I might just lose an eighth of an ounce. Talk soon, much love and give me your news. I feel bereft when I haven't heard the latest antics from down under for over a week. Much love Sue xxxx

Dear Diary,

Bank Holiday Monday. It's soooo amazing not having to get up for school on a Monday in the middle of a term. They ought to have one bank holiday Monday a month, just so that we could all catch up on our sleep. I'm beginning to make plans for my birthday. I'm going to be 15 in six week's time and 15 sounds so much older than 14, don't you think? Easily more than a year older, almost a woman. I want a party, but Mum says that's for when you're sixteen and legally able to do things, like buy cigarettes and have sex (maybe Chattie and I will on my sixteenth birthday, if we're still going out by then), plus it's a way of celebrating GCSEs when they're over. She even said she'd look into hiring somewhere clublike. Dad suggested we could go away somewhere and I could take a friend, since my birthday's a Sunday, which would be great if I could take Chattie, but he'd never agree to that, doesn't even know of his existence yet. When you're fifteen you wanna celebrate with your friends, not just your family, but it was sweet of him to try and think of something special I suppose. Great shopping potential. Mum says that if I manage to give up smoking by my 15th birthday she'll give me

£100, and that if I'm still not smoking by my 16th birthday she'll make that £500!!!! Now that's gotta be worth a try . . . imagine what you could buy with that kind of money . . . hard though with exams and everything.

Ruby, Chattie, Fran and I are going up to Kenwood House in Highgate today for a picnic, so I'll ask them what they think I should do. Ruby's birthday's a week before mine, so maybe we could do something together.

Dear Diary,

Bank Holiday Monday night. Wouldn't it be just absolutely and incredibly amazing if I could have my sixteenth birthday party at Kenwood! It's the most amazing large white house on top of a hill overlooking fields and a lake, and in June it would almost like be midsummer, so we could be outside with flares and fireworks and things.

From: Sue James
Sent: Thursday 9 May 21.16
To: Angela James
Subject: Re: Hi

Could you put them in separate rooms for a
while, so that they get back into the habit of
sleeping through the night and not waking
each other up? Or wouldn't they hack that,
being twins? It sounds to me like they're
getting into bad habits if this is now
happening every night, and you've got to be
really tough about it. Try ear plugs and a lock
on their door if you get really desperate. They
won't be traumatized for life, just a bit tired
in the morning, but they would be anyway. If
it's really getting to you, and you're knack-
ered, stand firm, and make sure Spike's
entirely with you on this one. Sorry to be
bossy. Motherhood's tiring enough without
losing the sleep that you deserve.

Went out to a dinner party last night, my first
since Tom. One of Matthew's clients so I was
very much Mrs Wilcox and a little nervous.
Dressing was a bit of a problem. I think I took
longer deciding what to wear than Frankie

does, which is saying something. In fact she had to help me in the end, which was sweet. Left Toyah (F's tutor) babysitting, in the hope that she'd fall in love with Tom – shrewd of me, no? – still lobbying her hard over childcare. I'm even thinking of offering to contribute some-thing towards her round-the-world ticket as an extra incentive – do you think that's taking things too far?? Anyway, dinner was indescrib-ably boring. These people were REALLY weird – rich, rude and they don't even do their own cooking for dinner, which I think is cheating. They brought in this Italian cook so the food was at least delicious, if fattening. I sat next to a good-looking man on my right, who clearly thought I wasn't worth bothering with, because he never once turned to talk to me and flirted incessantly with the woman on his right. On my left I had my lunatic host, who didn't have much to talk about other than the food and who did I think was likely to win the FA cup on Saturday, which is of limited interest, so I asked him what he did for a living and he looked so shocked by my question you'd have thought I'd asked him something really out of order like 'Does your wife give you blow jobs?' (I doubt it somehow.) He then did something so shocking I practically choked. He produced a camcorder and walked round the table, filming each and every one of us intensely. For one horrifying moment I thought he was expecting us each to do a turn – sing a song or recite a poem or something. I was on the verge of saying something flippant like, 'I hope you have some model release forms handy to stop us from suing,' when I caught sight of Matthew from the other side of the table, willing me to be silent with his eyes. Honestly, it is hard to really enjoy a tiramisu when you've got a camcorder pointed halfway down your ear. Is this a new after-dinner pastime that I've somehow missed because I've had a baby and been out of the loop for a while? Do they do this in Australia?

Must catch the news before I crash. Talk soon. S xxx

Dear Diary,

Friday. Talked to Ruby last night for over an hour about our birthdays while Mum and Dad were out. My ear actually hurt when we finally stopped talking and we came to no firm conclusion as to what to do, but it was fun running through all the things we COULD do, from ice skating to cinema to mass sleepover. Chattie says he'll ask his parents if we could all go down to his house in Wales for the weekend, which would be so cool, but I don't think Mum and Dad are going to like that much because Dad doesn't even know of his exis-tence, and Mum doesn't know we're back together, and they're going to want me to be here for my birthday. I think we're too young for that. He even says he wants to meet my parents and Lola, which feels a bit premature, but I'll see. Toyah reckons I ought to just mention him a bit, get them used to the idea that I have actually like got a boyfriend, so that they don't get too much of a shock.

Dear Diary,

Sunday evening, late. We snogged so hard on the Common this afternoon under our favourite tree that my lips are actually sore!! Just remembering what we did makes me feel hot and really randy. He ran his hands down my body, really nervously. I could feel his hand shaking as he felt my tits, and I didn't feel at all ashamed about them and their size, it was just so weird having someone else touch something so private. The fact that he seemed to like touching them made them feel bigger somehow. When he rubbed at my crotch I almost died it felt so good, I just didn't want him to stop. Each time we meet and touch I feel better about being close to him, and being touched by him, and each time I seem to like it more.

I hope Mum never reads this. I've decided the best hiding place is underneath the mattress of my bed. The very best hiding place would be to keep my diary with me all the time, but if it got discovered by one of the others at school I think I'd just die of embarrassment. I've made her promise me that she won't ever read it again, and she's said that she can give me her word on that. She also said that if I had talked to her about how I was feeling, then maybe she wouldn't have needed to read it in the first place, which is a fair point, so I've promised to try and talk to her about things in the future. I want to talk to her about Chattie, but I'm not sure how.

From: Sue James
Sent: Monday 13 May 10.03
To: Angela James
Subject: Truth, Privacy and Betrayal

Ange, darling,

I've been thinking about how difficult it is to
respect the boundaries of privacy, which every
individual is entitled to even within family life,
and yet remain truthful and honest with each
other. Matthew still hasn't expressed any
interest in sex, and while I'm relieved because
I'm still feeling fat and too shagged by Tom to
be gagging for it, I am beginning to wonder
whether this isn't something that we ought to
be talking about. But then what would he
say? I'd only be inviting him to say that he
finds me hideous and unappealing sexually,
and then I'd feel hurt, and that's hardly likely
to improve things between us.

Frankie made a very telling comment
yesterday about truth. I keep telling her that I
want her to be able to talk to me about
things, that I may be able to help her, and

479

I've promised her that whatever she tells me would remain private. But she said that that was only possible if she felt that I was strong enough to take the load, to take whatever she tells me, that she needed me still to be strong for her, make some essential decisions for her, and not to be shocked if she told me something that I didn't like. She's right, of course, because I haven't been strong enough for her this past year. You can't be when you're in the throws of the menopause and then have a baby at the age of 43. I'm soft, gooey, vulnerable, tearful, overanxious, sleep-deprived, my body image is at an all time low and my immunity is non-existent. I've a permanent cold, and I even think I may be bored enough to want to leave Tom and go back to work.

Sue x

From: Sue James
Sent: Wednesday 15 May 23.02
To: Angela James
Subject: Re: Truth, Privacy and Betrayal

Dearest, You're absolutely right about being more proactive. There's nothing like doing it to create desire. It's like the body needs a kick start to be sexual, and that means the mind has to force it to go to places that it doesn't think it wants to go. I'll have to pick my moment though, and feel really confident and strong about it, but I'll also have to work up a sexual appetite, fantasize about somebody young and athletic for an hour or something beforehand to get that tingle going . . .!

You were also dead right about asking Frankie about Chattie. Thanks, Sis. He rang tonight and I got to the phone first, so I asked her if they were 'dating' when she got off the phone and she blushed. How wonderful! And I said that, and that he was a very lucky boy, and that he'd better be treating her well and that I'd love to meet him, why didn't he come over at the weekend? She said she'd think about it, and

481

then said, 'How do you know, Mum, when you're in love?' I was so thrilled by such a question, that she wanted to ask me at all, that I forgot to be shocked. So I told her all the obvious things, about not being able to sleep, eat, think about anything but him, how if he made her feel good and she trusted him, then love would grow deeper, and I resisted the temptation to add that at her age this was far more likely to be a crush or an obsession, and she skipped up the stairs to her room happy with my answer.

I told Matthew about it, but came on really strong with the privacy aspect, said that he had to be so cool about it that she wouldn't notice the difference. He said that he was glad that someone at least was having sex in this house, to which I said she isn't, but she's probably thinking about it. There were to be no jokes or jibes with Frank, he wasn't to even let on that he knew, and then, whenever Chattie came round, he was to treat him as if he were just a friend. I don't want any of those embarrassing 'are your intentions with my daughter honourable' sort of thing. I also said that there were to be absolutely no jokes with Frank over his name, like 'Does he like to talk a lot?' or 'What sort of name is that for a boy?' and that it was bad enough him going on about having a flower living next door, and that if he behaved I might give him a blow job (!). How's that for a segue!!! He almost looked shocked, but then couldn't resist a smile and even hugged me.

Masses of love Suexxx

PS Mum has nearly finished her painting of you and the twins. Hope Spike isn't offended by the fact that he isn't in it. I'm going down to see her next weekend, and if it's finished I've promised to take it away and ship it out to you. She's been working on it for the best part of a month she says – do you think that means it should be good, or terrible? Matisse spent longer than that on his masterpieces surely? I think he even reworked them dozens of times, so don't expect a Matisse and you might be surprised . . . I'll let you know.

Dear Diary,

Friday. I can't believe it, I actually got an A for my maths homework this week and it's all because of Toyah. She's really helped bring my confidence up, and I understand the point of fractions now!! Saskia's being a complete bitch about me needing a tutor, but I'm managing to hold back from lashing back. Whenever she says something bitchy to me, I just imagine Chattie kissing me and how he doesn't kiss her, and then I feel strong enough not to bitch back, and that makes me feel good about myself too, that I don't need to be horrible to her to make myself feel better.

Dear Diary,

Sunday. Chattie came over today and met Mum and Dad by accident. I was so nervous when he did that I almost wet myself!!! Mum and Dad went to see Granny in her old people's dump, and came back early with this enormous hideous painting of Auntie Angela and the twins. Honestly, Granny really should give up painting, she's terrible at it. It was lucky that they did have it though, because they made such a noise dragging it in through the front door that Chattie and I were able to separate BEFORE they came into the sitting room and found us snogging. I think they were like as embarrassed as we were. They stood there gawping silently, and then Lola came in too and stared at us, and said, 'Have you two been snogging?' I introduced them, 'My Mum, my Dad, my Sister Lola; Chattie'. And then he managed to get Lola back by saying, 'Is this your sister??? Is she adopted?' which made them all laugh because she looks so unlike me. Even Lola laughed, so I guess she kind of likes him, not that I care. I dragged him up to my room before anybody got a chance to say anything else. Although not before Mum managed to raise the subject of food, inviting him for supper. He couldn't stay that long thankfully.

From: Sue James
Sent: Sunday 19 May 22.27
To: Angela James
Subject: Painting

Dearest

It's totally and utterly hideous as well as
ENORMOUS so enormous that we couldn't
get it into the back of the car and had to tie
down the boot with a rope. How did she
even manage to buy such a large canvas in
the first place??? Is THAT what we're
paying this home for? It also weighs a ton, so
I'm going to send it by the slowest, cheapest
boat available and hopefully it'll sink without
trace somewhere in the depths of the Pacific
and you'll never have to look at it at all. I'm
not sure that you'll even have wall space for
it. Got a garage??? But you'd better write to
Mum anyway, and express your excitement at
the prospect of seeing it . . . then you can
blame me if 1 do manage to get the ship to
capsize on the way. Perhaps I should insure
it as a valuable work of art?!

Our big news is that we met Chattie quite by chance this afternoon because we set off home extra early because of the painting. He's sweet I think, not much taller than she is and quite good-looking, but it never occurred to either of us that he might be black. Frank never mentioned it. He's not exactly black, more mixed race. Not sure what I think about that really. A bit too shocked to say, and since I promised Frank that I wouldn't be shocked by anything, so as not to close any doors between us, I'm trying really hard to pretend that everything's just normal . . . so he's black . . . but I could feel Matthew staring so hard at him that Frank began to suspect something, and I had to elbow him really hard in the side and tell him to come and help me with the supper in the kitchen. 'Do you eat meat, Chattie? We've got some steak for supper, good fillet steak,' I said, as Frank bustled him away up to her room. 'Love it,' he replied, 'only I need to get home for dinner, Mrs Wilcox.' So he's polite and a good boy I think, and the really good news is that he isn't a vegetarian – kids need protein to help them grow. At least Frank never went down that route.

I'll keep you posted. Sue x

Dear Diary,

Tuesday. Fuchsia has said that now I'm nearly fifteen I can babysit Clare, and has asked if I'm free this Friday. They're going out to a party and will be back late, which means lots of money. I really need the money, but I hate the thought that I might be missing something like a party. I said I'd tell her tomorrow. If Chattie could come and watch TV with me, then that would be great, but do you think they'd let me do that????

From: Sue James
Sent: Wednesday 22 May 12.23
To: Angela James
Subject: Re: Any news on that blow job?

Bingo! Sorry not to have kept you up to date with that important news. The earth didn't move shall we say, but we're definitely closer. He's also been remarkably sane when it comes to Frankie for a change. I lie awake, worrying about the fact that Chattie is black, and worrying about the fact that I worry about it at all when it oughtn't to be an issue for me – why should his colour be an issue for me? It isn't an issue at work, or at dinner parties, or on the bus. Yet, when it comes to my daughter I lie awake. Why? Matthew can't believe that I can be getting myself into such a state over her first boyfriend. 'She's only 14 for Christ's Sake, she's hardly going to settle down with the lad and have ten babies . . .' He's right of course, and it's a silly thing to lose sleep over. Maybe it's just the fact that she's got a boyfriend at all, and the fact that he's black gives me an issue to cling to. Maybe if he were white with red hair I'd be

490

lying awake worrying about the red hair. Matthew's also right when he says that it's fantastic that she doesn't even consider it to be an issue, and that it's a symptom of how middle-aged we are if we do. One really good thing is that he doesn't smoke, so I'm hoping he'll persuade Frank to give it up.

My big news this week is that Toyah has agreed to work for us full time for 6 months from the end of term. I don't think Iris minds – it was all a bit much for her, and Frankie's thrilled, says it's like having a big sister, and I think she's really helping to boost her confidence at school. Tom's asleep, so I think I'll try and catch up on some kip too. I was so tired this morning that I put the tea bags back in the fridge and then spent the best part of an hour trying to find them.
Love Sue x

Dear Diary,

Thursday. Mum and Dad have said I can have
a party here on the Saturday night before my
birthday, and that at midnight, when it's my
actual birthday, we'll have cake and fireworks in
the garden by candlelight!!! I'd love a DJ and
lights and things, but Dad says we haven't got
the room. It's three weeks on Saturday, so I've
been making mixed tapes and a list of people.
I'm allowed 20–30 max, which is kind of hard,
to choose who I mean. The main thing is that I
really really don't want Saskia to come because:

a) she's a mean bitch to me
b) she'd find out about Chattie and
c) that means I'd only be able to have 29 other
   people.

AND it means that I can't talk about it at
school at all, which makes life really difficult
because I WANT to be able to talk about it all
the time. Nothing's more interesting at the
moment than my birthday!!!! Egomaniac or
what??? I wish Saskia would just stop being so
difficult about all of this and find somebody
else that she likes more than Chattie, so that we
can just be friends again. It makes things so

difficult for Ruby, Fran and Serena because they know and they can't tell Saskia. She came into school today wearing this amazing skirt and matching top from Selfridges. It must have cost a fortune, but the really really said thing about it was that it made her look just like a miniature version of her mother. I mean that's not how you want to look when you're fifteen is it?? She was happy though, said she'd been approached by a model agency in Top Shop and that she was going to see them for some test shots next week. Lucky bitch.

Mum thinks it's fine for Chattie to come and see me tomorrow night while I'm babysitting, so that's cool. She also said she'd give me the money to go to the video shop on my way home from school, so that we can watch something good. They're being so nice to me, they even seem to like Chattie. Mum invites him for supper every time he rings, even though he keeps on telling her that he can't on a weekday. Perhaps this early memory loss is a sign of Alzheimer's. She hasn't forgotten the giving up smoking that I was supposed to think about, though. Every single day she says, 'Thought any more about that £100 I'm offering? Fifteen's getting closer!!' It's worth giving up just to have her NOT say that all the time.

Dear Diary,

Friday. Clare is in bed, the house is creepy because it's sooooo tidy and quiet, and I'm waiting for Chattie to come and keep me company. I've had a good look around and Mum's totally right, the woman's weird. Everything in the fridge is wrapped in clingfilm, Clare wears clean pyjamas every night, has to FLOSS her teeth before she goes to bed and then use a mouthwash (she won't have any enamel left by the time she's 20) and there are no 'things' in this house – no books, newspapers, games, silly little crap bits of plastic that lie around because nobody thinks to throw them out – so it's sort of cold and unfriendly. What I don't understand is how Clare and Lola can be such good friends when they clearly come from such totally different backgrounds. I've made about 5 lists of names and there are ten people who are always on them, so they're definitely coming to my party. It's just that the others keep changing. I wish Chattie would get here and help me with this. Maybe I should talk to him about Saskia and get it all out in the open.

Dear Diary,

Saturday. I feel I can really look forward to my party now because Chattie says he's going to talk to Saskia for me, tell her that we're going out, that I'm having a birthday party and that we'd both like her to come if she can behave. It needs to come from him, she won't believe me if I tell her. It'll make things easier at school. Fuchsia came back early from her party, which was a real pain because we hadn't finished watching our film and it had just got to the good bit, and it meant I was £5 short on the money I thought she was going to give me.

From: Sue James
Sent: Sunday 26 May 21.22
To: Angela James
Subject: HND

We've had a complete return to the neighbour from hell, just when I was beginning to think that I actually quite liked her. Frankie babysat for her on Friday night, which was nice of her, even if she was getting paid, and Chattie kept her company. But judging from the way she's been behaving you would think that Frankie had invited in a whole load of tramps and homeless junkies off the street to sit on her immaculate white sofa and sip her sherry. She slipped a note through the letterbox saying that she thought it was unacceptable for a babysitter to have a boy there. I slipped back a note saying that this wasn't just a babysitter, this was her next-door neighbour and the sister of her daughter's best friend, and that this wasn't just any old boy, but her boyfriend and a thoroughly nice chap. Two hours later back comes a note saying that they had left the kitchen in a mess and consumed a whole packet of biscuits in the sitting room and smudged chocolate crumbs into her sofa. I sent back a note saying that the biscuits went with the job, that she never cleans the kitchen when she babysits here, and that she is allowed to eat in front of the TV in our house, but that she should explain her house rules to her in future. She then scribbled angrily across the bottom of my note that there wasn't to be any future babysitting dates, and that no wonder I was having problems with her if that was the way I allowed her to behave, which of course made me want to hurl bricks through her living-room window and set fire to her house.

Matthew just laughed and said I shouldn't take it personally, but how can you not when the woman's that insulting???

Frankie says she couldn't care less, but that babysitting was such a good way of earning money and revising at the same time during the week, and that she was going to put leaflets through people's doors to see if she could get some more work.

I think the woman's a snob and racist. If Chattie was a blond pop idol she'd have offered him a drink.

Picture went by slowest post on Friday, so hopefully it'll never arrive. I had to hire a van to get it to the shipper's.

Tom very grungy with a slight temperature, probably teething, but otherwise we're all just fine. Love to everyone. Sue xxxx

Dear Diary,

Wednesday. Saskia's been a lot nicer to me all week. I don't know what Chattie said to her, but she's coming to my party, and it's just such a relief because we can talk about it at school and it means we've all got something concrete to look forward to. She's going to the model agency tomorrow and thinks she's about to become a star, so maybe that's why she doesn't seem to care about me and Chattie. I can't believe it's that easy to get famous, and if it's true I'll be jealous as hell, but at least I've got Chattie. So all we talk about now is her modelling career and my party, but now I'm worried that if we talk about it too much, word'll get round the whole school and there'll be 150 people there and Dad'll go mad.

Dear Diary,

Friday. Saskia's going to lend me her karaoke machine, so that's really cool, and she says she's gonna film the party on her camcorder and give me the tape as a present. Dad says he'll get beer and wine, but no Bacardi Breezers or vodka, and I'm cool about that. It's two weeks tomorrow and next Saturday I'm going shopping with Mum . . . GOOD . . .

Dear Diary,

Sunday. Lola's been driving me mad all weekend because she wants Clare to come to my party. She doesn't understand that this is not a kids' party, but almost a grown-up one. I'm nearly FIFTEEN for fuck's sake. AND if Clare comes it'll just be like having a little spy in our midst, and Fuchsia'll know EVERY-THING the next day, and that'll make Mum even more tense than she's bound to be the day after a party when the place'll be in a mess.

Had a really lovely day with Chattie. I went to his house!!! It's huge!!! With this massive conservatory out the back full of tropical plants. His mum was really nice to me, and he's got this really nice double bed which we spent most of the afternoon lying around on! I could lie in his arms all day. I just love the way he makes me feel about my body. Every time he touches my boobs it's as if they really exist, they like even grow when he touches them, it's amazing! He buried his face into them this afternoon and that just felt SOOOOO SEXY!!! Every time we kiss, I just wanna go that little bit further with him, but I'm not ready for full sex yet. I don't think so anyway.

Haven't smoked since Tuesday. That's five

whole days. Maybe I really could give up for that £100. Time to go to sleep. School tomorrow.

From: Sue James
Sent: Monday 3 June 11.17
To: Angela James
Subject: Blooming June

It's busting out all over the place – fab weather, really hot, and I spend a great deal of time lying around on a rug with Tom in the back garden. We've even got some good roses this year . . . can't think why, when I haven't done anything different with them.

Beginning to get cold feet about this birthday party we've said Frankie can have on the 15th. I mean, what do we do if a whole load of kids gatecrash and start to trash the place?? Call the Police? And if things do go wrong, it could set back family relations by months . . . Matthew'll go bonkers, Frankie'll feel as if she's let us down and can't trust her friends . . . but she has had a tough year and done so well pulling herself out of her hole. Her school work's really picking up now (she's drawn up a coursework timetable and getting good grades), and she seems happier in herself, so I think she deserves our trust on this one. I

503

also think that if we try and treat them a bit more like grown-ups they might behave like that, so I'm going to get in some good party food, and a piñata for them to bash the hell out of in the garden, so they can let off their high spirits out of the house.

Feeling slightly sad about the fact that these are my last few weeks off work. It's been fun and good for us all, but if I were to stay off work any longer I'd probably start doing absurd things like baking cakes or actually getting it together to sew name labels on to the children's socks, so I'd better get back to the real world of the sick, miserable and hypochondriac before that happens. Anyway, we need the dosh now with three kids.

Taking F shopping on Saturday for her birthday, and I've decided that rather than dreaming about losing enough weight to get back into my old clothes, I'm just going to splash out money on some new bigger ones, and let Frankie counsel me on the style. Matthew's looking after Tom and Lola for the whole day, so I'm planning to really spoil her and have a good time with my precious, grown-up first-born darling child. Can't believe that it's a whole year since we last went out together. So much has happened in the meantime.

Complete silence from next door, and she's been avoiding me at the school gate. Her loss – but it's not healthy for Clare and Lola, so I'm trying hard not to talk about it at all. Mum absolutely fine by the sound of things. She's made friends with an 'old bugger' called Graham who she says makes her laugh a lot. Hope we're not about to be brides-maids at a second wedding and lose all our inheritance. Time to get out into that sunshine.

Love Sue xxx

Dear Diary,

Wednesday. The idea of this party is really like exciting AND frightening at the same time. People keep coming up to me and asking if they can come, people I don't even know, and I'm really worried that there are going to be too many people there and that Dad's going to go apeshit . . . Talked to Mum about it, and she suggested dressing up Dad to look like a bouncer and putting him on the door. HA HA, VERY FUNNY MUM. She thinks that's hilarious, how sad is that? But she did also say that I shouldn't worry about that. If there were people who showed up who hadn't been invited, and I wanted them to go, she would ask them to leave and she would deal with it so that I wouldn't have to lose face with them at school. That might work. I think I want to get a really sexy black no-sleeved dress that hugs my hips on Saturday, make myself look like Audrey Hepburn for the party, the classic look.

From: Sue James
Sent: Saturday 8 June 22.28
To: Angela James
Subject: What a wonderful day!

Ange, darling,

I've had such a blissful day with Frankie. It was like I was stepping out with a young woman instead of a little girl or a grumpy teenager, and I just felt so proud to be with her. We wandered around arm in arm in the sunshine and I could just feel that she was happy to be with me, not the surly, reticent, greedy girl she was just a year ago. We did that thing that girls do of taking masses of stuff into the changing room, just to try anything on, and I haven't done that in years. It was such fun. We laughed so much at one point over a swirly sixties style top I tried on that I split the side of the fabric. I thought I ought to pay for it; she said don't be silly Mum, the fabric's crap, and hung it up on the rail outside the changing room. I spent an absolute fortune on her, but I don't care. She's worth every penny, and it was easy to do because she didn't ask for anything, was grateful for everything I bought, and I suppose I felt I owed her a real splash after everything we've been through together this year.

She was also unbelievably supportive of me, took me into several shops and made me try on things I would never have even looked at if I'd been shopping on my own, and she was right about 90% of them. So I now have a whole new look, thanks to her (and some amazingly flattering black drainpipe trousers), and I know it sounds sentimental but I feel as if we're starting out on a whole new life, the five of us.

When our feet were so sore we could barely stand any more, we climbed into a taxi with all our bags and I took her to The Ritz for tea, and as we sat there stuffing our faces with cucumber sandwiches and the most delicious cream slice I have ever eaten, she started asking me questions about work, questions she's never asked me before. What did I like about being a doctor? How did I know that I wanted to be a doctor? What did I hate about it? Did I think she'd make a good doctor? So I answered everything with more honesty than I ever have before, as if I was talking to you rather than one of my children, and she came out with all this amazing stuff, really sophisticated thoughts about her future. I had no idea she was thinking that way at all. She said she wanted to do something with her life that would make her feel good about herself, and wanted to help other people who were less fortunate. If she did Science A levels she could aim for medical school, and if that didn't work out she could think again. I remembered how Mum had trashed the idea of me being a doctor when I told her that I wanted to try for medical school (she said I wouldn't have the stamina or the empathy), so I told Frank that I thought she'd make a very fine doctor, a better doctor than I was, and that I'd pull every string to help her get there. I felt so proud of her, Ange, really proud, but it wasn't because she said she was interested in following in my footsteps, because she's bound to change her mind ten times before she gets to university (if indeed she ever goes), but because she seemed like such a focused and independent young woman who intended to get what she wanted out of life without my having to do much to help her. I was never that sure of myself at 15. She also said she hadn't smoked a cigarette for ten days, which made me so ecstatic I squealed so loudly that everybody looked round, and she blushed and said 'Mu-um' and looked like an embarrassed teenager again. We may be closer than we have been in years, but some things about being a mother never change.

Masses of love S xxx

Dear Diary,

Sunday. Mum bought me stacks of really cool
clothes yesterday, so I've had a real clear out this
morning to make room for them, but the best bit
of all was that she took me to a proper bra shop
for a fitting, and for the first time in my life I
feel comfortable about my its because I have a
black bra and a white one and they really fit and
flatter my figure. The woman who measured me
was really nice. She said I was a 34C, the perfect
size for my height, and that I was a very pretty
and lucky young woman to have such a figure
and would I swop? I wore the black bra for the
rest of the day and it meant that everything I
tried on looked better somehow. It was so nice to
have Mum for the day all to myself, she's so
much nicer, more relaxed, cooler when she's
away from all of the others.

Dear Diary,

Monday. I think about 150 people are coming to my party. I've tried to persuade Mum and Dad to go out, but they're not buying it.

Dear Diary,

Tuesday. Ruby came over after school to look through my clothes and thinks the Audrey Hepburn dress is really cool. She's going to wear my new slashed top.

Dear Diary,

Wednesday. Fuchsia has been spreading rumours about us outside school, although Mum won't tell me what she's been saying, so I suspect it's about me and Chattie. Mum says under normal circumstances she would warn neighbours that we were having a party, but that as far as she is concerned we can play the music as loud as we like!!!!!! Good old Mum.

Dear Diary,

Friday and tomorrow is party day and I'm only
TWO DAYS OFF BEING 15!!!!!

From: Sue James
Sent: Saturday 15 June 22.35
To: Angela James
Subject: The party

Ange, darling, well it feels like there are about 150 screaming teenagers downstairs, rather than the 30 we said she could have, but what the hell. Matthew's standing guard at the moment and I've sneaked up for a little break . . . we've chucked out about 20 kids that Frank said firmly were not welcome and the rest seem to be hehaving well . . . so far . . .

HND has been round twice already to complain about the noise because Clare can't sleep. I said, 'Sorry, but you're only 15 once, and they'll all be going home at half past twelve,' and I shut the door. The woman's been telling other mothers at Lola's school that Frank's been off the rails, drinking, smoking and shoplifting . . . what a bitch. I can't believe she could do that, particularly now, when everything is beginning to go so well.

Gotta go, the cops are at the door, she must have made a complaint about the noise . . .

From: Sue James
Sent: Sunday 16 June 16.27
To: Angela James
Subject: Re: The party

Thanks darling, I've told her your lovely message and she's thrilled with the parcel – I kept it for her until this morning. More make-up than you find in your average Boots. We've been busy clearing up the beer cans and the crisps trodden into the carpet, but mercifully there was only one round of vomit – on the bathroom floor, they must have missed the loo – which Matthew dealt with. It was quite a good party actually. I had to stop myself from dancing because I really didn't want to embarrass Frank, but Matthew and I had a quick boogie together on the landing when nobody was looking (I hope). The fireworks at midnight were spectacular. I spotted Clare looking out from her bedroom window and waved at her. Apart from the fact that there were at least double the number of guests, everything went well – no rows, no violence, no closet vodka drinking and, perhaps most surprisingly of

517

all, no dope. Don't they smoke these days??
She's been on the phone all day having a
post-mortem with her friends behind closed
doors. I've promised to try duck à l'orange
for supper, so I'd better get going.

Talk soon. Sue xxxxx

Dear Diary

16th June 11.30 and my fifteenth birthday is almost over. The party was really cool, Ruby and Chattie think it was the best ever, and what's really weird is that they think Mum and Dad were 'fun to be with'. Is that weird or what?? The best bit though was at about 3 this afternoon when I thought it was all over. Dad produced a present, a motorbike helmet, and asked me if I wanted a ride. I looked at Mum and she just smiled at me. 'Hang on tight,' she said, 'but if you come off and break a leg I'll kill you.' She also told Dad to make as much noise as he liked as we left – 'Bugger the neighbours, it's her birthday.' It was so cool. Soooo sexy and not at all scary like I thought it might be. I loved just hugging on to Dad like that as we toured the streets . . . haven't felt that close to him in ages. He took me to the river and we walked along, holding our helmets, and watched the tourist boats chugging up and down.

I feel much older somehow, and I've been reading back over this diary because I can't sleep, and thinking back over my fourteenth year. So much has happened. I've really changed. I get on better with Mum and Dad and my friends, I'm doing well at school, and not only is there Chattie in my life but sweet little Tom. He stuck his fist into my mouth this afternoon and chuckled, just like Lola does, when I tickled him under his arm. So I'm not sure that I need to share my thoughts with you any more. I think I'll put you away for a while, and maybe only look at you again when I have my own children and need to remind myself how they might be feeling. If I need to that is.